In the Shadow of the Arch

Also by Robert J. Randisi

In the Shadow of the Arch

Robert J. Randisi

St. Martin's Press ❧ New York

A THOMAS DUNNE BOOK.
An imprint of St. Martin's Press.

Design by Nancy Resnick

Library of Congress Cataloging-in-Publication Data

Randisi, Robert J.
In the shadow of the arch / by Robert J. Randisi. — 1st ed.
p.   cm.
ISBN 0-312-18115-9
I. Title.
PS3568.A5315   1998
813'.54—dc21   97-34708
                                                              CIP

First Edition: January 1998

10 9 8 7 6 5 4 3 2 1

To Marthayn,
for being the one who finally gave me a reason
to put my work second.

Acknowledgments

I WOULD LIKE to acknowledge the following people for their assistance in putting this book together: Major John Connelly of the Richmond Heights Police Department, who set me up with Sergeant Rick Vilcek, who was the source for most of the police procedure described in the book. Also my thanks to Ken Ryan, not only a police investigator but a fine writer himself. He introduced me to Major Connelly—and the wheels went round and round.

Special thanks to Barbara Lutz, who read the manuscript for St. Louis accuracy, and who made several other fine suggestions as well. Hopefully, she kept me from sounding like a hopeless tourist—even though I have now lived in St. Louis for four years.

Last, but certainly not least, I would like to acknowledge the editorial efforts of Marthayn Pelegrimas who, in four short years of cohabitation, has made me a better man, and certainly a better writer.

In the Shadow of the Arch

Prologue

HE PICKED SUMMER to start, because the young mothers wore shorts and sundresses in the summer. They walked through the malls, thinking nothing of showing acres of firm, young flesh. In fact, he had one spotted right now. She was blond, in her twenties, walking through the mall holding a young child by the hand. The child was a girl, also blond, about six or seven.

In her brightly colored sundress the young mother was all well-toned arms, shoulders, and legs, and as she passed him he saw that her whole back was naked. Throbbing, he turned and followed her.

Galleria was St. Louis' largest and classiest mall, but while a lot of people complained about getting lost inside he knew his way perfectly. Rather than following right behind her he circled the large fountain because he knew from the route she was taking that she was going to use the south entrance.

The woman had to walk at the child's pace, so it was easy to stay ahead of her. He took a look behind twice, each time to make sure she didn't take an escalator. He considered cutting through Lord & Taylor to get far ahead of her, but there was a chance that she'd take that last escalator before heading for the exit, and he didn't want to risk it. Instead he circled the fountain, passed between the St. Louis Bread Company and the Rendezvous Cafe, and got ahead of her.

As he passed the California Kitchen he knew she was behind him, heading for the south parking lot. He went out through the automatic doors and sat down on one of the metal benches to wait.

He watched as she came through the doors a minute after he did and once again admired his choice. She had a wonderful body, tight and sleek except for her breasts, which were large. He couldn't wait to pull the string behind her neck that would allow the dress to fall away from her bosom. As she walked past him he could see the sunlight illuminating the blond, downy hairs on her arms, giving her a sort of glow.

He allowed her a small head start and then followed her into the parking lot. Unlike some of the other malls in the city it was rare to find empty spots in the Galleria parking lot, whether you used the surface lot or the covered. He had decided to use the surface lot because he didn't like being closed in. As marvelous as this woman was, if she had headed for the covered parking he would have let her go and chosen another.

He trailed behind her as she tugged the little girl along. He was watching the woman's legs, which had solid calves, and he loved her walk. He knew that if it wasn't for the child holding her back she'd be striding proudly, her shoulders back, her chin high, her chest out. He risked a look around and saw that there were no people in their aisle. A man was walking toward the mall one row to their left, but there was no one on the right. Everything was going perfectly.

Finally, she reached her car, a small red Toyota Tercel, and he closed the gap between them, timing it so that she had her keys in her hand. He would be using her car to drive them away.

"Just stand still and don't move, honey, until Mommy opens the door," she was saying to the child when he reached them.

"Hey . . ." the woman said as he approached.

She was afraid. He could see it in her eyes which—he also saw—were a beautiful green. Up close he could see that her face wasn't that pretty after all, but from the neck down she was so beautiful that he was throbbing, afraid that he might come in his pants. Her body looked just the way it did in the movies he watched every night.

"Give me the keys," he said.

"But I—"

"Just give me the keys and the little girl won't be hurt."

"Oh, God," the woman cried, "don't hurt my baby—"

"I'm not gonna hurt—"

"Run, honey, run!" the woman shouted, and the little girl obeyed.

"Hey, wait—" he shouted, annoyed, but too late to stop her.

The little girl screamed as she ran, a high-pitched sound that hurt his ears.

"Damn it!" He wanted to tell the mother that she'd made a mistake, that he had no intention of hurting her damned child—he didn't want the *kid*, that would be *sick*—but in that moment he knew that he was the one who had made the mistake.

"Help!" the woman shouted, but he was running between the cars already, swearing that next time he would choose a mother who was pushing a stroller or carriage, and not one who had a kid who could *run!*

One

July 24, 1997

THE LITTLE BOY was about three years old, and as he entered the Richmond Heights police station on Big Bend Boulevard at 9:00 A.M., his Dr. Denton's left bloody little footprints behind him.

The first cop who saw him looked behind the boy, expecting a parent to be following. When he realized there was no adult with him he wondered what the hell a child was doing alone in the station.

Joe Keough was the second person to see the boy, having entered the station from another door. He stopped and stared, as the first cop had done. The boy saw Keough and headed for him like a small, towheaded guided missile.

"What the hell—" the cop said. "What's that on the floor?"

Keough looked behind the child and saw the wet footprints.

"That's blood," he said. "Officer . . . ?"

"Horton," the young uniformed cop said.

"Horton, I'm Detective Keough. Check outside and see if anyone's there. Somebody must have dropped him off."

"Right."

Keough dropped into a crouch as the child reached him. The boy's eyes seemed slightly unfocused as he approached. Never having been a father, Keough had no idea if that was normal for a child of this age.

Several other people had seen the child now and started coming forward, some cops in uniform, some civilians.

"Don't go anywhere near the footprints," Keough called out to everyone. Not caring how chauvinistic it might have been, he looked around for a woman. There were no female officers in this station, and no female detectives that he knew of, but there were clerks. Unfortunately, he didn't see one. He was going to have to deal with the child himself.

"Hi," he said, for want of something better to say.

"Hi," the boy replied, shortly.

"Where's your mom and dad?"

The boy looked around for a few seconds, then looked back at Keough.

"Got a cookie?"

Keough remembered that the station vending machine

had chocolate chip cookies. He'd noticed that when he first came in for his interview.

"Sure," he said, "we've got cookies. Why don't you come with me. Okay?"

"Okay," the boy said, his eyes still wandering, his hands idly clapping together soundlessly.

He looked at another uniformed cop and said, "Officer, get someone from social services over here, an ambulance, and see if you can get me a female clerk who's got some experience with kids."

Keough picked the boy up, but held him at arm's length so as not to get blood on himself from the child's feet, which were still dripping.

"Who are you?" the cop asked.

"I'm Detective Joe Keough. Is there a captain on duty?"

"Sure, the watch commander."

"Get him, too, will you? Tell him I'm in the kitchen with the boy."

"Right."

"Oh, and get me some pajamas."

"Pajamas?" The man frowned.

"Yeah, we've got to get these footie things off him and send them to the lab."

Looking helpless, the officer said, "Where am I gonna get pajamas?"

"Go to a store," Keough said. "Just get me some."

"What size?"

"Look at him," Keough said, holding the child toward the cop. "Use your judgment."

"Okay," the cop said, but he didn't sound very enthusiastic.

As Keough started for the kitchen, Officer Horton came back in and walked along.

"Anything?" Keough asked.

"There's nobody out there, Detective."

"What about bloody footprints on the sidewalk, or the steps?"

"None."

Keough frowned. Someone must have not only dropped the child off, but placed him right in front of the doors. They were taking a big chance that someone would see them. Somebody must have seen something. The quicker they did a canvas of the area the better.

Canvass

"Horton, do me a favor?"

"Yes, sir?"

Having recently moved from New York to St. Louis, Keough was not used to that kind of deference from a member of the uniformed force. It was going to take some getting used to.

"See if there's another detective in the building and get him over here for me."

"Yes, sir."

Horton went off to complete his task and Keough entered the kitchen, opening the door with his back, still holding the child at arm's length.

This was a hell of a start for his first day on the job.

Two

KEOUGH'S CAREER WITH with the New York City Police Department had dribbled to an end after a particularly messy case. He could have stayed on if he wanted to, but there was a lot of bad blood and it wouldn't have made much sense. Still, he might have hung on if he hadn't gotten an offer from a friend of his in St. Louis.

"Heard what happened to you, man," Mark Drucker had said on the phone one night. "Bad break."

Drucker was a minor politician or something in St. Louis—actually, the assistant to a minor politician—but he swore he could get Keough onto one of the smaller municipal police departments in St. Louis.

"There's tons of them here, man," Drucker said. "Every ten blocks you're in another city with its own police department, and they need experienced detectives."

So Keough had come to St. Louis, gone to the Richmond Heights Police Department for an interview with Chief Harold Pellman, and gotten the job—after answering some questions.

"I know what you went through in New York, Detective," Pellman said at that first meeting.

He was a tall, slender man in his early fifties who had stood to shake hands, and then reseated himself, inviting Keough to sit.

Keough didn't reply to the statement.

"Why would things be different here?" Pellman asked.

"I don't know that they would be, Chief," Keough answered. "I can only tell you that I would do my job."

"I don't need trouble here, Detective."

"I'm not here to bring trouble, sir."

"What I do need is an experienced detective," Pellman said. "I've finally succeeded in getting money from the city to increase the number of detectives we have on the force."

"How many do you have?"

"Three," Pellman said. "With the extra money we're going to hire three more. In fact, I'm going to promote two officers to detective. They're being tested tonight. I'll expect you to show them the ropes."

"Will I be in command?"

"No," Pellman said. "In addition to the three detectives there's also a detective sergeant, and he'll be in command. I will, however, need you to guide the others with your expertise."

"I understand."

"Even the detectives who have been here awhile could benefit from your knowledge."

Keough nodded, but he was hoping he could avoid having any of the existing detectives resent him.

"Once you're here and we see how things go," Pellman said, "then we might talk about a promotion."

Keough shrugged at that. He just wanted to be a detective and do his job.

"Okay," Pellman said, "what do you say we try it?"

Keough had smiled and asked, "When do I start?"

They figured it would take two weeks for him to get settled. When he arrived in St. Louis with his belongings, he had taken a small furnished apartment in Soulard and then started looking for something more permanent. During those two weeks he also went to see the Arch, the botanical gardens, the President Casino on the Admiral Riverboat, University City, the Central West End, just some of the things he might not have time for when he started the job.

Again, through his friend Mark Drucker, he found a place to live. A friend of Drucker's who owned one of the large homes in the Central West End was going to Europe for two years and needed someone to house-sit.

"Most of the house will be closed up," Drucker said, "but you'd have use of the living room, den, and kitchen downstairs, and one of the bedrooms upstairs."

There were twelve rooms, but four out of twelve was plenty for Keough and he liked the Central West End. It reminded him of Greenwich Village in New York, with its shops, bookstores, and restaurants and sidewalk cafes. That's how he came to live on Pershing Place, one of the West End's private streets.

On his first day as a detective on the Richmond Heights Police Department, Keough stopped at the Tuscany Cafe, the newest coffee emporium—nobody called them shops anymore—in the Central West End. He had coffee and a danish, never suspecting that in less than an hour he'd be in the station kitchen—he had to remember to call them stations and not precincts—with a three-year-old boy who had blood on the feet of his Dr. Denton's pajamas.

He sat the boy on the table and looked up when the door opened. A uniformed officer entered with one of the female clerks who worked in the city hall. One of the things Keough learned about St. Louis is that the smaller police stations like Richmond Heights shared a building with the city hall, and sometimes even with the fire department. Richmond Heights Fire Department, however, had its own building, right behind city hall. Behind that was the local library.

"Officer," he said, "would you go to the vending machine and get me some chocolate chip cookies, please?"

"You want cookies now?"

Keough stared at him and said, "They're for the boy."

"Oh, right . . ."

As the door closed behind the officer, the woman approached Keough and the boy. She was in her thirties, dark-haired, slightly overweight in an attractive way.

"What's your name?" Keough asked her.

"Joyce Wilson."

"Joe Keough. Do you have children, Joyce?"

"Yes. Three."

"Any boys?"

"One."

"Then maybe you can help me."

"You seem to be doing all right."

"I'd just like to have a woman present."

"Sure. Can we clean his feet?"

"No," Keough said, "not until we have another pair of pajamas. I've sent one of the men for a pair."

"God knows what he'll come back with."

"Is there any milk—" he started to ask.

"Not in the building," she said, then spotted the small refrigerator in the corner. "Unless there's some in here."

She opened the door, saw a quart container of Pevely milk. She picked it up and shook it, found a glass, and poured the milk out. There was just about a half a glass. She brought it to the table where Keough was sitting on a chair facing the boy, still trying to avoid his bloody feet.

"Are you thirsty?" she asked the boy.

He nodded and said, "Cookies."

"The cookies are coming, pal," Keough said. "How about telling us your name?"

"Brady." The boy dug at his nose.

"Brady," Keough said, "what's your last name?"

The boy didn't answer.

"Where are your mom and dad?"

"Gone."

"Gone where?"

The boy shrugged.

"How old are you, Brady?" the woman asked.

The boy thought a moment then laboriously displayed three fingers of his right hand. At that moment the door opened and the officer stepped in with a bag of cookies.

"Thanks," Joyce said, taking them.

"Any sign of the captain?" Keough asked.

"He's on his way in."

"Bring him in as soon as he gets here, will you?"

"Yes, sir."

The officer withdrew as Joyce opened the cookies and gave the boy one.

"Brady?" Keough asked.

"Yeth?" he said, with a mouthful of cookie.

"Do you know where you live?"

"Yeth."

"Where?"

The boy started to swing his feet and drops of blood flew from them, narrowly missing Keough. He put his hand on the boy's knees to stop him gently.

"In a houth."

"A house?"

The boy nodded.

"Yeth."

He pushed the rest of the cookie into his mouth and looked at Joyce, extending his hand.

"Swallow what you have first, Brady, and have a sip of milk," Joyce said. "Then after you answer Joe's questions you can have another cookie."

The boy chewed and chewed with great concentration, then Joyce gave him a drink. He wiped off the milk mustache with the back of his right hand.

"Do you know where your house is, Brady?"

"Yes."

"Where?"

The boy pointed, his index finger slightly bowed.

"Where are you pointing to, Brady?"

"My house," the boy said, reasonably.

"Do you know the address of your house?"

The boy looked confused.

"The number on your house, Brady," Joyce said, helpfully. "Do you know the number on your house?"

"No," he said, shaking his head.

"What about the street?" Keough asked. "Do you know the name of the street you live on?"

The boy nodded.

"What is it?"

"It's Wise Street."

"Where is that?" Keough asked Joyce.

"A couple of blocks from here."

"We'll have to do a house to house."

"Maybe not," she said. "Brady, what color is your house?"

He pushed at his nose with his palm, flattening it momentarily, and then said, "Yellow."

Keough looked around. There was a yellow lined pad on the other end of the table. He grabbed it.

"Brady, look at this, then look at my shirt and at Joyce. Point to the color yellow."

Keough's shirt was blue, and Joyce's blouse orange.

The boy touched the yellow pad with one finger, then looked at Joyce and asked, "Cookie?"

Joyce looked at Keough, who nodded, and she gave the boy another cookie.

This time when the door opened, the uniformed officer was wearing captain's bars.

"What have we got?" the man asked.

"I'll tell you outside," Keough said, and left the boy with Joyce to step out of the room with the captain.

Three

"DETECTIVE JOE KEOUGH," Keough said to the captain when they were outside the kitchen.

"Captain Frank Bose, Watch Commander," the other man said, extending his hand. This was something else Keough was going to have to get used to. "First day, huh?"

"That's right."

"How'd you get stuck with this?"

"I walked into it."

"Lucky you. Run it down for me."

Keough did, quickly.

Bose listened intently and did not interrupt. He had intelligent eyes. He was in his fifties, with slate gray hair and a slight paunch, otherwise he looked like he kept himself in good shape.

"A yellow house?"

"That's right."

"Did you get the boy's last name?"

"I asked, but he didn't answer."

"I'll take a ride over there," Bose said. "You want to come along?"

"I haven't even signed in yet."

"You can take care of that later."

They both turned as a man in plain clothes approached them.

"Cap?"

Bose studied the man for a moment, then said, "Haywood?"

"That's right, sir," the man said, "Detective Haywood."

Haywood was a well-dressed black man, light-skinned and very handsome, probably in his late thirties.

"Joe Keough, Haywood," Keough said, extending his hand.

"Anthony," Haywood said, shaking hands. "What's up?"

"A small boy . . ." Keough started, running it down for him. He would later find out that Anthony Haywood was one of the newly promoted detectives.

"There's a woman in there with him now," Keough said, "Joyce . . . something."

"I know Joyce."

"Good," Keough said. "Stay in there with her and the boy. One of the men is bringing fresh pajamas for him. When you get them you can take off the bloody ones and bag them." Keough looked at Captain Bose. "What do we do for lab boys around here?"

"Request them from county."

"Can we do that?"

"Sure," Bose said. "I'll take care of it once we get in the car." Bose looked at Haywood. "We're going to try to find that house. Stay with the boy, as Keough said."

"Yes, sir."

"When the lab gets here give them the boy's pajamas, and have them look at the bloody footprints in the foyer."

"Yes, sir."

"And get some men on this street to canvass the area," Keough said. "Somebody had to have seen the boy being dropped off."

"Got it."

"Come on," Bose said to Keough, and they both left the station and went to the captain's car, where his driver was waiting for them.

"This is Officer Bennett, my driver," Bose said as he got in the front seat and Keough got in the back. "Bennett, meet Detective Keough."

"The new guy? From New York?"

"That's right," Keough said.

"Welcome to St. Louis."

Bennett looked like an experienced man. He was in his forties with some gray at the temples of his dark hair, and from his position in the front seat of the car he looked beefy.

"Where we goin', Cap?"

"We've got to find a yellow house on Wise Street."

Bennett frowned.

"I know of a couple," he said, finally. "Just hold on."

As Bennett started the car, Bose picked up the radio and requested the lab boys Keough wanted.

Keough was unfamiliar with the area except for the fact that it was supposed to be fairly affluent. Big Bend Boulevard itself did not look like much, but when Bennett turned down the street they wanted he saw the large homes.

"There's a yellow one," Bennett said, slowing down.

"Not that one," Keough said.

"Why not?" Bose asked.

"It's too big," Keough said. "I just don't think that boy came from that home. His PJs weren't expensive enough."

"The other one is further down," Bennett said, "where the homes aren't quite as big."

"Let's check that one first, then," Keough said.

"Do it," Bose said to Bennett.

"Yes, sir."

They drove down another block and a half and then Keough saw the house. This one seemed more appropriate. It was a well-kept home, clean and manicured, but not as ostentatious as the first one.

"This looks more like it."

Bennett pulled the car in front, staying off the driveway at Keough's request.

"I want to check it for blood," he explained, as they got out.

The three men walked the driveway, studying it for any sign of blood.

"I don't see any," Bose said.

As they approached the front of the house Keough said, "Officer Bennett, why don't you go around the back?"

"What am I looking for?"

"Blood on the outside," Keough said, "or a way in."

"Gotcha."

As Bennett broke off and went around the house, Keough and Captain Bose approached the front door.

"Shit," Keough said.

"What?" Bose asked.

Keough nodded at the door. The captain looked and saw the same thing he had—there was blood on the door-knob.

"Dis muz be da place," Bose said.

Four

"How do we get the door open without touching the knob?" Bose asked.

"We probably don't," Keough said, "but let's try."

He put one elbow against the door and pushed, but it did not give.

"Too much to ask for," he muttered. He put his hand in

his pocket and came out with a knife with a three-inch blade. "You're not seeing this, Cap."

He jammed the blade between the door and the door jamb and popped the door open. He put the knife away.

"Not much of a lock for this neighborhood."

"Some people just don't think trouble will ever find them," Bose commented.

"These people were apparently pretty damn wrong, weren't they?"

"Apparently."

Keough nudged the door open with his toe and entered the house, Bose close behind him. As soon as they entered they saw blood on the hall carpet, and on the walls.

"Jesus," Bose said, "you can even smell it."

"Yeah," Keough said, wrinkling his nose against the coppery scent, "there's a lot of it. Cap, can I ask you to go back outside and call for some more lab boys? We're going to need them here."

"All right."

"Also, get your driver from around back. We don't need him busting in."

"Okay. What are you going to do?"

"I'm being paid to detect," Keough said. "Why don't I?"

While Captain Bose was outside, Keough took a walk through the house. He wanted to run through it one time casually before he started looking in earnest for something. Besides that he really couldn't look as closely as he might have wanted to. He didn't have any gloves or plastic bags to put on his hands to protect the evidence.

There was blood in the living room and down a hallway leading to the master bedroom. In the bedroom there was a lot of blood on the bed. Someone had been attacked while in the bed, then had probably run down the hall to the living room and into the entry foyer. There, judging by the amount of blood, they must have been attacked again.

Some framed photographs were on a mantel in the living room. One of them was of the boy, Brady. He was a few months younger, but recognizable. People always took pictures of their small children every month, and then every few months until they got older. The photo of Brady told him he was definitely in the right house. Later he'd remove the photos from their frames to see where they were taken.

There were no other photos of children, just two adults, apparently Brady's mother and father. The mother was very pretty, with blond hair and blue eyes and—if the photo wasn't touched up—great skin. The father looked slightly overweight, with brown, thinning hair and a handsome, boyish face. They both seemed to be in their early thirties.

He found Brady's room. No blood there, but small red footprints in the hall led from the master bedroom to the living room. Brady had either been in the room during what happened, or immediately after. Keough wondered if the boy had seen what happened. He was not used to dealing with children this young. The unfocused look he had seen on Brady's face could have been normal for a three-year-old, or—as he had thought fleetingly earlier—could have been the result of some drug. Now he was thinking that maybe the boy was in shock, but that would be for a doctor to say.

"Keough?" Bose's voice called out.

"I'm in the master bedroom," he called back. "I'm coming out." He didn't want Bose compromising the scene.

As he came into the living room Bose asked, "Anything back there I should see?"

Keough picked his way across the bedroom, avoiding the bloody trail. He noticed that Bose was standing in a dry spot in the foyer.

"Blood," he said, reaching the man, "lots of it in the master bedroom, and on the bed."

"Are we in the right house?"

Keough nodded. "Photos on the mantel confirm that."

"What about the boy's room?"

"No blood, but he was in the master bedroom. His tracks lead from there to the living room.

Both men looked down at the floor of the foyer.

"It doesn't look like he got this far, though," Keough said.

"Poor kid," Bose said. "I wonder what he saw?"

"I wonder if he'll be able to tell us what he saw."

Bose shrugged. Keough looked at his watch.

"How long does it take for a lab crew to show up?"

"I don't know," Bose said. "To tell you the truth I haven't ever had to deal with a homicide scene before."

"You've been lucky."

"Up until now," Bose said.

"Yeah."

"I guess I'll leave you alone in here to do your job," Bose said. "I'll go outside and wait for the crew."

"Is there a grocery store nearby?"

"There's a Schnuck's not far from here."

"Would you send your driver over there to get me a box of sandwich bags?"

"Sandwich bags?"

"Yes, the little plastic bags for—"

"I know what they are," Bose said, without rancor. "What are you going to do with them?"

Keough held up his hands and wiggled his fingers.

"Of course," Bose said. "I'll send him right away."

"Tell him to get the cheapest he can find," Keough said. "The expensive ones will be too thick."

"Right."

"Also, we might need a car or two here when people realize it's a crime scene."

Bose nodded. "I'll request some help from Maplewood."

"Good," Keough said, and Bose walked gingerly to the door, avoiding the blood, and went outside.

Keough knew that Maplewood was one of the adjoining municipalities. He still had trouble thinking of these places—Maplewood, Clayton, Brentwood, Ladue, Richmond Heights, and others—as cities, with their own fire and police departments, and their own mayors. In New

York the individual boroughs—Brooklyn, Manhattan, Queens, Bronx, and Staten Island—have their own borough presidents, but there was only one mayor, one fire department, and one police department.

There was going to be an awful lot to get used to here.

Five

OFFICER BENNETT ARRIVED with the sandwich bags and Keough started to look around in earnest. If what Bose said was true he'd have plenty of time before a lab crew arrived.

He started in the living room, this time picking up the framed photographs from the mantel and examining them. He noticed that one of the frames with Brady's photo had a smudge of blood on it. He hoped the lab would be able to get a print from it. He set it aside to point out to them.

He studied the blood on the floor of the living room. Some of it came from tracks, and it looked to him like three sets. Brady's were easy to make out. Another set were bare feet, small adult prints, probably a woman. Brady's mother? The third set were a man's shoes. Could have been Brady's father, but it could have been another man. The bare feet had to be his mother. What other woman would be barefoot in the master bedroom?

He placed his foot next to one of the man's prints. They were about his size, which meant the man was average.

Next he went to the kitchen. There was no blood here, but one drawer was open. He walked over to it and found that it was the silverware drawer. There were the usual forks, spoons, and knives in a rubber holder. Next to the holder were a couple of larger knives with black handles and serrated edges, one larger than the other. He wondered if there was a third lying somewhere with blood on it? Or did the doer bring his own knife?

On the counter he found steak knives in a holder. They were the kind with holes through the handles so that they'd hang. There were eight slots, and each slot had a knife. None were missing. He lifted each knife out to examine it for blood, but they were all clean—at least as far as the naked eye could see.

He looked at the phone hanging on the wall, took it off and gave a listen. When he heard the dial tone, he replaced it. There was no blood on the phone. He went to the kitchen door and found it locked. Also no blood on it. There was no sign that the kitchen had been involved in the action.

He left the kitchen and stopped in the dining room. No blood on the floor, or on the table or chairs. The woman had obviously run straight from the bedroom to the living room and tried to get out the front door. The doer caught her there. Keough wasn't thinking of him as a killer yet, but he didn't think it would be long.

He walked down the hall to Brady's room and stepped inside. The wallpaper was decorated with characters he didn't recognize. The sheets on the bed featured Power Rangers. He studied the bed and floor intently, but they were clean. Brady had not returned to the room after stepping in the blood.

He left Brady's room and before going to the master bedroom checked out the third room, probably a guest room. The bed was neatly made. There was a dresser, but the drawers were all empty. It didn't look as if anyone had been in that room for some time.

He left and went down the hall to the master bedroom. He was going to spend the most time here, and come away with some sort of sequence of events constructed in his head.

The bed was queen-sized. There was a dresser with a mirror, and a chest of drawers. Also a night table on each side of the bed, each with its own lamp. There was a phone on one of them, the one to the right.

The bed was soaked with blood, more on the right side than the left, as he faced it. He went around to the right and saw that the floor was also soaked. The floor on the left side was clean. Barefoot tracks led from the blood on the right side to the door, and into the hall.

Brady's mother had been in bed, lying on the right side, when someone—Brady's father?—attacked her with a knife. Badly hurt, bleeding profusely, she nevertheless had the strength to bolt from the bed and into the hall, still bleeding badly. She bled enough that the attacker had stepped in it and left tracks of his own.

Instead of following the tracks he continued to look around the room. He looked in the drawers of both the dresser and a chest of drawers. The dresser was the mother's, while the chest was the father's. This was pretty traditional.

A look in the night table on the right confirmed what he'd thought, that Brady's mother slept on that side. He had to step carefully to avoid the blood while getting the drawers open. He noticed that there was a vibrator in the bottom drawer. He picked it up and turned it on. From the way it ran he figured the battery power was still high.

He went around to the other side and found, among other items, condoms in the top drawer. The brand was Ramses. It was a box of twelve and there were five left. Also of interest was an empty holster, no gun, and no shells to indicate what caliber it might have been. From the shape of the holster, though, it was probably a pistol, not an automatic.

He walked to the master bedroom and reminded himself to look for another bathroom, probably down the hall. The tub and sink were clean and dry. He opened the medicine cabinet and didn't find anything out of the ordinary. The family apparently favored both Tylenol and Advil. There were also some children's liquid aspirin.

There was a can of Vanilla Essence air freshener on the toilet tank and an odd contraption in a holder on the wall that looked like an electric toothbrush. On the counter around the sink was one container of toothpaste, one plastic cup, and two toothbrushes. The area under the sink was open. There were several plastic baskets under there, almost like laundry baskets, but smaller, filled with items like hair rollers, pins, and a hair dryer, implements designed for the care of hair and nails, as well as some makeup.

He left the bathroom and took one last look around the bedroom. He checked the closet, which had two sliding doors. He noticed that the closet was two-thirds filled with women's clothes, and a third filled with men's. The ratio of shoes was much higher than that, with many more women's shoes than men's. Up on top he saw a collection of baseball caps. Two of them had the logo or name of riverboats in the area, the Casino St. Charles, and the Casino Queen. There was a St. Louis Cardinal hat, a hat that said "Highlander" on it, another that said "Sunset Express," and still another from a casino, this one in Vegas, the Luxor. There was also a Chicago Cubs hat, a St. Louis Blues hat, and a hat that said Chicago Police.

Was Brady's father a cop? A former cop? He'd seen nothing else in the house to indicate this.

There were shoe boxes on the other part of the top shelf, but he did not go through them. He would have someone do it, though, sometimes people kept a gun in a shoe box.

He closed the closet and left the room. He walked down the hall, careful not to step in the blood, and found the other bathroom. It, too, was clean, with nothing remarkable in it.

Just outside the bathroom was a linen closet. He opened it and found it filled with neatly folded towels and sheets, except for one shelf. Here a towel was unfurled, partially hanging down off the shelf, as if one had been snatched from atop it hurriedly. This led him to believe that a towel may have been used to try to staunch the flow of blood. Did the doer change his mind after stabbing her and try to save her? A husband who attacked his wife in a frenzy and then came to his senses might have done this. There were also sheets and pillowcases in the closet, but he couldn't tell if any were missing.

Keough completed his examination of the house, ending up in the front foyer again. There wasn't much more he could do until the lab boys got there, at which point he'd go through the house again with them, so he went outside.

Captain Bose and Officer Bennett were both leaning against the car with their arms folded. Some people—passersby, neighbors—had already begun to gather in front of the house.

Keough walked to the car and both policemen straightened up.

"What did you find?" Bose asked.

"Not much," Keough said. "I tried reconstructing the crime scene."

"How do you do that?" Bennett asked, with obvious interest.

"You just try to read the evidence, construct a sequence of events."

"So how does it look to you?"

"This is preliminary," Keough said, "but I think Brady's mother and father must have had a fight which resulted in the father attacking the mother with a knife while she was in bed. The footprints indicate that she ran out of the room down the hall with him after her. He must have caught her in the front foyer."

"And the boy?" Bose asked.

"He either entered the master bedroom before or after. We'll know more when I question him further."

"Jesus," Bennett said, "you mean he might have seen his father kill his mother?"

"Maybe," Keough said, "but maybe he only stabbed her." He told them about the towels in the linen closet.

"Maybe that towel's been hanging there for days," Bennett suggested.

"That could be," Keough said, "but the house is spotless, with everything in its place. Whether the lady of the house cleaned it herself, or had it cleaned, I don't think that towel would hang that way for very long."

Bennett shook his head.

"I don't think I would have thought of all that," he said, admiringly.

"With some training and experience, you would."

"That must be why they're giving you the big bucks."

"Bennett, can you do me a favor?"

"What's that?" the officer asked.

"How about seeing if any of these people saw anything? And if so, get their names and addresses. We'll take statements later."

"Sure," he said. "I can do that."

"Cap, will you wait here for the lab and those other cars?"

"Sure," Bose said, "but what are you going to do?"

"I'm going to start canvassing some of these houses," Keough said, "the ones on this block, and the one behind the house. I want to see if anyone heard any commotion last night or this morning—probably this morning."

"What about the names of the people who live here?"

"A check of the deed to the house will give us that, but somebody here might tell us before then."

"I'll see if I can find out," Bennett said.

"Thanks."

Keough started toward a neighbor's house as Bennett approached the crowd and asked, "Anybody know the names of the people who live here?"

Six

KEOUGH WAS TEMPTED to stay at the house to instruct the lab crew, but he chose to believe that they would know what they were doing. After all, St. Louis was a major city with a major police department—at least, the *city* had a major department—which had dealt with crime scenes before. Keough's friend Mark Drucker had warned Keough about coming to the Midwest with a New York attitude. Keough's first reaction had been "What New York attitude?" but he quickly realized that he had done all right so far by listening to what Drucker had to say.

He'd noticed, of course, that the language was different in St. Louis. Oh, it was English, but while people in New York waited "on" line, in St. Louis they waited "in" line.

There were other subtle differences, and he noticed many of them while he questioned the neighbors who lived around the Sanders house.

The first neighbor, to the immediate left, had told him that the Sanders had been living there for about four years.

"They're real nice people, Mr. and Mrs. Sanders," Mrs. Wilhemina Arnette told him. She was in her sixties, wearing what he'd called a house dress—he didn't know what they called it in St. Louis. "Quiet."

"Did you hear any noise last night or this morning, Mrs. Arnette?"

"I told you they were quiet, didn't I?" she asked, peevishly.

"Yes, ma'am, you did."

"Then I didn't hear any noise," she said. "I never hear any noise from them. They're nice, quiet, young people."

"Can you tell me their first names?"

"Her name is Margaret, I think . . . or is it Margo? One of those."

"And him?"

"He's hardly around," she said, "always working. I don't talk to him at all, only to her to say hello."

"I see. Well, thanks for your help, Mrs. Arnette."

"What's happened over there, anyway?"

"We're not sure, ma'am," he said. "That's what we're trying to find out."

He left her before she could ask any more questions and went to the neighbor's house on the right. No one answered the door, which didn't necessarily mean that no one was home, but he decided to try again later.

He was coming back from the second house when he saw a couple of cars pull into the driveway of the Sanders house. Several men were getting out as he approached them.

"Who's in charge?" one of them asked. He was carrying a metal case like the one television repair men when they used to come to your house.

Keough and the captain started to speak at the same time, but Bose was the one who stepped back.

"I'm Detective Keough. It's my crime scene. This is Captain Bose, of the Richmond Heights Police."

"What have we got?" the man asked.

"What's your name?"

"Kendricks."

"Are you a crime scene technician, Mr. Kendricks?"

"I am."

"How many of you are there?"

"Three," Kendricks said. "The others are Holman and Carter."

"All right. I'll take you all inside and show you what we've got. It's not a pretty sight."

"I don't see a meat wagon," Kendricks said. He looked to be forty or so, perhaps old enough to still use the term *meat wagon*.

"No bodies," Keough said, "but a lot of blood."

"Let's go, then."

As they walked to the door Keough took out the box of bags again, removed two, and slid them over his hands.

"Nice touch," Kendricks said. "Are you new?"

"First day on the job in St. Louis."

"From where."

"New York."

"I thought you were a little old to be a rookie."

"Far from it."

Keough and Kendricks entered the house, followed by the other two techs.

"In case you're wondering," Kendricks said when they were inside, "we know what we're doing."

"I was going to assume that."

All three techs put down their "tool boxes," took plastic gloves from their pockets, and slipped them on. Keough noticed that all three men were already sweeping the room with their eyes.

"How many hot spots?" Kendricks asked.

"The master bedroom, the hallway leading there, the living room, and this foyer."

"Right."

Kendricks quickly turned and split the job among the three technicians. Keough noticed that he took the master bedroom himself.

"I'm going to go outside and let you boys do your jobs," Keough said.

"We appreciate that, Detective," Kendricks said.

"There's just one other thing," Keough said. "There's a picture frame on the mantel with the photo of a little boy in it. There's blood on the lower right-hand corner of the frame. You might get a good latent."

"Well take a look at it," Kendricks promised.

"Fine," Keough said. "Like I said, I'll get out of your way."

Keough went outside and slipped the sandwich bags off his hands. The first thing he was going to do when this was finished was get himself his own rubber gloves.

Seven

AS EXPECTED, THE area in front of the house became like a circus. Several uniformed officers worked at keeping the crowd back, while a couple of others helped Keough canvass the neighborhood. Ordinarily Keough would have liked to have experienced detectives doing that, but he was forced to work with what he had.

It was remarkable to him that no one appeared to have heard any commotion. Had the man and woman made it to the front door and not outside? In spite of the fact that there was blood on the doorknob?

From across the street Keough regarded the house again. When he did he felt stupid. He crossed over and was intercepted by Captain Bose.

"I've got a message for you, Detective Keough."

"From who?"

"Major O'Connell." Keough hadn't met O'Connell yet, but he knew the man was also the assistant chief. "He wants you to come in and brief him on what's going on."

"That'll have to wait."

Bose looked incredulous.

"What?"

"There's one more thing I have to do."

"B-but the chief said as soon as possible."

"That's what I intend to do," Keough said, "get to him as soon as possible."

Obviously, Captain Bose had never failed to jump at an order, and would never ignore one.

"Keough—"

"Captain," Keough said, "this is my crime scene. Before I can leave it I have to make damn sure it's secure. I'm sure the major will understand that."

Bose looked confused. Keough felt sorry for the man having to deal with Keough's New York attitude.

"Uh, should I, uh, radio him and tell him—"

"Negative," Keough said. "I'll tell him myself when I go in. Okay?"

"Uh, well, o-kay, I guess . . ."

"Just one more thing, Captain," Keough said, "and I'll be done."

Bose scratched his head and watched Keough approach the front door and go inside the house. He felt rooted to the spot, not sure what to do.

Keough entered the house and slid two bags on his hands again.

"Are you Holman?" he asked the technician on his hands and knees in the foyer.

"No, sir, I'm Carter," the man said, without looking up.

"Mr. Carter, has anyone located the garage door?"

"Sir?"

"The door that leads from the house into the garage?"

"Oh, no, sir."

"I'll find it."

He started to open a door at hand, and Carter said, "Sir?"

"Yes?"

"That's a closet."

"Oh."

"In these houses," Carter said, "the door leading to the garage is usually in the kitchen."

"Thank you, Mr. Holman."

"Sure."

Keough worked his way around the man without getting blood on his shoes and walked to the kitchen. From across the street he had spotted the garage and realized that he had not gone inside to check it. Because he'd walked head on into this investigation five minutes into the job, he felt he wasn't thinking straight. He should have checked the garage right after he finished with the house.

He walked across the spotless kitchen and was faced with two doors. Naturally, the first he opened was a pantry. The second, however, led to the garage.

"Shit," he said, as he walked through the door.

There was a small puddle of blood on the floor of the two-car garage. There was also a car there, which surprised him. He expected to find the place empty. Maybe the Sanders had two cars.

This one was a BMW, a year or two old from the look of it. It was dark green in color. He took a deep breath before walking over to it, fully expecting to find the body of Mrs. Sanders inside. Either in the back seat, or in the trunk.

The BMW was a two-door model; he tried the door on the driver's side first, and it opened. He stuck his head in and looked at the back seat. Seeing that it was empty, he released the breath he had been holding. As he straightened up he noticed there was some blood on the passenger seat, but not a lot. Certainly not enough for a wounded person to have sat there—unless she had sat there with a towel wrapped tightly around the wound.

The other possibility was that the blood had been left by Brady's feet. If someone had used this car to drive Brady to the police station, had the other car been used to transport Mrs. Sanders, alive or dead? And if so, were there two drivers? For the first time he considered there might have been two attackers. Both male? Or one male and one female? Did Mr. Sanders have a girlfriend who'd been in on this?

He withdrew from the car and closed the door. He'd have one of the technicians come out and go over it.

He looked again at the puddle of blood on the floor. It was approximately where someone might have been standing by the other car, perhaps waiting to get in. How had they gotten out here without leaving any blood in the kitchen?

He walked around to the back of the BMW. The trunk was tightly shut, and he was going to have to get inside. Once again he felt himself holding his breath. Was Mrs. Sanders in the trunk?

He went in search of the trunk release so he could find out.

Eight

"I DON'T WANT to start having trouble the first day, Keough."

"Neither do I, sir."

"When I call for a man to come in from the field," Maj. John O'Connell said, "I expect him to come in forthwith."

"I understand that, sir."

O'Connell was about five ten, wiry, with gray hair and intense eyes. He appeared to be about fifty.

"Then why was it necessary for me to wait half an hour for you to show up?"

"Sir," Keough said, "it was necessary for me to secure my crime scene before I could leave it. Normally, I'd be working with a partner. If that was the case I could have left that task to him and come in sooner."

"Well," O'Connell said, "you don't have a partner, Keough . . . at least, not yet."

"I realize that, sir," Keough said. "That's why I couldn't leave—"

"Detective Keough," O'Connell said, cutting him off, "who is in command here?"

"You are, sir."

"Can we keep that firmly in mind as we move forward?"

"Yes, sir," Keough said. "That's my intention."

O'Connell sat down behind his desk and heaved a sigh. Keough was not used to being in the presence of a major. It was not a rank that was used in the New York Police Department.

There was a second man in the room. He was Sgt. Dick Bilcheck. He was wearing a white shirt with his detective's shield pinned to the pocket. He was also under six feet, only just, and looked to be in his midforties. He and Keough had only met a few moments ago, and had gone into Major O'Connell's office.

"Detective," O'Connell said, with a glance over at Bilcheck, "have a seat and tell us what we've got."

* * *

Keough ran it down for the major and for his own immediate superior, Sergeant Bilcheck, right up to the point
where he opened the trunk, expecting to find Mrs. Sanders
inside.

"Was she there?" O'Connell asked.

"No," Keough said, "and there was no blood in the
trunk. If he drove her from there he did it in another car."

"But the blood in the front seat."

"I think it was left by the kid."

"He used one car to drive the woman, and the other to
drive the kid?"

"It's a theory."

"So where's the woman? And the car?"

"I'll check the hospitals for the woman," Keough said.
"If he wrapped her wound in a towel, maybe he decided to
take her for treatment."

"Or maybe he took her and the car and pushed them off
a bridge."

Keough shrugged and said, "That's a theory, too."

"Where's the boy?"

"I left him with Joyce, um, Wilson, a woman who works
next door. I'll have to go and check and see if social services has come for him, yet."

O'Connell sat back in his chair, folded his hands in
front of him, and regarded Keough.

"I hate to say this," the older man finally said, "but I'm
impressed."

"I'm just doing my job, sir."

"Maybe," O'Connell said, "but you're doing it a whole

lot sooner than you expected. You walked into a bad situation and took it over. Do you always react so well under pressure, Detective?"

Keough smiled. He thought, at that moment, that he still had not found a place to fly his kites. If he didn't soon, *then* there'd be pressure.

"Yes, sir," he said, "every time."

Nine

LATER THAT DAY Keough sat at his desk staring at a brown leather phone book in a plastic evidence bag.

Once he had made sure that the boy, Brady, was in the proper hands with social services, he'd gone back to the Sanders house to see how the lab was doing. After they'd finished up and promised him results by the next day he'd gone through the house again. He found two things of interest. One was a safe deposit key in a small red envelope, and the other was the Sanderses' phone book. He'd picked each up with a bag on his hand, then bagged both by turning the bags inside out and took them back to the station with him. Instead of putting them in a property room, though, he kept them at his desk for a while.

The detective's squad room was in the basement along with a captain's office shared by two captains, a turnout room for the patrol officers, a booking room and two two-man cells. At the moment there were three desks in the squad room. They were going to bring in three more, at some point, which would make the room pretty crowded, but at the moment there was plenty of room. Bilcheck, the sergeant, had an office on the first floor, next to the assistant chief. The chief's office was on the second floor, with the mayor's and some other dignitaries.

Detective Haywood had gone out on a burglary call when the responding car had called for a detective. Keough was nearing the end of his shift and took the phone book and safe deposit key out of his desk drawer.

He opened the bag and took the book out. He'd leafed through it earlier, but now he went slowly, taking a better look at each page.

He didn't want to have to phone everyone in the book. He was hoping that he'd be able to separate friends from acquaintances, family members from professional contacts. He still didn't know what Mr. Sanders' business was. He'd gotten their last name from the neighbor, but finding some of their mail in the house had enabled him to find out their first names. He was William. The neighbor, Mrs. Arnette, had been wrong about the woman. Her name wasn't Margaret or Margo, it was Marian.

In addition to the phone book Keough had removed

the Sanderses' most recent phone bill from the house. He had tucked it inside the book, and took it out now.

He spent a few minutes leafing through the book, but the Sanders did not differentiate in any way the business numbers from their friends or families. Neither was Keough able to find any other Sanders listed in the book. If he had known Marian Sanders' maiden name, that might have helped him find a family member in the book, but he didn't.

He took the phone bill out of the envelope and spread out the pages. There were eleven. Apparently, the Sanderses made a lot of long distance calls, as well as calling card calls. Local calls were not listed, but Keough began to make a note of the most frequently called numbers on a yellow lined pad, especially if the duration of the calls exceeded ten or fifteen minutes. Calls of that length usually indicated family or friends.

When he was done he had ten phone numbers. He set the phone bill aside and looked around the room for the Yellow Pages. When he couldn't locate them he picked up the Sanderses' phone book again and looked inside. In the front of the book was a page with a map of the country and a listing of all the area codes. Using that he wrote down on the pad, next to the numbers, the state each call was made to.

The ten numbers reflected calls to six different states: Florida, Pennsylvania, Ohio, Kansas, Colorado, and California. It was pretty evenly divided between the East Coast, the Midwest, and the West Coast.

When that was done he looked at his watch. He was

about ten minutes from the end of his shift. If he started making phone calls now he'd have to put in for overtime. He didn't think that would be wise, not on his first day. He was debating whether or not to take the book home when Det. Tony Haywood came walking back in.

"Thought I'd be late," Haywood said. "The boss doesn't like unnecessary overtime."

"I'm glad you said that," Keough said. "I was just wondering what to do. How'd the burglary go?"

Haywood made a face.

"They didn't really need us there," he said. "The people insisted on seeing someone, though, and I had to explain the futility of taking fingerprints at the scene of a burglary, especially when the people had four kids, like these did. We would have had to fingerprint the kids, as well as the parents, and the woman got all upset about that. Seems she thought anyone who gets fingerprinted has a criminal record."

"What did you tell them?"

"I told them we'd do the best we could," Haywood said with a shrug.

"Sounds like you handled it just right."

At that point two men entered the office and Haywood introduced them to Keough. They were Detectives Lou Merchant and Frank Leslie. Keough stood to meet them, tucking the phone book into his pocket as an afterthought.

"We've been looking forward to meeting you," Merchant said. He was the oldest man in the room, about fifty. He was gray-haired and thickly built through the middle. It was obvious somebody needed to give him tips on what "plain" clothes meant. He was wearing a lime green sports jacket over a purple silk shirt.

"I hope we get a chance to work together," Frank Leslie said, shaking Keough's hand. Leslie was in his late twenties, the youngest man in the squad. He had gone the opposite way of his partner, and was wearing different shades of brown. Keough decided to wait and see if the men made a habit of dressing this way before he said anything.

"I'm sure we will," Keough said.

It was time to go home and call it a day. His first day as a Richmond Heights police detective had been, to say the least, eventful.

Ten

KEOUGH HAD BEEN living in the house in the West End for only a week. The house stood on the corner of Pershing and Euclid, Euclid being the main street that cut right through the West End.

The Central West End was where St. Louisans did their shopping until stores like Saks Fifth Avenue and Montaldo's moved away in the seventies. Since then the area had been built up again and now sported all sorts of shops, cafes, and restaurants.

What impressed Keough about the West End were the choices available to him, and he was only too glad to house-sit the house on Pershing for as long as the owners wanted to be away.

He arrived home in the evening, when it was no longer necessary to put coins in the parking meters. He had developed the habit of parking on Euclid, instead of driving through the gates onto the private street. Somehow, he didn't quite feel entitled to that, yet.

He parked and got out of his car, a 1993 Oldsmobile Cutlass Supreme he had purchased when he first arrived in St. Louis. He admired the huge, ornate streetlights which belonged to another era as he walked to the gateway that led into Pershing Place. The wrought iron was moored on each side to big concrete pillars, and to either side of each pillar was a small entryway. Once through there he mounted the steps to the house and let himself in.

There was no two ways about it, the house was a mansion. It had three floors, with two stairways, one which led to the kitchen and the other to the large entry foyer.

The living room was to the right and the dining room was on the left. The dining room, however, was one of the rooms closed off, the furniture covered with sheets. When he ate in the house he did so in the kitchen, which was large enough to have a good-sized table in the middle of it. He used the living room and kitchen on the first floor, and the bedroom and den on the second. He never used any part of the third floor. The den was actually one of the five bedrooms which had been converted into a den and office. He'd only been there a week and still had boxes in the living room, den and bedroom to be unpacked. He probably should have worked harder at getting settled during that week, because it was going to be slow going now that he was on the job. Truth be told, though, it had been too long since he'd been on the job, and he was anxious to get back to it. Of course, he didn't know that he'd be back in it five minutes after walking into the building.

As he entered the house, he went into the kitchen and opened the refrigerator. He pulled out a beer, a Pete's Wicked Ale, which he had discovered since moving here. One beer at home, he thought, and then he'd wander down the block for some dinner.

He popped the top off the beer and sat down at the kitchen table to drink it. He became aware of the phone book in his jacket pocket and pulled it out. The yellow lined sheet of paper he'd written the most often called phone numbers on was folded up inside.

He had not been able to locate any members of Mr. or Mrs. Sanders' families. Tomorrow he'd ask the boy, Brady, what he knew, but he didn't really expect to get much out of a three-year-old.

When he'd returned to the station the first time the boy had still been there, dressed now in new pajamas. Keough still didn't know the name of the officer he'd sent for the pajamas, but it was obvious the man knew nothing about kids because he'd brought back a pink pair. Joyce had removed the bloody ones and given them to Detective Haywood to bag, and then had dressed Brady in the new pair.

The second time Keough returned to the station the boy was gone. Tomorrow he'd go down to wherever they were holding him and try to question him further.

Meanwhile, he sipped his beer and leafed through the phone book, looking for some hint of whom to call. He wasn't about to start making long distance phone calls from the phone bill on his own phone. He'd do that from the station.

By the time he finished his beer, his stomach was growling. He decided to take the phone book with him to Dressels, where he'd have a few more beers with dinner.

Dressels was small, dark, and comfortable. They served food downstairs, while the upstairs was reserved strictly for drinking and, when they had it, entertainment.

The walls downstairs were covered with framed sketches and drawings of literary and theatrical figures, and there were similar sketches on the front of the yellow menu. Classical music played constantly, and a collection of cassette tapes was clearly visible behind the bar.

It was an oval bar and it dominated the place, stuck right in the center of the room, with tables all around it. He grabbed a table toward the front and ordered a Newcastle Brown Ale from the waitress, whose name was Dawn. She was one of the reasons he liked the place. She was mature, attractive, and greeted him warmly the second time he had been there. This was now his fourth visit and she greeted him again like a long-lost friend—or, at least, a regular customer.

"How are you getting along in St. Louis?" she asked, when she brought him his beer.

"Just great."

"Finding your way around?"

"Well," he said, "I can get to work, and I can find my way back here to the West End."

"That' not bad for, what, two weeks?"

"Starting my third. In fact, today was my first day of work."

"How did that go?"

He looked up at her. She was slender, and he knew she kept herself in shape with exercise from conversation he'd heard during his other visits. Although they'd talked a little each time he came in, she still did not know that he was a policeman.

"You don't want to know."

"That bad, huh? Maybe a good meal will fix that."

He ordered some of Dressels' homemade potato chips, and the contents of the crock pot, which changed every day.

Dawn brought the basket of chips and Keough worked on them and the Newcastle while going through the phone book again. He turned over the piece of paper on which he had written the long distance calls and wrote down three local numbers. One of them was for a Dr. White, another was for Jenny Rasmus, and a third was for a YWCA. The phone book was apparently Marian Sanders', not her husband's. If he was a businessman, it was likely he had a phone book at work, or even carried it with him.

Thinking of business Keough went through the book yet again, looking for a number that might be Mr. Sanders' work number. There were two in the book that looked likely, and he wrote them down just as Dawn brought his dinner. He tucked the book away in his pocket, ordered a second Newcastle, and devoted all of his attention to dinner.

Keough left Dressels after dinner, saying good-bye to Dawn. He was well fed, but in the mood for coffee. He thought about crossing the street and going to the Tuscany Cafe but instead decided to stop at Left Bank Books, the Central West End—and one of St. Louis'—oldest bookstore. There were two entrances to the place, one which led directly into the store, and the other into their coffee shop, which appeared to be a new addition. He decided to browse a bit, and bought a mystery novel called *Lukewarm* by a local writer. The book featured a private detective who lived and worked in Florida. Keough had never read this writer before, but the book sounded interesting.

He read a couple of chapters over a cup of coffee and then left the store and walked home.

When he got home he took a shower and went into the den. He was greeted by the sight of boxes stacked against one wall, small and medium in size. He decided to ignore them for now.

There was a leather armchair there, which he had

begun to use for reading. He briefly considered leafing through the phone book again, but decided to leave that for the next day, when he was at work. Tonight he'd do some reading for pleasure, before turning on the television to watch CNN or ESPN, or maybe even both.

He could do some unpacking tomorrow, after work.

Eleven

AT NINE-THIRTY the next morning Keough was sitting at his desk with the phone book and the numbers he'd written on the yellow lined pad in front of him. He knew he shared the desk with one of the detectives who was working the later shift, but he didn't know which one. The squad was working only two shifts, so that the midnight-to-eight shift was without a detective. If one was needed, each member of the squad would take turns being on call. It was the detective sergeant, however, who would be awakened first, and who would make the choice of whom to call.

Whichever man he was sharing the desk with had left crumbs on the top of it, probably from his dinner. Keough had to go to the men's room for a damp paper towel to clean it off before he sat down. He was going to have to have a talk with his deskmate.

Once the desk was cleaned he got down to business, trying to find Mr. Sanders' place of business.

The first number he called was a place called Kaufman, Coolly & Fine, Attorneys-at-Law. They did not, the receptionist told him, have a man named Sanders working for them. Was he an attorney? Keough hung up without identifying himself, and without telling her that he didn't know. He had found nothing in the house that reflected Sanders' profession.

The second number was for a place called First Choice Realty. He called and asked the woman who answered if a man named William Sanders worked there. The answer was yes.

"Is his wife named Marian?"

The woman hesitated, then said, "Why, y-yes, it is—"

"And do they have a little boy?"

"Y-yes, Brady—what is this about, please?"

"What is your name, ma'am?" Keough asked, preparing to write it down.

"I'm Miss . . . Miss Bonny," the woman said, starting to sound nervous. "Is—is something wrong? H-has something happened? Who is this?"

"My name is Detective Joseph Keough, ma'am, I'm with the Richmond Heights Police—"

There was a sharp intake of breath and then the woman said, "Police!" letting the breath out at the same time.

"Yes, ma'am. Is there a manager I can speak to, please?"

"H-has something happen to Bill—uh, Mr. Sanders?"

"I'd rather talk to a manager, if you don't mind, Miss Bonny."

"Of course. I'll connect you to Mr. Riverside."

He waited through a series of clicks and then a man came on the phone.

"Hello, is—is this a policeman?" The voice was timid, quavering slightly. Keough wondered if this was normal, or the result of talking with a cop.

"Yes, sir, my name is Detective Keough, I'm with the Richmond Heights Police."

"Is something wrong?"

"Well, I'd like to come and talk to you about William Sanders, Mr. Riverside."

"Has something happened to Bill?"

"He seems to have disappeared."

"Disappeared? That's terrible. Did Marian report—she must be frantic."

"Well, Mr. Riverside, Mrs. Sanders seems to have disappeared, as well."

"What? Look, I don't understand. What about the boy? What about Brady?"

"We have the boy, sir."

"Look," Riverside said again, "I don't understand." His voice had become much firmer, now, as if he was taking control of himself.

"Mr. Riverside, may I come to your office to talk to you?"

"Well . . . of course, if it's about—I mean, I want to help, but I don't know what I can—"

"I'd just like to talk to someone who knows the Sanderses, sir. The neighbors don't seem to be able to help me."

"That's because they're very private people."

"I see. Do you know them well, sir?"

"Er, fairly well, I suppose."

"How long have they—look, I'd really like to come to your office and ask these questions. In about two hours? Can you arrange to be there at, say, eleven-thirty?"

"Well, I have a meeting, but—well, of course, yes, I'll be here."

"Where is your office, sir?"

Riverside gave him an address on Clayton Road.

"Can you give me a landmark, sir? I'm sort of new in town?"

He gave him two landmarks, the Cheshire Inn—which was either a hotel or a restaurant, Keough wasn't sure which—and a huge Amoco gas sign.

"It's the biggest double-sided, free-standing gas sign in the country," Riverside added.

"I see."

"We're across the street."

"I'm sure I'll be able to find you, then. Thank you, Mr. Riverside. I'll see you at eleven-thirty."

Keough hung up, pleased that he had found someone to talk to about William Sanders so soon, and so easily. He intended to push his luck later, though. After lunch he intended to start calling the long distance numbers, choosing to do it then because of the time differences involved.

He didn't have time to talk with Brady Sanders before his meeting with Riverside, so he looked at some of the paperwork that was on his desk.

A couple of incidents from earlier in the week were represented, both occurring before he was even on the job. They'd been held for him, though, because there had been no one else to refer them to. One was an assault case, where the victim had ended up going to the hospital with a head injury that was serious, but not life threatening. He wondered what kind of reception he'd get from the family showing up at the hospital four days after the fact.

The second incident was a burglary, and he felt sure that all he'd have to do was the same thing Haywood had done the day before, talk to the people, soothe them, and assure them that the police were on the case.

He decided to take care of the latter before seeing Riverside, and the former on the way back. After that he'd go downtown to wherever they were holding little Brady Sanders and see if the child could answer any of his questions.

Twelve

HE SPENT ABOUT twenty minutes talking to the woman who had been burglarized. Her husband was at work, but she assured Keough that the home was her responsibility.

Her husband brought home the check and she dispersed it as was necessary.

"I know it sounds like an old-fashioned relationship," she said, protectively, "but it works for us."

She offered him coffee, which he accepted, and while he drank it he assured her the police would do their best to get her belongings back. She said that the police officer who had responded to her call told her to make a list, and she handed that list to Keough. He told her he would attach it to her report.

Before leaving the station house he had gotten directions to Clayton Road, near the Cheshire Inn. The desk officer told him that all he had to do was pull out of the station parking lot, turn right on Big Bend and take it to Clayton.

Eight minutes later the address he wanted was just about a hundred feet further on his left, a house with yellow shingles and green trim. The Amoco sign was further up the block, on the right, past the Cheshire Inn. He parked in front of it. The one shingle that wasn't yellow had the name of the company on it: First Choice Realty.

He walked to the door. There was a handwritten sign on a small piece of cardboard that said, "Ring and walk in."

He did and found himself in a small waiting room with chairs and magazines. To his right was a window, like in a doctor's office, only there was no glass separating him from the woman who stood behind it.

"Yes?" she asked. "Can I help you?" She had been seated at a desk but stood up to ask the question. She was young, in her early thirties, and very attractive. She had long brown hair, large, luminous eyes, a pretty mouth, and a long, lovely neck.

"Yes, my name is Detective Keough." He showed her his ID. "I called about speaking with Mr. Riverside."

"Of course," she said. "I'll tell him you're here."

"Just a minute," he said, stopping her before she could pick up the phone. "Are you Miss Bonny?"

"That's right."

"We spoke on the phone, also."

"Yes."

"Can you tell me anything about Mr. Sanders?"

"L-like what?" she asked, nervously.

"Well, what kind of guy he is? How well you knew him?"

"We work in the same place, that's all," she said, growing even more nervous. It was pretty clear to Keough that something had been going on, maybe a crush, perhaps even an office romance. He decided to leave it for later.

"Okay," he said, "you can ring Mr. Riverside now."

She nodded, picked up the phone, buzzed Riverside, and announced Keough.

"It's just through that door at the top of the stairs," she said, hanging up.

"Thank you."

He went through the doorway she indicated, directly across from the entrance, and saw the stairway. There were a couple of small offices behind the stairs, but he didn't see anyone in them. He went up the stairs and they wound around once before he got to the second floor. He was facing a large office and there was a man standing in the doorway.

"Detective Keough?"

"That's right."

The man put out his hand. He was about forty-five, very tall and thin, pale-skinned and sickly looking, but his handshake was very firm.

"I'm Carl Riverside, Detective," he said. "Please, come in."

They both entered the room. Riverside went behind his large oak desk, and Keough sat in a chair across from him.

"I hope I can help you," Riverside said.

"How long has William Sanders worked here, sir?" Keough asked, taking out a small notebook.

"Er, can you tell me something of what's happened, Detective Keough?"

"Not much, Mr. Riverside," Keough said. "It's an on-going investigation."

"I didn't, uh, see anything in the newspaper today."

"We haven't released anything to the papers," Keough said. "I'll just need you to answer some questions."

"Surely."

Keough hated when people said that.

"How long did he work here?"

"He's been here five years."

"Coming from where?"

"I'm not sure," he said. "Out of town, I think. I was not the one who hired him."

"I see. Would that be in his personnel file?"

"Why, yes."

"Could we get a copy of that up here?"

"Of course. I'll ask Miss Bonny to bring it up." He picked up the phone, buzzed downstairs and asked for the file.

"She'll be up shortly."

"That's fine. Uh, how long has Miss Bonny worked here?"

"Miss Bonny?" The man looked puzzled. "What does she have to do with—"

"She's very attractive."

"Yes, I suppose she is," Riverside said. "She's, uh, been with us about eighteen months."

"That's all?"

"Yes."

"Did you hire her?"

"As a matter of fact, I did."

"And did she work with Mr. Sanders?"

"She works with everyone in the office, at one time or another."

"I see. I assume she's single?"

"Look here," Riverside said, "I thought you were here about Bill Sanders?"

"I am," Keough said, "but like I said, Miss Bonny is very attractive."

"I don't think you should, uh, well—yes, as a matter of fact, I do believe she is single."

"Did she and Bill Sanders have something going?"

"I don't believe Miss Bonny would be, uh, seeing a married man."

As if on cue Miss Bonny appeared at the door. She stopped short, as if realizing she was the subject of their conversation.

Keough saw that her body matched her face. She was what he called not skinny. She was well built, with full breasts and solid legs and thighs, and she probably never spent time in a gym. She was certainly not built for a modeling runway, but bedrooms probably came to the minds of most men who saw her.

"Just give me the file, Miss Bonny, and you can go back to work."

"Yes sir."

Both Keough and Riverside watched her as she crossed the room, handed Riverside the file, and then walked out, again.

"What about Sanders?"

"What about him?"

"Does he go right home, or does he stop at a bar? Pick up a girl?"

"I don't know, Detective Keough."

"What about in the office?" Keough asked. "If not with Miss Bonny, maybe one of the other girls?"

"We only have two female employees in the office," Riverside said, "and Nora Downes has been married for thirty years."

"What about customers? Female customers?"

Riverside hesitated and Keough knew he had something.

"Sanders did—does very well with our female customers."

"I see."

"I'm not saying he sleeps with them to sell them houses."

"I understand."

"I'm just saying that he is charming. We usually let him handle the women who come in alone."

"So that was his specialty?"

"Inasmuch as he has one, yes."

"What about his overall sales record?"

Riverside shook his head.

"Not good," Riverside said. "He doesn't sell well to men, or to couples."

"Why has he worked here five years, then?"

"As I said before, Detective Keough," Riverside said, "I do not hire, and I do not fire."

"Aha," Keough said, "then who does?"

"Mr. and Mrs. Bentley."

"And who are Mr. and Mrs. Bentley?"

"They own this company."

"I think I see," Keough said, but just to make sure he asked, "How old are Mr. and Mrs. Bentley?"

"Jason Bentley is sixty-two," Riverside said, "and Cynthia Bentley—his second wife—is thirty-eight."

"I see," Keough said, standing up. "Would either of the Bentleys be here right now?"

"No," Riverside said. "Mr. Bentley rarely comes in."

"And Mrs. Bentley?"

"She is usually here, just not today. She, uh, is pretty much in charge of the day-to-day operations of the office."

"And what is your job?"

"I'm the manager."

"Mr. Riverside," Keough said, "I get the feeling you don't like Bill Sanders."

"Not very much, no."

"And his co-workers?"

"I can't think of anyone who actually likes Sanders," Riverside said, "except . . ."

"Except Mrs. Bentley?"

Riverside nodded.

"Can I get a look at Sanders' desk?"

"Of course," Riverside said, reaching for the phone. "I'll tell Miss Bonny to show it to you."

"Thanks for your time, Mr. Riverside," Keough said, standing and shaking the man's hand. "I'll see myself out."

Thirteen

WHEN KEOUGH GOT back downstairs he approached Miss Bonny's window.

"Mr. Riverside said you'd show me Bill Sanders' desk."

Her head had been bowed and at the sound of his voice she jerked it up and stared at him. Her eyes looked red, as if she'd been crying or, at least, holding tears back.

"Of course," she said. "This way."

She came around from behind her window and walked him back to the steps and to one of the offices he had seen beneath them earlier. There were two desks in the office. She walked to the one near the window and touched it.

"This is his," she said, her hand lingering. More and more Keough was getting the feeling that if there wasn't something going on between Sanders and Miss Bonny, she wished there was.

"Thank you," he said, moving around behind the desk. She didn't leave and he looked at her.

"I—I think I should stay."

Keough smiled at her and said, "Fine."

He went through the desk drawers and didn't find anything unusual for an office.

"What kind of man is Mr. Sanders?" he asked while opening and closing drawers.

"He's . . . a very nice man."

"Was he well liked in the office?"

"I . . . don't know what you mean."

Yes, she did, but she didn't want to say anything against the man.

"I was just wondering if he got along with the other salespeople, the other office workers."

"I'm . . . sure I wouldn't know."

"Well, how about you?" He finished going through the drawers, stood up straight, and looked at her. She wanted to stick around, so he figured he'd put some pressure on her.

"I . . . don't know what you mean?"

"I mean, you're a very pretty woman, Miss Bonny," Keough said. "Did Mr. Sanders try anything with you?"

One hand drifted up to her throat.

"He's a married man, Mr. . . . . Detective."

"Married men have been known to fool around a bit, Miss Bonny," he said. "Do you think Bill Sanders fooled around?"

"I . . . I should get back to work."

"I'll be done here shortly," he said.

She nodded, turned, and left, moving as if she was under water.

The woman was either in love with Sanders, or they were lovers. Nothing else would explain her attitude toward Keough.

Keough sat behind the desk and started examining the top. There were odds and ends, pens and pencils, slips of paper with notes written on them. He examined each piece, but there didn't seem to be anything that would be helpful to him.

He turned his attention to the man's Rolodex. He didn't know what he was looking for, but figured he'd know it when he saw it. Unfortunately, he didn't see it.

He thought about stealing the Rolodex, but he still had Marian Sanders' home phone book. He decided simply to go with that.

He left the office and went back out to the waiting room, where Miss Bonny was sitting behind her desk with her head down, one hand to her forehead.

"Just thought I'd let you know I'm finished," Keough said startling her again.

"Oh!" Her eyes were still red, and wet.

"Miss Bonny, is there something I can do for you?" he asked, gently.

"I . . . no . . . well, yes . . . is Bill—Mr. Sanders—is he . . . dead?"

"I don't honestly know," he said. "Mr. and Mrs. Sanders are both missing."

"I see. And Brady?"

"He's safe."

"That's . . . good."

"Miss Bonny, is there something you'd like to tell me before I leave?"

"N-no," she said, stammering a bit, "nothing I c-can think of."

He grabbed a business card from the counter and turned it over. He wrote his name and the number at the station and handed it to her.

"If you decide there is something you want to tell me, please give me a call."

She accepted the card.

"What's your first name?"

"A-Angela."

"Maybe Bill Sanders will need a friend, Angela. If he should call you, it would be in his best interests for you to call me."

"I—I don't know—"

"Just keep my number, Angela," Keough said. "We'll talk again another time."

He left the young woman with a blank, somewhat stunned look on her face.

Fourteen

Before going back to the Richmond Heights station Keough stopped at Barnes Hospital to see the victim and family of the victim of the assault. Their name was Foster.

The hospital was on the fringe of the West End, which he hadn't realized, or he might have waited to hit it on his way home.

The family was rightfully incensed that it had taken the police so long to come and talk to them. Keough saw no need to take the blame for it. He explained that he had just received the case, although he did not tell them that this was only his second day as a St. Louis cop. That would not have instilled confidence in them.

He questioned the victim, who was seventeen, and found out who had assaulted him. He made his notes and assured the victim and the family that he would make an arrest as soon as possible. After that it would go to the courts.

"Wait a minute," the mother said, putting her hand on her husband's arm for support. She was in her forties, overweight, with upper arms that flapped even when she breathed. Her husband was if anything, even heavier. The boy in the bed was obviously their son, and might possibly have been beaten up for it.

"Ma'am?" He looked up at her from his notebook. Her round face was flushed and there was a sheen of perspiration on her forehead and upper lip.

"You mean we have to go to court?"

"When I make an arrest, yes, ma'am. Your son will have to testify against the boys who beat him up."

"I ain't gonna," the boy said.

"Shut up!" the father said.

"But . . . he told you who they was," the woman said. "Why does he have to go to court?"

"Because he's pressing charges, ma'am," Keough said. "Somebody has to press charges against these boys."

"Don't the police do that?" she asked.

"No, ma'am," Keough replied, "the victim has to do that."

The Foster family exchanged glances, uncertainty etched on all their faces.

Keough put away his notebook. The boy's injuries were painful, but not serious. In fact, he had no broken bones.

"Why don't you all talk about it and let me know what you want to do?" he suggested. He opened the notebook again and wrote down the phone number of the Richmond Heights station, which he had already memorized. He tore the number out and handed it to the wife.

"Give me a call."

"We'll do that," the woman said, crumpling the piece of paper in her damp palm.

Keough felt certain he would not hear from them again.

When Keough got back to the station Detective Haywood was sitting at his desk.

"Saw you signed in this morning," Haywood said. "I was wondering where you were."

"There were two cases on my desk," Keough said. "I went out and did interviews. I also talked to someone about that case yesterday."

"The kid's parents that disappeared?"

"Right."

"What'd you find?"

"Somebody to talk to about the husband," Keough said. "I found where he works and talked to his boss."

Keough related his conversation to Haywood, making it short. He also told him about Miss Bonny, and his feeling that Sanders was a player when it came to women.

"You did all that today?"

Keough nodded.

"Got started early. Anything come up while I was away?"

"Nothing," Haywood said. "I was just getting caught up on some paperwork."

Keough understood that Haywood had started as a detective yesterday, same as he had. How much paperwork could there be to catch up on?

"What's your next move on the kid's case?" Haywood asked, curious.

"I've got to talk to him again," Keough said. "Where would they have him now?"

"That'd be downtown somewhere."

"Well," Keough said, "I'll have to find out."

"Day's almost over," Haywood pointed out.

Keough looked at his watch and saw that his shift was an hour from over. The three interviews he'd conducted had taken most of the day and he hadn't even stopped for lunch.

"Any good places to eat downtown?" he asked Haywood.

"Plenty. There are some great restaurants down in Laclede's Landing, by the Arch."

"I guess I'll check it out."

"Want some company?" Haywood asked.

Keough didn't want Haywood along. He didn't want the man to know he would be seeing the kid on his own time.

"That's okay," he said, "I think I'm just going to wander around down there and get the lay of the land. Maybe I'll have time to see the kid before the shift is up."

"But . . . you'll have to come back here to sign out."

"You can sign me out, can't you?" Keough asked. It was something that was done in New York all the time, but he didn't know how that would sit with Haywood.

"Well . . ."

"I'll owe you one, Haywood," he said. "The day will come when you'll want to get out of here early."

"What if I get caught?"

"Tell the truth," Keough said. "I went to interview the

kid and wanted to save having to come all the way back here. Who's going to mind?"

Haywood hesitated, then said, "I guess I could do it."

"Thanks," Keough said. "I appreciate it."

Keough checked his desk drawers and found a white pages phone book. He started looking for a number, paused at the child abuse and neglect hotline, then continued on until he found the Family & Children's Services listing. Under that heading he found the Missouri Division of Family Services. He made a call and found out where Brady Sanders would have been taken. He closed the book and returned it to the bottom drawer.

"Thanks again, Haywood."

"Sure thing, Keough," Haywood said. "I hope you find out something helpful."

"So do I," Keough said, and left the office.

Fifteen

IT WAS JUST about shift's end when Keough managed to locate Brady Sanders. There was a family services building on South Grand, which was not as far downtown as Haywood had indicated.

Keough presented himself at the building and showed his ID. He explained his involvement with the boy then waited for a family service counselor to come down and talk to him. The wait turned out to be well worth it. The counselor was a woman in her thirties, very smartly and attractively dressed in a blue skirt, white blouse, and medium heels. She had dark hair cut short and knew how to use makeup to make the most of what she had. She highlighted her lovely eyes and managed to de-emphasize a nose which some might have thought too big. Not a classic beauty, but certainly a head turner. She was tall, slender, high-breasted, with the kind of figure and movements that suggested exercise.

She introduced herself as Valerie Speck, and Keough noted when they shook hands that she wore no rings.

"How's Brady doing?" Keough asked.

"He seems to be doing quite well," Valerie Speck said.

"You sound surprised."

"To be frank, I am," she said. "Children this age usually ask for their parents very often."

"And Brady isn't?"

"Not once."

"How do you explain that?"

"I can't."

"Could it be the result of the trauma?"

"That's another thing I wondered," Valerie said, then paused abruptly. "I assume you want to see the boy?"

"I do."

"Can we go to my office first and talk?" she asked. "This is a very unusual case."

"Maybe Brady is just a very unusual boy."

"That's a possibility, Detective, that I have considered. Follow me, please."

Keough did so, with pleasure.

When they got to her office Keough thought that it was the equivalent of his, only she didn't have to share it with anyone. With the two of them in the room it seemed crowded, but he didn't mind. She was wearing a perfume he found particularly pleasant.

"Can I get you some coffee?" she asked.

"That'd be nice," he said. "Black. I missed lunch."

"Working hard?"

"Yes," he said. "Second day on the job."

She left the room and returned quickly with a mug of coffee, then sat behind her desk.

"You'll pardon me," she said, "but you seem, well, a little old to have started as a detective only yesterday."

"I started as a St. Louis detective yesterday," he said, and then explained that he had recently moved from New York and the New York City Police Department to St. Louis, and the Richmond Heights department.

"That explains the accent."

"Brooklyn," he said.

"St. Louis must seem rather tame by comparison."

"Not when you consider what I had to deal with yesterday, roughly one minute after I walked into the building."

"Could you tell me how this all started?"

"Sure."

He gave her an abbreviated explanation, starting with

Brady walking into the station with bloody feet and ending with the discovery of the blood-spattered house. He didn't pull any punches because he had the feeling that this lady didn't warrant it.

"My God," she said. "That's fantastic. And you can't find them?"

He shook his head.

"Do you think they're dead?"

"I think she might be," he said. "If she is, she'll turn up before he does."

"Why?"

"Because if he killed her, he's on the run and she's in one place. Somebody will stumble onto her, eventually."

"That's horrible."

"Yes, it is."

"But now I'm totally confused."

"About what?"

"About Brady's reaction."

"And exactly what reaction is that?"

"He's not exhibiting any kind of shock."

"Well," Keough said, "maybe he didn't see anything."

"But why isn't he asking for his parents?"

"Maybe," Keough said, "he doesn't care to see them again."

"If that's the case," she said, "it's even sadder."

"Can I see him?"

"Why?"

"I need to ask him some more questions."

"Of course," she said, "but I want to be present when you do."

He smiled at her and said, "I wouldn't have it any other way."

She made a phone call and then led Keough through a series of corridors to an interview room. It was furnished comfortably, with a sofa and a chair, a television, and a small plastic, yellow-and-blue child's table with toys on and around it. Brady was sitting at the table as they entered.

"Brady?" Valerie said.

The boy looked up at the sound of her voice, smiled when he saw her, then lost the smile when he saw Keough.

"Brady," Valerie said again, crouching down by him and touching his arm, "do you remember this man?"

Brady stared at Keough with wide eyes.

"I gave you a cookie yesterday morning, remember?"

The boy's eyes brightened and he said, "Cookie?"

"That's right." Keough put his hand into his jacket pocket. Before leaving the station he had gotten a package of chocolate chip cookies from the vending machine. He took it out now. "Would you like a cookie now?"

"Cookie," the boy said, nodding firmly.

"May I?" Keough asked Valerie.

"Of course."

Keough guessed from the way Brady looked at Valerie that she had already built up a rapport with him. He crouched down next to Valerie so that their shoulders were touching, and her scent was strong in his nostrils. He opened the pack of cookies and gave one to Brady.

"Brady, can you answer some questions for me?"

With his mouth full of cookie the boy nodded his head.

"I'll sit over here, on the sofa," Valerie said, and withdrew. Keough didn't know if she was speaking to him or to the child. He wondered if that was the secret to her success with children.

"Brady, did you see your mommy and daddy yesterday morning?"

The boy nodded. The question was simple, but Keough had no idea if the boy had any concept of yesterday, today, and tomorrow.

"What were they doing?"

Brady shrugged.

"Brady, did you see your daddy hit your mommy?"

Brady looked at Valerie. Keough did not turn his head to see what sort of response she was giving him.

"Brady? Did your daddy ever hit your mommy?"

Brady looked at Keough, swallowed his cookie, and nodded.

"Did he hit her yesterday?"

Brady stared at Keough and then said, "Cookie?"

"I'll give you another cookie after you answer, Brady."

That didn't seem to sit right with the boy, and suddenly Keough sensed him closing up.

"That wasn't a good idea," Valerie said.

Now Keough turned and looked at her.

"I guess not."

He handed Brady another cookie and the boy took it and then turned his attention to the toys in the room.

"You've lost him," Valerie said.

Keough turned his body now to face her.

"I really need to get some answers."

"I might be able to get them for you," she said, "if you tell me what the questions are."

She was sitting on the couch, her skirt riding up her thighs somewhat, her knees together. Nice knees.

"How about if I tell you over dinner?" he heard himself ask.

She gave him a slight frown, studied him for a moment, and then said, "I'll have dinner with you so we can talk about Brady."

"I understand."

"Do you?"

"Completely," he said. "Besides, I'm hungry and I have no idea where to go to eat."

"I know a few places," she said, standing up. He stood as well. "Will you wait here while I take Brady back?"

"Sure."

"I won't be long."

She waked over to Brady, spoke soothingly to him and picked him up.

" 'Bye, Brady," Keough said.

The boy waved good-bye to him, but did not speak as Valerie went out the door with him.

Sixteen

WHEN VALERIE SPECK returned she had put a jacket on over the blouse. It was the same blue as her skirt; it had gold piping, though, on the lapels and around the pockets.

"Do you like Korean food?" she asked.

"I like any food that's good."

"Grand Avenue is a haven of small ethnic restaurants. They're mostly Mexican or Asian."

"That's fine. We can take my car, and then I can bring you back here."

"Okay," she said, smiling. "Let's go."

She led him back through a maze of corridors and then downstairs until they were outside the building. He took the lead and led her to his car.

"Just keep driving straight," she said, when they got into the car. "It's about ten blocks and on the right."

"Okay."

As he started driving she asked, "Do you have children?"

"I've never been married."

She laughed and said, "That's not an answer these days."

"I guess not," he said, laughing with her. "No, I don't have any children. Why?"

"You seemed fairly comfortable talking to Brady."

"Did I?" he said. "An old cop's trick. I wasn't comfortable at all."

"You don't seem like such an old cop."

"I learned the trick from an old cop."

"Ah," she said, "that explains it."

Keough took a look at Grand Avenue while he drove. Left and right he saw little curio and antique shops, a lot of ethnic restaurants as Valerie had said, some book stores, and junk stores.

"It looks like an interesting area."

"It is," she said, "especially when there are street fairs. You can get all sorts of food, buy lots of junk, and get your tarot cards or palms read. It's just up here on the right. Park anywhere."

Keough found a space and parallel parked.

"You did that real well," she said, impressed. "Parking is not my strong point."

She had her door open and had stepped out before he could come around the car and open the door for her. He wondered if she'd let him open the door of the restaurant for her.

She did.

The smells that greeted them made Keough's stomach growl. Most of his experiences with Asian food were with Chinese. He was looking forward to this.

They were seated and a waiter came to take their order.

"I'll have what the lady is having," Keough said, waving away the menu.

"You'd like me to order for both of us?" she asked.

"Please."

"All right." She spoke to the waiter in dialect, which impressed Keough.

"How many languages do you speak?" he asked when the waiter left.

"I speak Castilian Spanish," she said, "which means I can get by with Mexicans, Cubans, Puerto Ricans, and Spaniards. Also a smattering of German, Italian, and very little Greek . . . and some Chinese."

"Didn't you just speak Korean?"

"No," she said. "The restaurant is Korean, but that waiter was Chinese."

"But you enjoy different ethnic foods, then?"

"I love them."

"And there are enough restaurants in St. Louis to keep you satisfied?"

"There are tons of restaurants in St. Louis," she said. "You'll find out."

"And is there a husband in this picture?" he asked.

"There was a husband at one time," she said, "but he is no longer in the picture."

"Deceased?"

She made a face and said, "From your mouth to God's ear."

Right then and there Keough decided he liked Valerie Speck a lot—in fact, maybe a little too much.

Seventeen

THE MOOD AFTER the comment about her husband could have been somber, even awkward, but they managed to avoid that. Valerie even asked Keough to explain how he had come to move from New York to St. Louis.

"It doesn't sound like a typical New Yorker's move," she said.

"Maybe I'm not a typical New Yorker," he replied. "What is a typical New Yorker, anyway?"

"Someone who was born there—"

"Guilty."

"—lived there all their life—"

"Guilty, to a point."

"—who couldn't imagine living anywhere else."

Keough hesitated.

"Guilty?" she asked.

"Up to a point."

"What point?"

He hesitated again before answering.

"The point where there's just no way you can continue in your job, and there's no other job you can do."

"Being a policeman you mean?"

"A detective."

"Oh," she said, "excuse me. I didn't think that was a sore—"

"It isn't," he said, "I'm just stating a fact. I came here to start over and to work as a detective. If they had wanted me to start back in uniform, I couldn't have done it."

"What would you have done then?"

"I probably would have gone on being a detective, privately."

"But luckily you got this job."

"Yes," he said, "but not without some help. I have a friend here in St. Louis who got me the interview."

"And then you got yourself the job."

"Yes."

"Good for you." She picked up her glass of wine and held it aloft. "Here's to starting over."

He picked up his wine, clinked glasses, and drank.

"I know something about that," she said putting her glass down.

"About starting over?"

She nodded.

"Ten years of marriage to the wrong man and I finally got it into my head."

"That marriage was a mistake?"

"Not marriage itself," she said, "marriage to Don."

"I see. So you'd get married again? Not that this is a proposal," he hurriedly added.

"I didn't think it was. Yes, I would get married again,

if and when I find the right man. Meanwhile I've got a job I like, that I'm good at . . . which I should be doing right now."

"Brady," he said.

"Yes. There's something very wrong with that little boy, Joe."

They'd moved onto a first-name basis during the first course of dinner.

"He seems fine."

"That's just it," she said. "He shouldn't be. He saw something—"

"Maybe he didn't."

"No, he did."

"How do you know?"

"I feel it. Remember, I said I was good at this."

"All right," he said. "He saw something. He probably couldn't have gotten that blood all over his feet and *not* seen something."

"You're going to have to find out what it was," she said, "or I am. I can find out from him, maybe, if I can get through to him."

"The only way I can find out is to find his parents," he said, "one or both."

"One or both may be dead."

"Yes."

"Then we'll both just have to go at it from our respective sides," she said. "One of us may be able to help the other."

"Yes."

"We'll work on it together, then."

He liked that idea. It meant he'd get to see her again.

"Yes," he said.

He drove her back to her building to get her car. They had split the bill at dinner since, she said, they were both working. He didn't bother to tell her that he was off the clock.

"What will you do now?" she asked, as she got out of his car.

"Keep looking for Sanders," he said.

"Not Marian?"

"I think Marian's dead, Valerie."

"Why don't you think Bill is dead?"

He hesitated a moment, then said, "The way I reconstructed things at the house, he's alive."

"If he is," she said, "you'll find him."

"I'll do my best."

"Keep in touch with me, okay?"

"I will."

"Together, maybe we can help this little boy."

"He's lucky to have you in his corner, Valerie."

She smiled and said, "I've been thinking that about you all evening, Joe. Goodnight."

She closed the door and he watched her walk to her car, a Toyota Camry, get in, and drive away. He almost decided to follow her to see where she lived, but decided against it. His third week in town, second day on the job, he really shouldn't have been thinking about a woman.

Not even one as attractive and interesting as Valerie Speck.

Eighteen

WHEN KEOUGH GOT home he took his mail out of the mailbox and carried it inside with him. He leafed through the ads and the bills, looking for something interesting. There were two items that caught his eye. The first was a letter from a little girl in Brooklyn. The other was a package from his friend, Mike O'Donnell.

O'Donnell had been a columnist for the *New York Post* while Keough was a New York cop. The same case had cost both of them their jobs. While Keough had come to St. Louis, O'Donnell had gone south to Florida—Key West. His aim at the time was to write the book about the case. He'd written true crime books before, and had made the best seller list once. His publisher was looking for him to do it again, and O'Donnell was hoping that the Kopykat case would do it.

Keough opened the brown envelope and took a book out. O'Donnell had called it *Kopykat*. The cover showed two silhouettes facing away from each other. They represented the two serial killers Keough had caught, the Lover and Kopykat.

Keough was surprised that the book was out already. It had only been a year since the two killers had been caught.

Inside the book he found a publicity release and a letter from O'Donnell. The release told Keough that what he had in his hands was an early copy of the book. The official publication date of the book was still a month away.

The letter from O'Donnell was two typed paragraphs:

Dear Joe,

Here it is, buddy. Just so you know all that effort wasn't for nothing. I appreciated your help. You'll notice that you are mentioned; although, as you asked, I didn't make you into a supercop—I don't think. Let me know what you think.

Hope all is well for you in St. Louis. Key West is quiet—maybe too quiet. I guess the same might be true for the Midwest, huh? Keep in touch. I should be at this address for another few months—I think.

Take care,
Mike

Keough turned the book over and looked at the back cover. There were some reviews and quotes from O'Donnell's past books. He looked at the front cover and saw a quote from another true crime writer saying how he enjoyed it.

Inside he saw more reviews and quotes: *The New York Times*, *Newsweek*, the *Los Angeles Times*, Mike McAlary, Anthony Bruno, John Dillman, and others. Keough was glad for his friend that the book had been received so well. Now he only hoped that it would sell well and get O'Donnell back on the best-seller list.

He put the book aside, vowing to read it later—or at least leaf through it to find his name and see what kind of treatment his friend had given him.

Now he turned his attention to the other letter.

It was from Cindy Valentine. She and her mother, Nancy, had lived in the apartment across from Keough's in his building in Brooklyn. He and the little girl had formed a friendship before the Kopykat case, but during it he and Nancy had grown closer. When the case was over it seemed like they were going to have something, but it quickly soured, and Keough knew why.

It only took a couple of weeks for O'Donnell to take the material Keough supplied him to his publisher and get the okay to do the book. It was a month later when the department found out that O'Donnell was doing the book. They tried to squash it, but O'Donnell's publisher stood behind him all the way.

Keough went through the motions of putting through his papers for early retirement, but he knew the checks would never arrive. Somehow they got fouled in the system. He could have hired a lawyer and taken the New York City Police Department to court, but he decided against it. O'Donnell told him he was nuts, and even Nancy Valentine told him he should fight, but in the end Keough just let it go. Thanks to O'Donnell cutting him in on twenty percent of his advance, he was able to relax for a while, until he decided what he was going to do.

"There'll be more, once the royalties and foreign sales start coming in—and if there's a movie," O'Donnell told him, "you'll be rich."

Keough didn't care much about the money, though. That wasn't what his life was about. He loved being a cop, specifically being a detective, but he couldn't do that anymore, not in New York.

From the point in time when he ceased being a cop he stopped being the Joe Keough who Nancy Valentine fell in love with. By the time he was ready to leave New York for St. Louis they were done. Cindy Valentine, however, did not give up as easily, as evidenced by the letter he held.

He read it quickly, two long, single-spaced paragraphs of sloppy typing telling him how much she missed him, what she was doing with her life, and asking him to write back.

He put the letter aside and picked up the book. What he held in his hand was the reason he was no longer a New York City detective. It was a conscious decision on his part. He did what he thought was right, knowing full well that it would cost him the job he loved. He'd lucked out getting this job in St. Louis, but what would he do if the same situation arose here? Would he do the right thing, or would he keep his job?

He put the book down next to the letter and went to the kitchen.

Nineteen

August 24, 1997

HE WAS IN the mall twenty minutes before he picked her out. She was a fine specimen, tall, firmly built, sporting just a little bit of belly, probably left over from her pregnancy. Given time he knew she'd firm that up.

He had become an expert on them, these young mothers with their long blond hair, fair skin, glowing embers of fine hairs on their arms and backs. He could tell from looking at them how long ago they had delivered, how old the child in the stroller was, without even looking at the child.

This mother was wheeling a three-month-old around the Crestwood Mall. Crestwood was real handy to Shrewsbury and Webster Groves residents. It was not as large as some of the malls, but it was extremely popular because of the arcade on the lower level.

He watched the woman for half an hour to be sure she was alone and there wasn't a husband, boyfriend, sister, or mother somewhere. Sometimes they were at the mall with a girlfriend, but this young mother seemed to be here all alone—just her and her baby.

Perfect.

* * *

Al Bennett was thirty-eight. He had worked for the Sumner Brothers' Hauling Company for the past eight years, and during those eight years he had learned to look before he dumped—especially when it came to Dumpsters in neighborhoods like Richmond Heights. In the past he'd found working televisions, VCRs, things people threw away you wouldn't believe.

This day, though, was the first time he had ever found a baby.

The phone on Keough's desk rang. He'd been sitting there hoping it would. It had been three days since a decent case had crossed his desk—and a month since the Brady Sanders case had been taken away from him. A month and still the father hadn't turned up, nor was there any sign of the mother, who he was still convinced was dead somewhere.

He'd done some surveillance on Miss Bonny from Bill Sanders' office, hoping that maybe she'd lead him to Sanders, but nothing had come of it, and he had to suspend it after a few days. He couldn't justify spending his time on it, and he wasn't yet so deep into the case that he was willing to spend his own time working on it.

All of that became moot, however, when he was called in by Detective Sergeant Bilcheck.

"The Sanders case," Bilcheck said.

"What about it?"

"It's being transferred over to Major Case."

"Why?"

"It's an obvious violent crime."

"Do they take all violent crimes?"

"Most of them."

"Why this one?"

"Because they want it."

Bilcheck did not seem happy about this, so Keough was careful to voice his objection without snapping at the man.

"It's been a violent crime right from the beginning," he said. "Why do they want it now?"

"I don't know, Keough," Bilcheck said. "I've been informed by the chief that the case is now in the hands of the Major Case Squad. I told him I didn't like it. I told him that you've done all of the preliminary footwork and should be allowed to continue with the case. Apparently, he didn't agree."

"Would it do any good to argue with him?"

"No," Bilcheck said. "You can try, but no. He's usually pretty inflexible about things like this."

And so the case went to Major Case, and it was no longer Keough's job to worry or wonder about Brady Sanders, his mother, and his dad.

But he did . . .

The ringing phone was insistent.

"Detective Keough," he said into it.

"Uh, yeah, this is Officer Foster, Detective, in Communications?" It was a woman's voice.

"What do you need, Officer?"

"Well, sir, somebody just called in that they found a body."

"Did you send a car to check it out?"

"I'm sending one, but I thought you might be interested in this."

"Why would I be?" Keough asked. Maybe it was a woman's body. Maybe Marian Sanders' body had finally surfaced. "Is the body male or female?"

"I didn't say body," Foster said.

"I could have sworn—" Keough started, then stopped. He looked around the empty room. He was still working with Detective Haywood, who had gone out on some kind of call. "If you didn't say body, Officer Foster, what did you say?"

"Baby, sir," Foster replied. "I said somebody found a baby."

Keough hung up and left his desk.

He got the address from Foster in Communications and took his own car. He'd been using a department vehicle, an unmarked Crown Victoria, but there were only two of them, and one was a clunker. It was first come, first serve with the cars and Haywood had gotten the good one that day. Keough had a hand-held radio with him and set it down on the passenger seat as he started his car.

The development was about a mile from the station house, across from the Galleria Mall, which was helpful. Keough had managed to learn the neighborhood pretty well during the past month—mostly because he'd been driving around the streets trying to find some sign of Bill or Marian Sanders.

He hadn't seen Valerie Speck since their dinner, but

he'd talked to her on the phone half a dozen times since then, mostly about Brady. Every once in a while, though, he managed to interject some personal information. He'd been pretty busy for a while, and then when things slowed down for him she became busy, and the time just never arrived for him to ask her out. He kept track of Brady, though, who had been placed with a foster family living in Arnold, wherever the hell that was.

Keough arrived at the scene and pulled his car into the parking lot of the development. He spotted the big green refuse truck, with a Richmond Heights police car parked next to it, as well as a St. Louis County car, both with the lights flashing. Everybody responded when a child was involved, that was the same in St. Louis as well as New York. A crowd had gathered, so he couldn't get near the truck with his car. He pulled into a nearby parking space, didn't bother to straighten the car, and walked over to where the crowd was assembled.

". . . ought to get it out of there," someone was saying.

As Keough got closer he heard the baby crying. The sound had probably been muffled by the Dumpster and the trash in it.

"Excuse me," he said, flashing his badge, "can I get by, please?"

Once he was through the crowd he hung his shield from his pocket and approached the two uniformed men.

"Is that baby still in the Dumpster?" he demanded.

"Yes, sir," one of the officers said.

"Why, for God's sake?"

"We were, uh, waiting for a supervisor," the other man said. He was the St. Louis County cop.

"Jesus," Keough said. "Give me a hand, will you?"

He approached the Dumpster and the two officers boosted him up into it. It was filled most of the way and solidly packed, so he was able to stand. The baby was lying on its back on a blanket, but it wasn't wrapped, the blanket was simply beneath it. It stopped crying when it saw Keough.

"How you doing, little one?" he asked.

The baby looked at him and started to cry again. The blanket was yellow, but the child's outfit was pink, which meant it was probably a girl.

"Who did this to you, huh?" He bent over and lifted the child, leaving the blanket, which was soiled, behind. As he stood up, the crowd broke into applause.

"What is it?" somebody yelled.

"It's a girl," Keough called back.

"Is she all right?" a woman asked.

"She looks fine, for now." He looked at the officers. "Did you call for an ambulance?"

"Uh, no," one of them said, "we were, uh, waiting for the captain."

"Call an ambulance now," Keough said.

They turned to go to their cars.

"One of you!" he shouted. "The other one can help me out of here with this baby."

The two men looked at each other, then one continued to his car while the other one turned back.

"Take the baby," Keough said. The man was from Richmond Heights, but he didn't look familiar. He was going to need more time before he got to know the men in the Richmond Heights station, even though there was only a total of thirty-nine, including the supervisors and chiefs. He'd worked single tours of duty in Brooklyn where there were thirty-nine people on duty just for that tour.

"Huh?" The man reacted as if Keough had asked him to hold a steaming turd.

"Hold her while I get out."

"I, uh, don't know how—"

"Let me," a woman said, as she stepped forward and actually pushed the officer aside.

"Thank you," Keough said, handing her the child and climbing out of the Dumpster.

The woman was in her forties, and held the child with practiced ease.

"Do you know her, ma'am?"

"No, I don't," the woman said, "but I wish I did. She's a cute little thing."

The child had stopped crying once Keough placed her in the woman's arms. He noticed that she had placed her fingers by the child's mouth, and the baby was avidly gnawing on them.

"This child is starving," the woman said.

"How about the rest of you?" he called out. "Does anyone know this child?"

The crowd moved forward so everyone could take a look, but no one could identify the child.

"What's going to happen to her?" the woman asked.

"Well, she'll go to the hospital first, to be checked out, and then we'll try to identify her."

"And if you can't?"

"Then the child welfare department will have to take over."

"Will you feed her?" the woman asked. "This child looks like she hasn't eaten in days."

"I'll see she's fed as soon as we get to the hospital, ma'am."

"Who would do such a thing to a child?" the woman asked. "It's a sin."

"It's a crime, ma'am," Keough said, "and we'll find out who did it."

Twenty

THE ANGER THAT went through him was intense. He'd planned so carefully, watched her for the better part of an hour, and just when he thought she was perfect this had to happen.

He'd followed the young, blond mother to the food court, thinking that she was going to have lunch alone, and suddenly she met another mother with a stroller. This one was not his type at all, though. She had black hair. He hated women with black hair, especially ones like this. Oh, she was pretty enough. She had a solid body beneath a blue denim dress, worn short to show off her athlete's legs. But she was the type who had dark hairs on her arms, and when she reached out to feed her baby he saw that she also had dark hair in her armpits.

This kind of woman made him sick, and now to top it off, she was in his way.

He decided to take a seat at a nearby table and see if maybe they would split up again after lunch. He tried to control his anger while he watched them, but he knew the only thing that would make it go away was if that woman went away.

"Geek alert," Marie Tobin said.

"Where?"

"Don't turn your head. He's sitting at a table to your right, behind the woman with the three screaming kids."

Debra Morgan turned her head slightly and saw the man her friend was talking about. He was wearing a T-shirt and jeans and had long, lank hair and a rather intense look on his face. He had very high cheekbones, which hollowed out his cheeks a great deal, and a thin-lipped mouth that was made even thinner by his expression. He wasn't eating anything, but was just sitting by himself. He appeared to be looking around, but his gaze always came back to them. This didn't surprise Debra. She knew that both she and Marie were pretty, but he was probably looking at Marie. She even admitted herself that she was slutty-looking, while Debra was more genteel in appearance.

"Of course," Marie had said to her once, "we could change all that with some makeup and an attitude adjustment."

Debra had declined her friend's offer.

"Oh, he doesn't look like such a geek," Debra said, kindly.

"Take my word for it," Marie said. "The only thing I don't know is if he's looking at you or at me. I guess that depends on whether he likes blondes or brunettes." She touched her dark, shoulder-length hair.

Her blond friend laughed and said, "I'm just as happy if he's looking at you, Marie."

The two women made sure their respective children—Marie's son Toby and Debra's daughter Alexa—had their bottles firmly in place before turning their attention to the Greek salads they'd both bought.

"Are things still bad at home, Deb?"

"They're not *bad* . . ." Debra said, lamely.

"Still no sex?"

Debra shook her head.

"Allan treats me like I'm his . . ."

"Mother?"

Debra nodded.

"It's not that you're like his mother, Deb," Marie said, "but that you *are* a mother. He's just looking at you differently."

"Did that happen with you and Will?"

"Oh, yes," Marie said, "it's still happening. Men are such children themselves, especially around a mother. You should do what I'm doing."

"What's that?"

Marie just smiled.

"You're not!" Debra said, shocked.

"I am."

"With who?"

"You'll never guess." Marie looked so smug.

"Who? Don't keep me in suspense." Debra was pleading. She needed some excitement in her life and she was too chicken to go out and get her own.

"The UPS man."

"No!"

Marie Tobin nodded, looking very satisfied with herself.

"Why? How? What's he look like? Oh, God, I want all the details," Debra said, over her shock but still excited by the news.

"I thought you would," Marie said, and leaned forward to give them to her.

He watched the two women put their heads together. He just knew they were talking about him. What were they saying? he wondered. Did they like the way he looked? Maybe they'd both be interested . . . but no. He couldn't even think about doing anything with the dark girl. The blonde, though, she was perfect. She looked just like the one in the movie—she *was* the one in the movie, with her hair down her back and her bare legs . . .

He willed them to finish their salads and go their separate ways. He had an erection that was almost painful, and swore he could *smell* the blond woman from across the room.

She was as ready as he was.

He knew it!

He watched them until they finished their lunch, and then they left the food court together. Instead of taking the elevator they took the escalator, even though there were signs clearly stating that strollers were not permitted on them. Why did people think they could just ignore signs like that? That kind of arrogance drove him crazy, and he was sure that it was the brunette's doing, not the blonde's. The dark-haired mother got on the escalator first, and the poor blonde simply followed her.

She was easily led astray. This made her even more precious to him.

He went up the escalator after them, keeping a safe distance. They walked together to the parking lot exit near the Pasta House Co. and left the mall together.

He watched as they went down one aisle and then he moved to the next and kept them in sight. There was still a chance that they would reach the friend's car first and then he'd have free access to the blonde.

But even in this she spoiled it for him. They reached the blonde's car first and the other one stood there with her, waiting for her to get in.

He was incensed! There was nothing he could do to quell it. It would eat him alive if he didn't release it somehow, and he knew just how to do it. The bitch deserved it.

As the blonde pulled her little Honda out of her parking space and drove off, the dark-haired bitch walked a little further to her car, which—of course—was a van. On top of everything else she was one of the legion of van bitches that had begun to pop up more and more. He *hated* van bitches. When he found the perfect woman for him he wouldn't touch her if she went to a van.

As he followed and watched her start to put her child in the van, he realized this was probably for the best. The urge had come too soon this time. It was only a few days since the last one, and this action probably would have gotten him in a lot of trouble. As it turned out, the bitch had probably done him a favor, but he still felt the need to vent his anger.

He reached her as she was putting the stroller into the van. She was parked out of sight of the mall and standing on the passenger side. No one would see what happened next.

He approached her and said, "Excuse me?"

She was half in the van and off balance as she looked over at him.

"Yes? Hey, you're—" she started, straightening up, but she had no chance to finish.

He punched her in the right eye.

She yelled, grabbed her eye with one hand, and fell to the ground hard. She put her other hand out to catch herself, and there was an audible snap of a bone as she landed.

"Bitch!" he spat at her, and quickly walked away, leaving her crying on the ground.

Twenty-one

"Is THIS GOING to become a habit with you?" Valerie Speck asked Keough.

"It's my way of getting to see you again."

There was silence on the other end of the line. Keough waited, and was about to speak when she beat him to it.

"If you want to see me again," she said, "all you have to do is ask."

"That means I have to call you at work."

Another silence, this one shorter.

"Here's my home number."

She gave it to him and he wrote it down.

"How's the baby?"

"She's fine," Valerie said. "Did you know that she's the second one?"

"Second one what?"

"Second baby found in a Dumpster."

"No," Keough said, with great interest. "I didn't know. Where was the other one found?"

"Wait . . ." He waited, wondering what the connection could be between two infants left in Dumpsters in different parts of the city—if they were found in different parts.

"Here it is," she said. "South County, Mehlville, to be exact."

"Where the hell is that?"

"South," she said, laughing.

"You're smart," he said. "I like that in a woman."

"Let me know what happens, will you?"

"You can bet on it."

They said good-bye and hung up. He turned in his chair and looked at Haywood.

"South," Haywood said. "There's a couple of ways you could go, but from here I'd say . . ."

Keough wrote down Haywood's directions and then asked, "Who covers that?"

"The county."

He then pulled out a phone book and looked up the number for the St. Louis County police.

"This is Detective Keough with the Richmond Heights department. I need to speak to a detective."

"Which one?"

"Whoever's on duty," Keough said.

There was a series of clicks and then a man's voice said, "This is Detective Womack."

"This is Detective Keough, from Richmond Heights. I'm trying to find out something about a baby that was found in a Dumpster out there."

"I remember that," Womack said, "but it's not my case."

"Can you tell me whose it is?"

"Hold on."

After a few moments of silence Womack came back.

"That was caught by Barry Gardner, but he's not on today."

"When is he working?"

"I'll check the chart . . . hmm, looks like he'll be back in two days. That's Friday."

"Listen, I need to talk to him before then," Keough said. "Can I get his home phone?"

"Can't do that," Womack said, "but I can call him and have him call you."

"Fine. Can you do that today?"

"I can try. Where are you?"

"I'm at the Richmond Heights station."

"I'll tell him," Womack said. "He'll call you there. He's got kids, too, and this case is tearing him up."

Good, Keough thought as he hung up, maybe Gardner would call back soon. He and Womack agreed that the Mehlville detective would leave a message with Gardner's wife if the man wasn't home.

"Give him my home phone, too," Keough said, and recited it.

"Got it," Womack said.

"Thanks."

"Sure."

Keough hung up.

"Think they're connected?" Haywood asked, from behind him.

Keough swiveled his chair around.

"I don't like coincidences," Keough said, "but they do happen."

"What if a third one turns up?"

"Then we'll have too much of a pattern to ignore," Keough said.

He turned and dialed Valerie Speck's number again.

"I'm flattered," she said, "you're calling again so soon. You don't have another baby, do you?"

"No, but I'm still interested in that first one."

"Did you talk to the detective from South County?"

Keough explained that he'd left a message, but he wanted to know from Valerie if there were any other Dumpster babies.

"Not here," she said, "but I can check around and get back to you."

"Thanks," Keough said. "I'll owe you dinner."

"I'll collect," she said, and hung up with the promise to call back as soon as she knew something.

At that moment a uniformed cop stuck his head in and said, "Keough?"

"Yeah?"

"Chief wants to see you."

"The chief, or the major?"

He still hadn't gotten used to calling somebody Major. Since Major O'Connell was also the assistant chief, he tended to think of him as "Chief."

"*The* chief."

The man withdrew before Keough could think of a dodge.

"Probably just wants to be briefed," Haywood said.

"Yeah," Keough said, standing up. "Listen, I'm waiting for some calls. If they come in—"

"Want me to take a message?"

"No," Keough said, "tell them to hold on and then come and get me."

"In the chief's office?"

"That's where I'll be."

"Why don't I just take—"

"Tony," Keough said, "just call over there and ask for me. You can talk to the chief's secretary."

"Okay," Haywood said. "Okay, I can do that."

"Thanks."

Keough left the office and started for the chief's office. The man probably wanted to know if Keough was intending to open a daycare center in the station. It was odd that the two cases which seemed as if they were going to require the most of Keough's time involved kids.

Twenty-two

As KEOUGH ENTERED the chief's office the man's head was down, examining something on his desk. He stood just in front of his superior's desk and waited. Eventually, Chief Harold Pellman lifted his head.

"Jesus," he said, startled, "are you always that quiet?"

"Sorry, Chief," Keough said. "You were, uh, occupied."

"Sit down, Keough."

"Yes, sir."

"Tell me about the baby in the Dumpster."

"My report will be on your desk in the morning."

"I'd like to hear about it now."

Briefly, Keough gave the story to the man, who listened intently and waited for the end to ask questions.

"No one was able to identify the baby on the spot?"

"No."

"What about reports of missing kids?"

"I'm checking that."

"Who'd do a sick thing like put a baby in a Dumpster?"

"A sick person. Oh, and there's another twist."

"What's that?"

"Well, apparently this is the second baby found in a Dumpster."

"In Richmond Heights?"

"No," Keough said, "the first one was found in South County, a place called Mehlville."

"That's the county. Have you talked with anyone there, yet?"

"I have a call in to the detective who handled that case," Keough said. "I'm waiting for him to call me back."

"Keep me apprised of the situation."

"I will, sir."

"Thank you," Chief Pellman said. "That's all."

"Yes, sir."

But Keough didn't leave.

"Is there something else?"

"Yes, sir, there is. The Sanders case."

"Which case is that?"

"The child who came walking into the station? The missing parents, with blood in the house?"

"What about it?" Keough still wasn't sure the chief knew what he was talking about.

"I was wondering why the case was taken away from me and given to Major Case?"

"That's what Major Case does, Detective," the chief said. "They investigate major crimes of violence."

"There's no evidence that a major crime was committed here, sir."

"There's the blood, and the missing parents."

"That's circumstantial—"

"We're not in court here, Detective. It was decided that Major Case would take over that case. That's all there is to it."

Keough bit his tongue. If this had happened in New York he would have given more of an argument, but he was new here and was still trying to fit in.

"Is that all now, Detective?"

"Yes, sir," Keough said, "that's all."

He stood up, and before he could even leave the chief's attention was turned back to whatever was on his desk.

When Keough got back to the squad office Haywood was talking to a woman who had a fairly recent black eye. She was brunette and young, wearing a sundress, and except for the shiner she was very attractive. He also noticed that her left forearm was sporting a cast.

She was sitting in a chair next to Haywood's desk, and next to her was an infant sleeping in a stroller.

". . . no provocation at all?" Haywood asked.

"None," the woman said.

"He just walked up to you in the parking lot and hit you?"

"He said, 'Hey,' or something like that. I turned and he punched me."

"Excuse me for saying this," Haywood said, leaning forward, "but you're a very attractive woman. Did he come on to you in the mall?"

"No," she said. "I never saw him before . . . well, yes, I did."

"Where?"

"In the mall, in the food court. He was watching me and my girlfriend."

"Watching you *or* your girlfriend? Or both of you?"

"I don't know," she said, annoyed. "That would depend on if he liked blondes or brunettes better."

"Your girlfriend is a blonde?"

"Yes." She bit the word off testily.

"What's her name?"

"Why do you need her name?"

"If he attacked you," Keough said, stepping in, "maybe he'll attack her if he sees her again. You wouldn't want that to happen, would you?"

She turned and looked over her shoulder at Keough. With her in that position Keough could see right down her dress. She was extremely attractive and well built. He could also see that her eye was swollen almost completely shut. Somehow it was even more painful looking at an injury on a beautiful young woman.

"No, I wouldn't."

"You give us her name and we'll see that she's warned."

"All right."

Keough nodded to Haywood.

"Hey," Haywood said to him, and then to the woman, "excuse me. That call you were waiting for came in."

"You didn't call me?"

"Couldn't," Haywood said, and inclined his head at his complainant. "His number's on your desk. He said he'd be there."

"Okay, thanks."

Keough sat at his desk and dialed the number of the detective in Mehlville. They arranged to meet at a restaurant in South County the next morning for breakfast.

As Keough hung up, Haywood was finishing with the woman.

"My husband's going to kill me," she said, standing.

"Why?" Haywood asked. "You can't help it if someone assaulted you."

"He's always warning me about . . . about strange men, and about going out alone."

"You were in the parking lot of a mall in the middle of the day for Chrissake," Haywood said, and then quickly added, "excuse me . . . but how can he blame you for this?"

"He will."

"Do you need someone to drive you home, ma'am?" Keough asked.

"I took a cab here," she said. "I can't do much driving with this arm and this eye."

"Detective Haywood here will run you home, ma'am. He can also talk to your husband, if you're worried."

Keough gave Haywood a look, and the young detective nodded and rose hurriedly. In point of fact, he welcomed the opportunity to spend some time talking to the young woman. Injury or no, she was a knockout as far as he was concerned. Maybe she wasn't completely happy with her husband and would welcome some extra-personal care.

"I'll be happy to do that, Mrs. Morgan."

"M-maybe that would be best," she conceded. She looked at Keough and said, "Thank you . . ."

"Detective Keough, ma'am."

"Thank you, Detective Keough. Do you think there's any chance you can catch this guy before he attacks someone else?"

"We'll do out best, Mrs. Morgan. I promise you that."

She nodded and Haywood ushered her out, following her, taking just enough time to raise his eyebrows at Keough and mouth a "Thank you."

Twenty-three

THE RESTAURANT WAS called Gingham's, and it featured family-style cooking. It was located on Lindberg Boulevard just off Lemay Ferry Road. Det. Barry Gardner was already there, sitting in a booth in the smoking section. He was a big, red-faced, white-haired man in his fifties, which was how he had described himself to Keough. The man was nothing if not accurate at self-description. Although he was off duty, he had agreed to meet Keough at a place of his choice.

"Detective Gardner?" Keough said, standing by the booth.

Gardner looked up and smiled.

"Keough?"

"That's right."

"Have a seat."

"Thanks."

Keough slid into the booth opposite the man.

"I understand you've got a case similar to mine," Gardner said.

"That's right."

"Tell me about it."

Before he could a pleasant-faced blond woman in her midforties appeared at the booth.

"You gonna eat today, Barry?"

"You know it, Dotty. I'll have the usual."

"Country-fried steak and eggs, and a short stack," the woman said.

"Right."

Keough's stomach turned as he thought about country-fried steak at that moment.

"How about you, handsome?"

"Just a short stack," he said.

"Something to drink?"

"Coffee, and orange juice."

"Are you a friend of Barry's?"

"He's on the job, Dotty."

"Don't that make you friends? I'll get your orders, guys."

As Dotty walked away, Keough told Gardner about the child that had been found in a Dumpster.

"Where was the Dumpster?" Gardner asked.

"In an apartment complex."

"Mine, too," Gardner said.

"Think we've got a serial here?" Keough asked. The word *serial* or the phrase *serial killer* were bad words in the New York City P.D. He didn't know if that would be the case here in Missouri.

"A serial what? Baby snatcher?" Gardner asked. "And what does he do with them before he puts them in the Dumpster?"

"Maybe nothing," Keough said.

"Then what—"

"Maybe he does something to the mothers."

"The mothers?"

"He's got to be snatching the babies from somebody," Keough said.

"The mothers," Gardner said again, as if mulling the suggestion over.

"Anyone claim the baby?" Keough asked.

"Not yet."

"Anyone report a young mother missing?"

Gardner rubbed his jaw.

"I didn't check."

They were silent for a moment.

"I feel like a horse's ass," Gardner said then. "We looked for the baby's mother and family, but only to claim it."

"Maybe you better check hospitals and morgues for young women in their twenties and thirties."

"Shit," Gardner said.

"What?"

"Women are havin' kids in their forties now, too."

"You're right," Keough said. "I'm going to do the same thing, mothers in their twenties, thirties, or forties."

"I'll do it," Gardner said.

"Let's also have someone canvass those apartment complexes. Maybe someone saw something, like a stranger poking around a Dumpster."

"Okay."

"Can we keep in contact on this, Gardner?" Keough asked.

"Yeah, sure," Gardner said, "I guess maybe I need a keeper."

"Maybe just some help," Keough said.

Dotty came with their food and Gardner asked Keough where he was from. He explained that he had come here from New York, and the New York Police Department, but didn't go into the circumstances. To his credit, Gardner didn't ask. He did ask how Keough was liking St. Louis, and Keough said he was liking it fine.

Gardner told Keough his life story, but Keough doubted he'd remember most of it an hour later. He had the habit of tuning people out when they started talking about themselves. They never seemed to notice, anyway. He'd hear about every other word, and when something seemed to need comment, or when the person stopped, he'd pay attention again.

All he really retained was that Gardner had been a cop for thirty years in St. Louis, and a detective for the past five years.

They each got separate checks and paid them at the register. Gardner waved good-bye to Dotty who, Keough had surmised, knew nearly everyone who was eating in the place at that time of day.

"Have a good day, guys!" she called out. "Come on back."

Outside Gardner shook hands with Keough.

"I'll get right on it at my end, Keough," he said. "Thanks for, uh, bringin' it to my attention."

"Hopefully, between the two of us we can solve this thing," Keough said.

"You really think it's the same perp, huh?" Gardner asked.

"I guess we'll know," Keough said, "if another one turns up."

Twenty-four

IT WAS THE first week of September when the first adult body turned up.

Keough had spoken with Gardner once since then. They had both finished their canvasses of the apartment complexes, and no one had seen anything—that is, no one had admitted to seeing anything.

Keough came in that morning, hoping to be able to call Valerie Speck to ask her out. He'd been meaning to since their last conversation, but he'd been so busy with the baby case, and others. He was even still thinking about the Dr. Denton's case, as he had come to think about it. He wished he'd had time just to tail Miss Bonny from First Choice Realty. He still thought she had something going with Brady's father.

He was alone in the squad room, going over some case

files, closing them out and filing them, when the phone rang.

"Detective Keough."

"Detective, this is Sergeant Piazza, in Communications."

"What can I do for you, Sergeant?"

"We've got a call from a detective over in Forest Park."

"Is that ours?"

"No, but there's a detective there from the Major Case Squad who asked for you."

"Why me?"

"They've got the body of a young woman," the sergeant said.

Marian Sanders, he thought. Brady's mother. He opened his desk drawer and took out her photo.

"Give me directions," he said, grabbing a pen.

Keough turned into the park off Skinker and followed the Sergeant's directions to a stone building where there was a gathering—a gaggle?—of St. Louis County and unmarked police cars, and plenty of yellow POLICE LINE tape. There was also a crowd of gawkers trying to get a look at what was going on.

Keough parked his car away from the action, slid his shield case into his breast pocket so his tin was showing, and then worked his way through the crowd until he came face to face with a uniformed officer.

"Where's Detective Steinbach?"

"Inside."

"Is that where the stiff is?"

"Yeah."

"Thanks."

Keough slipped under the tape and walked to the entrance of the park restrooms, past another cop. He started into the ladies' room.

"Not there," the cops said.

"What?"

"They're in the men's room."

Keough frowned a moment, then changed direction and went into the men's room. There were four men gathered around something that he couldn't see, their backs to him.

"Detective Steinbach?"

A man turned. He was in his thirties, slender, about five ten, well dressed, and clean shaven.

"That's me."

"Detective Keough, Richmond Heights."

"Oh, yeah," Steinbach said. He extended his hand and shook Keough's.

"You might want to take a look and see if this is your girl."

"She's not my girl, anymore," Keough said. "She's yours."

"Not mine," Steinbach said.

"Well, somebody from your squad."

"Would you take a look for me?"

"Sure," Keough said, grudgingly.

Steinbach and the other men moved aside to let him take a look.

The urinals were the old kind, the ones that went all the way to the floor. The woman was sitting in one with her back against the porcelain and her legs straight out in front of her. She was naked and, in life, obviously had a fine, healthy body.

"That her?"

"Give me a minute," Keough said. He took out the photo he'd taken from the Sanders living room, crouched down, and held it next to the dead girl. The lifeless face bore no resemblance to the smiling face in the photo.

"It's not her."

"Mind if I take a look?" Steinbach asked.

"Go ahead."

He passed the photo to Steinbach, who followed the same procedure. He looked over his shoulder at one of the other men, possibly his partner, and that man shook his head, as well.

"Too bad," he said, standing up and handing the photo back to Keough. "It looks like her, but it's not."

"Same type," Keough said, rubbing his jaw.

"Wonder why she was dumped in here instead of the ladies' room?" another man asked aloud.

"That's easy," Keough said. "She was dumped here by a man."

"Why do you say that?" the man asked.

"Because a man would dump her in the men's room. A woman would have used the ladies' room."

Steinbach looked at the other man and said, "That makes sense, no?"

"Maybe," the man said, grudgingly.

"You locate the husband of yours, yet?" Steinbach asked Keough.

"No. What about this one?"

"Nothing, yet," Steinbach said. "We've got to get her to the morgue and get her printed, check the missing persons reports. Lots of blondes turning' up missin', huh?"

"Looks that way," Keough agreed. "Will you keep me informed?"

"Think yours and this one are related?"

Keough shrugged.

"Probably not. Mine involves a missing husband, as well, blood all over the house, and an abandoned kid. Still, I'd like to know what you find."

"That was last month, wasn't it?"

"July."

"I'll put you on my list for copies of my reports, how's that?"

"Very cooperative of you, thanks."

"Sure, why not? Sorry to drag you over here."

"No bother," Keough said. "Thanks for thinking of me."

"Yeah . . . well, we got to get back to work."

Steinbach had not introduced the other men, and Keough didn't ask. As he was leaving, the medical examiner's truck arrived.

He worked his way back through the crowd and walked to his car. He got in but didn't start it up right away. He was suddenly back in Gingham's with Detective Gardner, talking about missing mothers and babies in Dumpsters.

He got out of the car and walked back to the men's room.

Twenty-five

THE ROOM WAS crowded, due in part to its smallness. Keough was there, along with his assistant chief, Major O'Connell. Detective Steinbach was there representing the Major Case Squad, along with his superior, Captain McGwire. Also in attendance was Det. Ken Jackson, Major Case's lead homicide investigator. Steinbach had responded to the scene of the dead woman two days earlier, but the case was being handled by Jackson. Keough had also found out that the man was in charge of the Sanders Dr. Denton's case.

"Jackson's not going to be happy about you being there," Steinbach had told Keough the day before, on the phone.

"Why's that?"

"Because he's got an ego so big you'd think he was from New York—oh, sorry."

"No problem."

Sure enough, when Keough was introduced, Jackson stared daggers at him.

"Let's get this meeting underway," said Captain Mc-

Gwire, who was in charge. "Detective Keough, it looks like you were right . . . sort of."

"What do you mean, 'sort of,' sir?"

"Well, we did as you suggested. We pulled all missing persons reports on blond women in their twenties and thirties, and their babies. There were four cases, citywide. One turned out to be the case of a woman who simply took her baby and left her husband."

"And the other three?"

"Legitimate missing persons. We called in the husbands and showed them the women, and the babies."

"And?"

"And we got a match."

"Where's the 'sort of' come in?" Keough asked.

"The woman was matched with the second baby found," Steinbach said, "not the first."

"So the first woman, the first baby's mother, is still out there, somewhere," Keough said.

"Looks that way," McGwire said.

"Is the baby back with the father?" Keough asked.

"No," McGwire said.

"Why not?"

"The father's a suspect," Jackson said. "We're not returning the baby to him just yet."

"Is there some sort of evidence against him?" Keough asked.

"Not much," Jackson said, "but he *is* the husband."

Meaning that he was a suspect simply because he was the husband. For a leading homicide investigator, Jackson seemed to like the shortest line between two points.

"I don't think he did it," Keough said.

"Why not?" Jackson asked.

"Because we found two babies," Keough said, "and there are three of them missing, along with the mothers. Do you think he had something to do with all three?"

"I don't know," Jackson said. "I'm still conducting my investigation."

"If you ask me—"

"I'm not," Jackson said.

"Excuse me?"

"I don't need some hotshot ex–New York detective coming here and telling me how to do my job."

"That's out of line," Major O'Connell said.

"Is it . . . sir?" Jackson asked, when he realized who had spoken.

"He's entitled to his opinion, Chief," Keough said.

"Captain," O'Connell said, "I think you should listen to my man's theory."

"I don't see why not," McGwire said. "Go ahead, Detective Keough."

"First I have some questions."

"All right."

"What's the dead woman's name?"

McGwire looked at Jackson, who answered grudgingly. "Janet Downing."

"Where was she last seen?"

McGwire gave Jackson a hard look.

"The West County Mall," Jackson said. "She and her husband split up. She took the baby. They were supposed to meet an hour later, but she didn't show up."

"So she was most likely grabbed at the mall."

"Yes," Jackson said.

"I'm guessing in the parking lot."

Nobody said anything. Keough suddenly remembered the woman who had reported to Haywood that a man had punched her in the parking lot. She had black hair, but she said she'd been with her girlfriend, a blonde.

"Detective Keough?"

Keough realized this was the second time Captain McGwire had called his name.

"Yes, sir, I'm sorry," he said. "Sir, I think we have a serial here."

"A serial what?" McGwire asked.

"Well, it looks like we have a killer," Keough said. "He grabs young mother with babies, dumps the babies, and kills the mothers."

"Why risk grabbing a mother and child?" McGwire asked.

"It would be easy to control a mother if you threatened her child."

"There's no evidence that this is anything but a one-shot job," Jackson said to McGwire.

"I agree, sir," Keough said. "There's no evidence to support my theory, but two babies have been found, and one mother. Why wait for the other mothers to turn up dead?"

"What do you suggest we do, Detective?" McGwire said.

"Well . . . in New York we'd form a task force to work on the serial killer case."

"And you'd like to head that task force?" Jackson asked, nastily.

"That wouldn't be my job," Keough said. "I don't have the rank—"

"You know," Jackson said, interrupting him, "I read your book."

That stopped Keough.

"My book?"

"What book?" McGwire asked.

"The book on the Kopykat killer," Jackson answered.

"I didn't write that book," Keough said, realizing what Jackson was referring to. "It was written by Mike O'Donnell—"

"I know O'Donnell's work," McGwire said. "He has a new book out?"

"Yes, sir," Jackson said, "he does, and it's all about Detective Keough here. He was a big hero in New York, caught two serial killers—but then he had to leave town."

"That was my choice," Keough said. "Besides, that has nothing to do with this."

"I agree," Major O'Connell said, although he had been looking on during this conversation quite confusedly. "What Detective Keough did or did not do in New York has no bearing on what we're discussing here."

"I agree, also," McGwire said, "but your man himself has said that there's no evidence to support his theory. I'm afraid we'll have to wait until there *is* some such evidence. Meanwhile, my man will continue to work on this case as an isolated incident."

And with that the meeting ended. Keough didn't argue, but he had several thoughts on the subject that he was going to pursue on his own. After all, the case of the first baby was originally his.

Keough walked out of the room with Detective Steinbach, but Jackson caught up.

"Keough."

Keough turned and looked at the man who, in a short span of time, he had come to dislike.

"Don't think I don't know what this is about," Jackson said.

"I'll bite," Keough said. "What's it about?"

"The Sanders case."

"What are you talking about?"

"You're pissed because they took that case away from you and gave it to me," Jackson said.

Well, Keough couldn't very well argue that point. He *was* pissed that the case had been taken away from him, but that had nothing to do with anything that had been said in that room.

"Have you had any progress on that case?" Keough asked.

Jackson snorted and said, "More than you," and walked off.

Keough turned to Steinbach, who said, "Don't believe him. He hasn't found out a thing."

"What's his problem?"

"A big ego," Steinbach said, "and a dislike of detectives from New York."

"Since when?"

"Since meeting you, I think."

They proceeded down the hall together.

"I'd like to see the reports on the three missing mothers and children," Keough said. "Is that possible?"

"Are you gonna pursue this?" Steinbach asked.

"I'd just like to see the dates on the reports."

Steinbach chewed the inside of his cheek and then said, "I'll see what I can do. Do you think this has something to do with the missing couple?"

That startled Keough.

"I hadn't thought about that."

"Well, was the mother blond?"

"Yes, but the child walked into the police station—and the father's missing, as well." Not to mention all the blood that was left in the house. "I don't think it's connected."

"Unless the father is our man," Steinbach said. "Give it some thought."

Outside Keough and O'Connell walked to their cars together.

"Thanks for the support in there."

"I always back my men, Keough," the major said. "Do you really think we've got a serial killer in St. Louis?"

"He stalks, then he kills, Chief. And he dumps the babies."

"Well, thank God the babies are alive."

"Two of them are," Keough said, "one probably isn't."

"What?"

"There are two more women out there, Chief. Probably one is dead and one is still being held."

"What makes you say that?"

"I haven't seen the reports, so I don't know the dates of the reports, and I don't know the sequence of events. Once again this is theory."

They reached O'Connell's car, but the man made no move to unlock it and get in. Keough took this as his cue to continue.

"This is the first dead woman, and she matches up with the second baby. That means that the first baby's mother is out there. There's also a third report on a missing mother and baby, and they've yet to show up. I think he's dumping the babies and keeping the mothers for a while. If I'm right, then he already finished with the first mother. Her body's still out there, someplace. Also, we've yet to find the third baby. When we do, I'm afraid that child will already be dead."

"Why do you say that?"

"Again, I don't know the date the third mother and child disappeared, but if I'm right he will have already gotten rid of the third baby, and we haven't found it yet." Keough hesitated then asked, "How long do you think a child that age can last in a Dumpster, Chief? Especially if someone's accidently buried it in garbage?"

Twenty-six

HE WATCHED THE women on the TV screen intently, watched them pushing their strollers with their sleeping babies into a corner, then taking off their clothes and joining the man on the bed. This was not his favorite scene. The women were beautiful, blond and firm young mothers, but the scene he preferred was the one they did without the man. He wondered for a moment what would happen if he grabbed two young mothers and brought them back here. Would they do the same things the women on the screen did?

He studied the faces of the women on the screen with great care, then looked at the woman who was tied up on his bed. In the beginning, when he first saw her in the mall, he was convinced she was one of the women on the screen. Now that she was here, in his home, he could see that she wasn't. Again, he'd wasted his time—but he wasn't in a big hurry. He knew that eventually he'd find them, the two women in the movie. The guy at the rental store told him that the women were from the St. Louis area. All he had to do was keep going to the mall, because that's where young, blond mothers with strollers all showed up, eventually.

Tomorrow, he'd try the Mid-Rivers Mall, but after that he was going back to Crestwood, to see if he could find that woman again, the perfect one the dark-haired woman had ruined for him. It had felt good to punch that bitch.

He looked at the woman on his bed and knew he'd have to get rid of her soon, before she started to smell. It was amazing how ugly and foul they were when they were dead, while in life they had been so pretty and sweet.

He untied her hands and feet and sat next to her on the bed, watching the movie. He was naked, and as he watched he touched himself, stroking himself and petting her smooth butt until he was almost bursting. He turned her over then, on her back, and spread her legs. He turned her around so he could continue to watch the screen as he pushed himself into her dry pussy. He started to grunt as he thrust his hips, watching the two women on the screen. It was no good, though. She was staying dry, so he withdrew and simply finished himself off, expending his seed onto the dead woman's back with a loud groan. Laying on her, his cheek pressed to her bare skin, he noticed she was growing colder with each passing moment.

It was happening too often, now. He was killing them too fast, forcing himself to get rid of them and go out and find a new one quicker. How many, he wondered, would he have to go through before he found the right one—and when he found her, how long would it be before he found the other one?

The Crestwood one, he was convinced she was one of them. After West County tomorrow, he'd go back there and wait for her.

He turned over, wiped himself on the sheet, then put his feet against her and shoved her off the bed. He rewound the movie so he could watch it again, but he drifted off to sleep halfway through it.

He awoke to the sound of static on the TV screen, opened his eyes, and looked at the snowy screen. He yawned, scratched his crotch, then rolled over and looked at the woman's body on the floor. He hadn't wanted to go out tonight, but he was going to have to get rid of the body while it was dark.

He grabbed his watch from the night table and saw that it was 3:00 A.M. There were still a few hours of darkness before morning.

He got out of bed, turned off the TV and VCR, and dressed in dark clothes. After that he took down the blanket—*the* blanket—from the top of the closet and rolled the body up into it, not giving her a second look.

He hoisted the rolled-up blanket over his shoulder and carried it out to his car, secure in the fact that there was no law against carrying a rolled-up blanket. He didn't care who saw him, as long as it wasn't a cop.

He put the blanket in the trunk of his '79 Gran Prix and got behind the wheel. The car started smoothly, as it always did, because he worked on it himself. All he had to do now was figure out where to take this one. The first one hadn't been found yet, but he had seen on TV and in the newspapers that the second one had. That meant he wasn't going to be able to go back to Forest Park. He was going to have to come up with someplace new.

The babies were easy. It made sense to leave them in Dumpsters in apartment complexes because they were always in use. He had nothing against the kids. He *wanted* them to be found alive, and so far two of them had. It was getting a little late for the third one, though. If they found that one dead it wasn't going to be his fault. He wasn't going to feel any guilt.

He thought for another five minutes and then it came to him. It was perfect. He put the car in reverse, backed out of his driveway, and drove off to dispose of number three.

Twenty-seven

THE NEXT DAY Keough asked Haywood about the report that had been filed by the woman who had been punched in the eye in the mall parking lot.

"Didn't I tell you?" Haywood asked.

"Tell me what?"

"It didn't happen here, it happened in Crestwood."

"So you sent the report over there?"

Haywood nodded.

"Did you call ahead?"

"No."

"So you don't know who caught the case?"

"No," Haywood said, "all I did was send it over."

"Do you still have a copy?"

"Sure, I've got a file copy."

Haywood went to a cabinet, opened a drawer, and produced the report. He handed it to Keough.

"Thanks."

"Want to try your luck?"

"What?"

"I think she plays around, but she wasn't interested in me. Maybe she doesn't like dark meat."

"Maybe she just couldn't see you very well out of one eye," Keough said. "If she ever sees you again she'll be sorry she missed out."

"You can say that again." Seriously, Haywood asked, "No, really, what's your interest?"

"When she was here she said she was with a blonde."

"So?"

"So the dead woman who was found in Forest Park was blond."

"There are a lot of blondes in St. Louis, Joe. Why look for a connection with this one?"

"I guess I'm just nosy, Tony," Keough said, instead of trying to explain it. "Thanks for the report."

"Hey, are you gonna put that back?" Haywood asked. "It's got my name on it."

Keough had intended to take it with him but instead he jotted down the woman's name, address, and phone number and then handed the report back to Haywood.

"I'll be back in a couple of hours."

"What do I say if somebody's looking for you?"

"Tell 'em I'm out having lunch."

The woman's name was Marie Tobin, and she lived with her husband and son in an apartment complex off Hanley Road, near Highway 40, not far from the Richmond Heights station. That explained why she reported the attack there instead of in Crestwood, where it had happened.

Keough recognized the woman who answered the door, even though both of her eyes were open. She still had the cast on her forearm, and the eye where she'd been hit still had some slight discoloration around it, but for the most part had healed. She was even prettier than he'd thought when he saw her the first time.

"Mrs. Tobin?"

"Yes?" She obviously did not recognize or remember him.

"Ma'am, my name is Detective Keough. I was in the police station when you were making your report—"

"Of course," she said, cutting him off before he could finish. "I remember, now. You were very nice to me."

Suddenly, with recognition, her body language changed. She had been wearing a sundress at the station but today she wore a pair of overalls cut into shorts, with a yellow tube top underneath. She was showing a lot of her arms and shoulders, her ribs—and her legs.

"May I come in?" he asked.

"Sure," she said, backing away. "My husband's not home, and I just put the baby down for a nap."

He entered the apartment and found himself in a pleasantly furnished living room. He could see further into the apartment—the dining room and kitchen. There was also a stairway leading to a second floor, where he assumed the bedrooms were.

He didn't know if she'd told him about the baby so that he could keep his voice down, or if it was an invitation of some kind. He remembered Haywood saying that he thought the woman played around. He hoped she wasn't sending him signals; that was not what he was there for.

"Can I get you something?" she asked. "Some iced tea or a beer?"

"No, thank you, Mrs. Tobin—"

"Marie," she said, "my name is Marie." She stood with her hips cocked. The way she looked, he was sorry that he made a habit of staying away from married women. He was suddenly very uncomfortable being there.

"Marie," he said, "how's your arm?"

"It's fine, thanks," she said. "Doesn't hurt too much."

"And how did your husband react when you told him what happened?"

"Oh, he yelled some about me goin' out dressed—well, like this—but then he bought me flowers. Everything's all right."

"That's good. Marie, I'm here to find out the name of your friend, the one who was with you at the mall the day you were attacked."

"Deb?" she said, frowning. "Why do you want to know about her?"

"I have reason to believe that the man who attacked you was stalking her."

"If he was stalking her, why'd he hit me?"

"I think because you got in his way. You see, I believe he was planning to snatch your friend Deb and her baby. She does have a baby, doesn't she?"

"Yes," Marie Tobin said, "the same age as mine."

"I think he hit you out of anger."

Now she looked confused and forgot about posing. She rubbed her bare arms, as if she were suddenly cold.

"Why didn't he . . . snatch me and my baby, then?"

"I believe it's because you have the wrong color hair. Is your friend Deb a blonde?"

"Y-yes, she is," she answered. "You mean there's some maniac out there kidnapping blond women and their babies?"

"I think so. Have you seen anything in the papers about babies found in Dumpsters?"

Suddenly, her hands flew to her mouth. Her cleavage was visible between the V formed by her forearms.

"I saw something on television about one," she said, her voice muffled. She seemed to realize what she was doing and moved her hands. "You mean there have been two?"

"Two found, so far. Also, a woman was found dead in a restroom in Forest Park—a blond woman."

"Oh my God!" she said. She staggered back a step and he moved forward, grabbed her arm, and guided her to the sofa.

"Are you all right?"

"Y-yes. Do you want Deb's address?"

"That's why I'm here."

She reached out and grabbed his hand, held it tightly.

"You have to warn her!"

"Yes, I intend to do that, but . . . you mustn't spread this around, Marie." He was starting to wish he'd taken a different approach with her. "I only told you this so you'd know how important it was to give me this information."

"But . . . people have to be warned."

"And we'll do that," he said, "as soon as we're sure that I'm right. Talking to Deb will help me determine that."

"A-all right," she said, releasing his hand. "Her name is Debra Morgan. I'll—I'll write it down for you."

"Thank you."

She went to the kitchen and came back a moment later with the name and address written on a slip of paper.

"Thank you, Marie. Do you think you'd be able to give a police artist a description of the man?"

"I could try."

"That's all we'd ask, Marie. Thanks."

"Would you like me to call Deb and tell her you're coming? I'd—I'd like to help."

"That might be a good idea," he said, "but just tell her it's about the attack on you—you did tell her about that, didn't you?"

"Yes, I did."

"Good. Don't alarm her, just tell her I want to talk to her about that, and to expect me."

"All right. Will you wait—"

"No, I'll start over there," he said. "Just give me directions." After she did, he said, "Thank you again for your help."

Keough left the Tobin residence, hoping Marie Tobin would keep her word and not spread what he'd told her about. He also hoped she wouldn't panic her friend before he could get to her.

Twenty-eight

WHEN KEOUGH REACHED Debra Morgan's home in an apartment complex in Shrewsbury, the woman was waiting for him at the door.

"Are you Detective Keough?" she asked, anxiously.

"That's right," he said.

"Come in."

"Let me show you my ID, Mrs. Morgan—"

"Just come in," she said, backing away from the door. "Marie described you to me. She's very good at describing men."

I'll bet she is, Keough thought.

He entered the apartment and found it much like the one he'd just left, despite the fact they were so far apart. Living room, dining room, and kitchen all seemed to be downstairs, while the bedrooms were upstairs. Townhouses, he supposed they were called. He'd never lived in one himself.

"I made some coffee after Marie called," she said. "You don't have to drink any. It was just something for me to do."

"I'd like some, thanks."

"Come in the kitchen, then," she said.

Debra Morgan was much like her friend Marie Tobin. Tall and athletic, she was wearing a T-shirt and shorts, showing lots of long, long legs. The T-shirt was tied beneath her breasts, which were full and firm.

"Where is your . . . daughter, is it?"

"That's right," she said. "She's asleep."

That made sense. Marie Tobin's child had been asleep, also. The same age, they obviously had the same nap time.

"Please, sit at the table. I'll get the coffee."

Watching her move around the kitchen he took back his original assessment. She wasn't like Marie Tobin. While she was obviously beautiful, with a firm, athletic body, she lacked something that Marie Tobin had—heat. Debra reminded him of an actress who had been popular some years back, although he couldn't see why. Daryl Hannah had always been beautiful, but Keough had found her cold, not sexy at all. Debra Morgan was like a supermodel, lovely but aloof, and unattainable. Marie Tobin was like a . . . well, a real woman. Sexy, vibrant, and judging from her flirtatious nature, available.

Debra Morgan brought two cups of coffee to the table and sat adjacent to Keough. There was already sugar and cream on the table, but he ignored them.

"Would you like something to eat with it?"

"No, this is fine," Keough said. "Why don't you take a long, deep breath, Debra—can I call you Debra?"

"Of course."

"Take a breath and try to relax."

"I can't relax," she said, sitting back and rubbing her arms. "Marie told me you think the man who hit her was stalking me."

"It's a possibility."

"What if he followed me home?"

"If he was stalking you, as I think, following you home is not his style. Besides, he couldn't have had time to hit Marie and then follow you, could he?"

"N-no, I suppose not."

"All I want to do is see if you can remember him, Debra. Describe him to me, think if you've ever seen him before, or since—"

"I haven't been back to the mall since that day—at least, that mall."

"Which malls do you frequent, Debra?"

"Why not make it Deb? Debra's too formal."

"All right, Deb," he said, "I'm Joe." He put his hand out and she took it. Her palm was cold. He took her hand in both of his and stared at her. "Relax. Just answer my questions and I'll catch this guy. Okay?"

She nodded, took her hand back, and said, "Okay, Joe. Where do we start?"

"Which malls do you frequent?"

After taking Debra Morgan through her last few visits to the Galleria, Crestwood, and West County malls Keough wasn't able to determine much. She and Marie did notice the man watching them at Crestwood, but Debra couldn't remember him from the other locations.

"I'm sure a lot of men watch you, Deb," Keough said. "Do you, uh, dress like you are now to go to the malls?"

"Sometimes," she said, "when it's really hot. There's nothing wrong—"

"Don't get defensive on me," he said, raising his hands. "I'm just asking questions. You do notice that men watch you."

"Of course," she said, "but men will watch any woman—"

"Almost any woman," he said, and she didn't argue.

"I'll have to tell my husband about this," she said.

"Deb, I'm working on a theory of mine that the rest of the police department doesn't necessarily agree on."

"I read about that dead girl, the one they found in the men's room in Forest Park. Are you working on that?"

"No, I'm not, but I was there."

"What did she look like?"

"She was blond, in her late twenties or early thirties—"

"In other words, she looked like me."

"A bit, yes."

He didn't bother telling her that other young, blond

mothers had been reported missing, along with their children.

"Would you suggest that I stay away from malls for a while?"

"Yes, as a matter of fact, I would—unless your husband goes with you. Does he ever?"

"Once in a while."

"Well, the next time you go, if you see the same man call security right away, then have them call me." He took out one of his new business cards and handed it to her. He had also left one with Marie Tobin.

"Okay," she said. "I don't mind telling you, I'm scared."

"I'll keep in touch with you," he said. "When something breaks, I'll let you know."

"Thank you, Joe," she said, then smiled for the first time, which made her that much more beautiful. "I do feel better now."

"I better get going. Thanks for the coffee."

She walked him to the door. At no time did he feel that she was posing for him, or coming on to him.

"Deb, I got the feeling when I was at Marie's that she was, uh, flirting with me."

"She is a big flirt."

"Does she ever take it further than that?"

"Why? Are you interested?"

"No," he said, shaking his head. "I make it a habit to avoid married women. That's not why I'm asking."

She hesitated, then asked, "Is it important?"

"It could be," he said, "but if you don't want to break your friend's confidence, I'll understand."

"No, it's okay," she said. "I want to help, and she'll understand."

"I won't repeat what you tell me."

"She just told me recently—in fact, that day at the mall—that she was, um, seeing someone."

"The man you saw at the mall, the one who hit her? Was he her type?"

She smiled.

"I love Marie, but *men* are her type, Joe, in general—but I'm pretty sure she didn't know him. She called him a geek."

"To his face?"

"Oh, no," she said. "We didn't speak to him."

"Was he a geek?"

He had taken down her description of him, which had been as precise as she could make it.

"Well . . . sort of geeky, if you know what I mean. I didn't think he was as bad-looking as Marie did."

"Okay."

He opened the door to leave and she put her hand on his arm. Again, there was nothing at all sexual about the contact.

"Joe, do you think if I hadn't been with Marie that he would have—I mean—"

"Don't worry about it now, Deb," he said, putting his hand over hers. "I'll be in touch."

"Thank you."

She watched him walk all the way to his car, and he waved at her before he got behind the wheel and drove away.

When he got back to the police station Haywood was excited.

"Joe, thank God you're back."

"Why?"

"You got a call," he said, "from Major Case."

"What'd they want?"

"They found another woman."

"When?"

"They called about an hour ago."

"Where?"

Haywood told him, and gave him directions. If they'd called an hour earlier they'd still be at the scene.

"I'm on my way." He rushed out of the office and back to his car, wishing he had called in before leaving Shrewsbury.

That's where the body had been found.

Twenty-nine

THE WOMAN WAS almost identical to the first, which meant she looked a lot like Debra Morgan. Her body was found behind a large supermarket, shoved behind a

Dumpster. Like the first baby, the body was found by a sanitation man when he lifted the Dumpster to empty it into the truck. She was naked, and had been strangled. There were ligature marks, indicating she'd been tied up, but she'd been strangled by hand. There were finger bruises on her neck.

"This is all the more reason I think everything is connected," Keough said to Detective Steinbach.

"I know," Steinbach said, nodding. "This guy likes Dumpsters."

They were both standing with their hands in their pockets, watching the coroner's people remove the body.

"And he strangles his victims," Keough said, "during sex."

The paperwork on the previous murder had told him that.

"I guess we'll need the coroner's report to know that for sure," the Major Case detective said.

"I don't," Keough said. "I know."

"How?"

"It would be too much of a coincidence otherwise."

"And you don't believe in coincidence?"

"I believe in them," Keough said, "but I don't like them."

"You're making assumptions."

"Based on experience."

"As a New York City detective?"

Keough looked at Steinbach.

"As a detective, period," he said. "Does it bother you that I came here from New York?"

"No, it doesn't bother me all."

They watched for a few more moments before speaking again.

"So you agree with me now?" Keough asked.

"*I* do."

Keough frowned.

"What's that mean?"

"Just what I said," Steinbach replied. "I agree with you."

"But no one else does."

"Nobody's going to okay the formation of a task force because of Dumpsters, Keough."

"What about Ken Jackson?"

"What about him?"

"Is he going to end up with this case, too?"

"No," Steinbach said, "not yet, anyway."

"Who gets this one?"

"As of now, it's mine."

"Can we work together?"

Steinbach gave Keough a long look. "Unofficially."

"Then let's get together, unofficially," Keough said, "because I have some information."

"About this woman?"

"No," Keough said, "I don't even know who this woman is, at this point, but I believe my information is connected."

"Okay," Steinbach said. "I've got to call those two husbands of missing women. One of them is going to ID her."

"What about dinner tonight?"

"Sure," Steinbach said. "Where do you live?"

"I'm in the West End, house-sitting."

"That's fine," Steinbach said. "I'm partial to Culpeppers."

"Seven?"

"See you at seven." The man started to turn away.

"Steinbach?"

"Yes?"

"What's you first name?"

"Al."

"Thanks for the call, Al."

"Sure," Steinbach said. "See you at seven."

Culpeppers did not spend a lot of money on ambience. It was a little bigger than your local bar, with two dining floors, the main and the basement. When Keough walked in he saw Detective Al Steinbach sitting at a table on the first floor. He had a beer in front of him. The other tables were all occupied, and so were the stools at the bar. Keough made his way between tables and joined Steinbach.

"Well, your friend got here," a waitress said, appearing at Keough's elbow. She was in her fifties, with a round, pleasant face. "What can I get you to drink?"

"Beer's listed on the menu," Steinbach said.

"I'll just have iced tea, thanks."

"Comin' up," the waitress said.

Keough sat down across from Steinbach, who was still wearing the same suit he'd had on earlier in the day.

"Did you get the ID made?"

"Oh, yeah," Steinbach said. "It was bad. We've matched

up the first two women and babies with the right men who reported them missing."

"Are the kids home?"

"Yes. The father who was a suspect has been cleared."

The waitress came with Keough's iced tea, and they paused while she set it down.

"So we're just waiting for the third mother and baby to show up."

"I guess . . . you said you had something you wanted to tell me?"

"You wanna order now?" the waitress asked.

They paused again long enough to order before Keough answered Steinbach's question.

He told the Major Case detective about Marie Tobin being attacked in the Crestwood Mall parking lot.

"Why do you think that's connected if she's got dark hair and she was just assaulted?" Steinbach asked, looking confused.

"Let me finish."

He told the man about Marie Tobin being with Debra Morgan, who was a look-alike for the dead girls.

"Aha," Steinbach said. "So you think he attacked the Tobin woman because she got in the way."

"Yes, that's what I think."

"Can she ID him?"

"She said she'll work with an artist."

"I'll take care of that," Steinbach said.

"There's something else I want to do."

"What's that?"

"I want to check with the mall security offices and see if there have been any other attacks like this one."

"You think our man misses as much as he hits?"

"Maybe."

"You'll need help checking the malls."

"Considering I don't know how many malls there are, yeah, I will."

"Which ones do you know?"

"Well, the Galleria, naturally. We have men and cars permanently assigned there. Then I know, uh, Crestwood and, uh, West County?"

"The bird mall."

"What?"

"That's what my wife calls it," Steinbach said. "The bird mall. They've got a dove on a pole above the parking lot. You can't miss it."

"Okay, so I'll take Galleria, Crestwood, and the, uh, bird mall."

"Fine," Steinbach said, "I'll handle Northwest Plaza, Mid-Rivers, South County, and the others."

"He's got to be using malls to troll for his victims because that's where you find mothers with strollers and babies."

"Shit," Steinbach said, as if he just realized something.

"What?"

The waitress came with the food and they paused again while she served them.

"What's on your mind?" he asked Steinbach.

"Why only malls?" the other man asked. "Why not

Toys'Я'Us, grocery stores, shopping centers—Jesus, schools!"

"He's not going to risk schools," Keough said, "but you're right about the other places."

"There's too many to check them all."

"Well, let's think about it. These places have parking lots, but they're a lot smaller than mall parking lots. It'd be too risky."

"You might be right," Steinbach said, and then added, "You *probably* are right. Why don't we just stick with the malls? At least until we see what we can find out."

"Agreed."

"It's just a scary thought," Steinbach said. "I mean, imagine this guy trolling Toys'Я'Us."

"I know what you mean."

They started eating.

"You got kids?" Steinbach asked.

"No," Keough said, "and I'm not married."

"I've got two, but they're both teenagers—and my wife's not blond."

"I wouldn't worry, Al."

"If this gets out . . ."

"Right now this is between you and me," Keough said. "You got a problem with keeping it that way until we find out more?"

"Hell, no," Steinbach said. "We're gonna need more before we go to the brass with this, anyway."

"What about Jackson? Do you want to bring him in on this?" Keough asked.

"No," Steinbach said, shaking his head. "He'll resist

this because it's your idea. I know him. He'll be an asshole to the end. I'll do an end run around him and talk to the captain."

"All right," Keough said, "when the time's right I'll talk to Major O'Connell."

"Okay."

They gave their attention to dinner at that point, exchanging some more personal information about each other.

"Kites?" Steinbach said, when Keough told him that he flew kites for relaxation.

"That's right," he said. "I find it calming. I know, you think it's for kids—"

"Hell, no," Steinbach said. "I used to enjoy flying kites with my kids, but they . . ."

"Grew out of it?"

"That's what I was gonna say, but—"

"Forget it. Do you have any idea where I could go around here to put a kite in the air?"

"Sure," Steinbach said, "Forest Park. In fact, there's a big kite fair once a year . . . I'm not sure of the time, though."

"I'll find out," Keough said. "I've been pretty busy with work, and with settling in."

"How'd you rate a house here in the West End?"

Keough explained about house-sitting, and about getting the job from a friend.

"Same guy who arranged my interview, by the way," Keough said.

"Uh," Steinbach said, "I've got something to show you."

"What?"

Sheepishly, the man reached underneath his chair and came out with a book. It was Mike O'Donnell's *Kopykat*.

"Jesus, where'd you get that?"

"Across the street," Steinbach said. "Big Sleep Books sells mystery and suspense books. They've got a small true crime section, and they had one copy. I bought it."

"Big Sleep?"

"It's from a Raymond Chandler novel."

"Oh."

"You don't mind if I read this, do you?"

"Hell no, go ahead," Keough said. "O'Donnell can use the royalties."

He didn't bother to mention that he was in line for a piece of the action, as well.

They finished dinner, paid the check—splitting it evenly—and left the place.

"I can walk from here," Keough said.

They shook hands.

"I appreciate the good faith you're showing, Al," Keough said.

"Hey," Steinbach said, "if what you're saying didn't make sense, I wouldn't be here. Let's get back in touch in a few days, or if one of us finds out something."

"Okay."

"See ya."

He watched as Steinbach walked to the corner and then turned left to go to the public parking lot down the street on Maryland. He wondered what questions the man would have to ask after he finished reading Mike O'Donnell's book.

He turned right and walked home, thinking about flying a kite.

Thirty

THE NEXT DAY Keough found out the names of the officers who were permanently assigned to the Galleria Mall. He drove to the mall early, before most of the stores were open, and was surprised to find people already inside. Actually, finding them there wasn't surprising, what they were doing was.

They were walking.

Maybe he hadn't been to enough malls, or maybe it wasn't a practice in New York malls, or *maybe* he simply was never in a mall this early before, but seeing people walking in sweat suits, some of them carrying hand weights, was not what he expected. He was surprised that the people who ran the malls would open them up to . . . what were they called? Power walkers? Mall walkers?

He located the security office and found a man on duty.

"Can I help you?" He was wearing a gray mall security uniform and sporting a belly that hung over his belt. His hair was white. He could have been forty with prematurely white hair, or a young-looking sixty, or anywhere in between.

Keough showed his badge and identified himself.

"Your guys are not in the office right now," the man said. "They got a desk and some file cabinets in a room in the back—"

"Actually," Keough said, "I wanted to talk to one of your guys first."

"Oh? Which one?"

"Anyone," Keough said. "Maybe you could help me out."

"I'm all ears," the man said. "The name's Cates, by the way, Pat Cates."

Keough shook hands with the man and said, "Joe Keough, Pat. Good to meet you."

"What can I do for you, Joe?"

"You can run down for me what happens when someone is assaulted on mall property. I mean, inside the mall, or in the parking lots."

"Well, that depends. If we see what's goin' on we interfere. If the victim reports it we'll take a look around the mall for the perpetrator."

"And what happens when you catch him?"

"We radio your guys to come and get them."

"Do you and the cops ever work together looking for somebody?"

"Oh, sure," he said, "your guys carry one of our radios

as well as their own units. We stay in touch and coordinate our efforts."

"And do you keep a written report on the incident?"

"Sure we do, and so do your guys."

With duplicate reports, Keough thought his job was probably going to be easier than he thought.

"Pat, I need to check out assault reports for the past two months or so."

"Okay," Cates said, "we have a clerical who could do that for you. Just assaults?"

"What do you mean?"

"You don't want to know about attempted assaults?"

Keough thought a moment, then nodded.

"Yeah, I do." A blown attempt by the perp might be as important as a successful one. "How soon can I get that information?"

"Well, that depends," Cates said, scratching his head. "The clerical comes in at eleven."

"What about the other files?"

"Your guys' files?"

"Yeah."

"That might take longer."

"What if I looked myself?"

"If you got that much time to spend," Cates said, "but you'll have to clear that with your boys."

"I'll wait for them."

"You got your radio on you?"

"I do."

"Why don't you get some coffee. I'll tell your guy to radio you when he gets here."

"Cup of coffee sounds good," Keough said. "Can I bring one back for you?"

"No thanks," Cates said. "I get plenty of coffee during the day, let me tell you."

"Where's the closest place?"

"St. Louis Bread Company. It's right behind the escalators by the big fountain. Can't miss it."

"Will they be open this early?"

"Sure," Cates said, "they do an early business selling the mall walkers drinks."

"Okay, I'll do that, then. See you later, and thanks for your help."

"Sure, no problem. Like I said, we cooperate with each other."

Keough found the St. Louis Bread Company with no trouble. They had all kinds of special coffees, which he had come to know from some of the other cafes he'd been frequenting, but he still ordered whatever was the closest to just a simple black coffee.

He took his coffee to a table where he could look out at the mall through a window. Some of the mall walkers were still at it, but they were mingling now with the shoppers who were coming in early to wait for the stores to open. They mingled out in the mall, and also in the shop where he was. He listened as people ordered everything from simple bottled water to all kinds of lattes and granitas.

At one point the automatic doors opened and a young blond mother came in pushing her child in a stroller. She was wearing high-waisted jeans, a white T-shirt, and black suspenders. She also had a pair of dark glasses on. She looked a step or two higher on the income scale than Debra Morgan and Marie Tobin. He wondered if she would make a likely target for the doer.

He realized then that he was already convinced that his theory was correct. He wondered if that was a manifestation of his New York attitude—which he didn't think he had. In any case, he was already thinking of this perp as his doer. He watched the woman advance into the mall and tried to think like the man he was trying to catch. He'd see her, determine that she was alone, and then probably follow her. Would he stay with her the whole time she was there? How many of them had he spotted right away like this, and how many when they were already in the mall a while, perhaps preparing to leave? He probably then followed the woman to her car and . . . and made his move.

What about witnesses? Hadn't anyone ever seen this guy when he grabbed the woman and her child? In order for that *not* to happen he had to move awfully quick. After a few minutes Keough decided he knew how. The guy probably watched and waited until the woman had put her child in the car. Maybe he even waited until she walked around to the driver's side. From there it would be easy simply to push her in, and make his threat against the child to insure her cooperation.

Now the question was, why pick women with children? Was it only to use the child as a hostage? When did he get rid of the child? Certainly not along the way. He probably waited until he had the woman secured, possibly even tied up. At that point he wouldn't need the child anymore.

Why didn't he kill the children? Why just put them in a Dumpster, where there was a good chance they would be found? Of course, there was no need to fear the children as witnesses. They were much too small for that. But if this was the kind of man who raped and killed women, what kept him from killing the children?

Keough was sure there was some kind of psychobabble to account for this, but as long as there was no one else working on this angle, as long as there was no task force, there would be no psychologists, and no FBI. Just him and Detective Steinbach.

He was about to get up for a second refill when his radio squawked and a voice called his number. Every member of the Richmond Heights department had their own number, even the patrol force.

"One seventy-three," Keough replied into his radio.

"Uh, this is one twenty-four, Officer Hartley. I, uh, I'm in the mall security office. I understand you wanted to see me?"

"That's right."

"Uh, who are you?"

"Detective Keough. Are you going to be there for a few minutes?"

"If you want me to."

"I'll be right up, Hartley. I've got something I need to talk to you about."

"I'll be here."

Keough clicked off, then looked around and saw that some of the mall walkers were standing with their lattes and fancy water watching him.

"Have a healthy day," he said, and walked out.

Thirty-one

OFFICER HARTLEY TURNED out to be a man in his thirties, tall and slender, with hair as black as shoe polish and a mustache to match. The black of his hair made his face look extremely pale. The two men shook hands and Keough told Hartley what he wanted.

"Come in the back with me."

Hartley led him down a hall to a small room with a desk and a filing cabinet.

"I have to be on patrol, but you're free to look through the files. You have to remember there's three of us working here, and we all, uh, have sort of different filing systems."

"In other words," Keough said, "I'll need all the luck I can get, right?"

"Right."

"That's okay," he said, "I'm used to relying on luck."

"I've got to get going," Hartley said. "I'm supposed to stay on patrol."

"Okay, thanks for your help."

Hartley started out, then turned and said, "Oh, there's one more thing you should know."

"What's that?"

"There's another man assigned to the Galleria besides the three of us who share this room."

"Who is he?"

"He's Narcotics, undercover. A place as big as this is perfect for drug deals to go down. I know your investigation doesn't concern drugs, but maybe he saw something while he was working."

"What's his name?"

"Taylor," Hartley said. "You can probably get ahold of him at the station. That'd be easier than trying to find him here."

"Okay," Keough said, "thanks again for your help."

"Sure."

Hartley left and Keough looked at the three-drawer file cabinet, wondering how long it would take to find what he wanted—if he found it at all.

He did, but it took an hour.

The report had been taken in July. Mall security had been called first, and then the Richmond Heights department was called in. The woman's name, address, and telephone number were listed. The case had been referred to Detective Merchant, who Keough knew was one of the three existing detectives in the department before he came on.

According to the report a man had approached a young woman named Katherine Fouquet in the south parking lot of the Galleria as she was getting into her car. He threatened to hurt her child if she gave him any trouble. The child—and here was the difference—was six years old, and when her mother called out to her to run away, she did, screaming. The woman then began to shout as well, and the man ran away.

"Son of a bitch," Keough said, out loud. "This was his trial run, his first try." Aware that he was talking to himself, he looked around and continued to work it out silently. Apparently, after this first try the doer had decided to approach only women who had children in strollers. That way, the children couldn't run away.

Keough called Detective Steinbach at Major Case and was told that he was out on a call. Keough left a message. "Tell him to look for cases involving children up to . . . uh, about six or seven years old—unsuccessful cases. He'll know what it means."

The woman sounded confused, but took down the message and promised to give it to Detective Steinbach.

Keough wrote down the woman's name, address, and phone number from the report on a piece of paper, and replaced the report in the files. Although the files *were* a mess, as it turned out if they had all been put together they would have filled one drawer of the cabinet completely.

As he was leaving the security guard he'd spoken to earlier asked, "Did you find what you wanted?"

"Yes, thanks."

"Do you still want our clerical to look in our files?"

Keough paused and thought, Why not.

"Yes," he said, and repeated to the man essentially the same message he'd left for Steinbach. Maybe the doer had made some other preliminary tries before he finally got it right. Who knew? And there were still other malls to check out. At least he could question this woman, in the meantime.

Katherine Fouquet had an apartment in a four-family building on Hanley Road in Clayton. Keough knocked and when the door was opened he blinked a few times. The woman was blond, well built, medium height. She could have almost been the twin of the other blond women he'd run into during the case, except for her face. If all the women were lined up side by side with their hair covering their face, or viewed from behind, they would have been considered identical.

"Mrs. Fouquet?"

"Yes," she said. "Detective Keough?"

"That's right."

"Would you mind showing me some identification?" she asked.

"Of course," he said, with a disarming smile.

He took out his shield and ID and showed them to her. She took the time to read the ID carefully. Keough had called ahead and asked if she would see him, and had gone to her apartment directly from the station.

"All right," she said. "You can come in."

She backed away so he could enter, then closed the door.

"Is your daughter here?" he asked, looking around.

"She's in school."

"Of course."

"Would you like to sit down?"

"Thanks."

She led him to the living room, and while she sat on the sofa he sat across from her in an armchair.

"You said on the phone you wanted to ask me about being attacked in the Galleria parking lot?"

"That's right."

"That happened a while ago," she said. "Why do you want to know about it now?"

"It might be related to something I'm working on."

"Has he attacked other women?"

"It's possible," he said. "Mrs. Fouquet—"

"Please," she said, "just call me Kate. It'll be easier."

"All right, then Kate," he said, "I am working on other cases involving attacks on other women, but they were women with infants, or toddlers, in strollers."

"My daughter is six," she said. "She ran when I told her to, screaming her head off, and I think he panicked. How could that be connected?"

"I think," Keough said, slowly, "that you might have been his first intended victim. I think after your daughter ran off and panicked him he decided to attack women with children who couldn't run away."

"Children in strollers."

"Yes."

"Why not attack women without children?" She frowned.

"I don't know that," he said. "Maybe when I catch him I'll find out that he has a mother fixation, I don't know. As it stands now he seems interested in beautiful, blond young mothers."

"Should I be flattered?"

"I don't think so," he said.

"Well, what can I do?"

"There are a couple of things. First, I need a description of the man, as precise as you can give it to me. Second, I'd like you to work with a police sketch artist to try and work up a likeness of him."

"Will I have to see him when you catch him?"

"You can identify him without him seeing you."

"I don't mind describing him," she said, "but can I talk to my husband about the rest?"

"Sure," he said, "no problem."

Keough took out his notebook and wrote down everything she could remember about the man.

"You seem to have a good eye for detail," he said, putting the notebook away.

"I just hope I've remembered correctly."

He stood up and she walked him to the door.

"I hope you catch him," she said. "I have to tell you I . . . I haven't been to a mall since that happened, and I'm very nervous in any parking lot."

"I don't blame you," he said. "With your help I think I can catch him, and maybe that will make you feel safer.

Here's my number." He gave her one of his cards. "Call me after you talk it over with your husband."

"I will," she said. "I promise."

"Thank you, Kate."

They shook hands and Keough left and walked to his car.

In the car Keough decided to try the other malls—Crestwood and West County, which he had come to think of as the bird mall—before going back to the station. When he arrived at their security offices he discovered they did not have offices there for the local police, nor did they have officers permanently assigned, probably because they were smaller than the Galleria—in the case of the bird mall, a lot smaller. Neither did they have many files, and he was able to skim through them fairly quickly—especially since he skimmed.

He did not come across any attacks similar to what he was looking for, just some purse snatches and pockets that had been picked. Both security departments offered all kinds of cooperation, and they agreed to have someone go over the records more thoroughly and call if they came across anything.

Keough returned to the Richmond Heights station too late to sign himself out at his regular time. It wouldn't do to look like he was trying to get overtime.

When he entered the squad room the two detectives looked up from their desks.

"Working late?"

By this time Keough had crossed paths with all of the other detectives. These two were Stine and De Noux. Stine was in his thirties, a native St. Louisan, while De Noux was apparently from New Orleans originally but had grown up and lived here most of his life.

"Getting back late," Keough replied to Stine.

"Hot case?" De Noux asked.

"Same old same old," Keough said. "Do you know if there are any messages for me?"

"If there are they'd be on the board."

There was a bulletin board on the wall, and the squad had taken to pinning messages up on it. Keough saw an envelope with his name on it. It wasn't sealed, so he took a peek inside and saw a greeting card of some sort. He put it in his pocket to open later and wondered if Steinbach had gotten around to checking his malls, yet. As an afterthought he left a message on the board for Detective Merchant and included his home phone number.

"Waiting for something important?" De Noux asked.

"No," Keough said, "just checking. You boys have a good tour."

De Noux was one of the detectives who had been in Richmond Heights when Keough got there, while Stine was one of the recently promoted detectives. Keough was getting along fine with Stine and Haywood, but the three detectives who had been in place when he got there—De Noux, Merchant, and Leslie—were still treating him with some reservations. When he worked in New York Keough would customarily discuss his cases with his partner, and no one else. Here the detectives weren't partnered up the same way. Two of them worked each tour, but they caught their own cases, often at the whim of Sergeant Bilcheck. For this reason Keough rarely talked about his cases with anyone except Haywood, with whom he worked most of the time, and even then only infrequently, if it was absolutely necessary.

"Playin' it close to the vest, huh?" De Noux asked.

Keough knew he could have taken the time to explain to De Noux that he didn't like to talk about his cases but he decided not to invest the time.

"Goodnight, fellas," he said, and left the squad room to go home.

He had bought a telephone answering machine a week earlier, and as he entered the red light was flashing four times. He pressed the Play button and listened to the messages.

Beep.

"Keough, it's O'Donnell. Did you read the book? Give me a call, man. I might be coming to St. Louis for a signing. We'll have to get together."

Beep.

"Detective Keough, this is Detective Steinbach. I checked with some of the malls and came up empty. Give me a call and let me know what you've been able to find out."

Beep.

"Detective Keough, this is Valerie Speck. I know this is short notice but I have tickets for the theater tomorrow night and I was wondering if you would, uh, like to go with me. You see, I'm terribly forward and I've grown tired of waiting for you to call me. You have my number. 'Bye. Oh, I *hate* talking to these machines! 'Bye."

Beep.

"Detective Keough, this is Detective Merchant, answering your message." Merchant went on to give Keough his home number. Keough returned this call immediately, but Merchant couldn't tell him any more than Katherine Fouquet herself had. He thanked the man for his information, though.

He didn't save any of the other messages. Tomorrow was Friday, and he didn't have anything planned. He wondered if he would be able to explain to Valerie why he hadn't called her yet. He wasn't sure he would, because he wasn't sure he even knew himself.

He called O'Donnell's number in Florida and got his message machine. Like Valerie Speck he hated talking to them, so he didn't leave a message. He knew this annoyed some people, but he figured he had the option to leave a message or not, and he chose not to.

When he called Steinbach's home number he didn't get an answer. He hung up, then picked up the phone to dial Valerie Speck's number, then put it down. He decided to have something to eat first, and during the meal he could decide what he was going to say to her.

Besides "Yes," of course.

Thirty-two

THE PLAY WAS *A Chorus Line*, with a no-name cast that did a fine job. It was, however, not the show that impressed Keough, but the Fox Theater. It was very old, but had been renovated not long ago and returned to its former splendor. Its marquee dominated its share of Grand Avenue.

The lobby of the Fox Theater was spectacular. The floor inclined slightly toward the back, where an elaborate staircase led to a private club. Flanking the staircase were two large lions painted gold with ruby eyes. The ceiling was at least fifty feet high, and a stained glass window rose above the front doors. On either side of the oblong room bars were set up, manned by tuxedoed bartenders.

Because Valerie had to work late they had arranged to meet at Duke's, a restaurant near the Fox that catered to the theater crowd.

"I'm sorry I haven't called," he said when they were seated and had ordered.

"I'm more interested in *why*," she said, frankly, then added, "at least to inquire about Brady."

Keough made a face. "I was taken off that case."

"I know. I talked to the new detective, a very unpleasant man named Jackson."

"Then you know why I haven't called."

"That explains why you didn't call about Brady, not why you haven't called me."

The question was a good one—even better considering how wonderful she looked in her blue silk suit. A single strand of pearls caught in her cleavage as she spoke and he tried to concentrate on her clear eyes as he said, "I'm stupid?"

"I don't accept that," she said. "Do I scare or intimidate you?"

"No."

"I didn't think so. Do you like me?"

"Very much."

"I like you, too, but I hate stupid men."

"You're right," Keough said, "I'm not stupid. I picked up the phone to call you a dozen times."

"Then why didn't you?"

"I couldn't think of a good explanation as to why I let Brady's case be taken away from me."

"How about you didn't have a choice?"

"I didn't, actually," he said. "That is, I wasn't given one. I could have argued, but—"

"But you're new in town and at that job, and it wouldn't do to rock the boat just now. You know, all of that is understandable."

"It is?"

"Sure. I didn't get stubborn about my job until I was

there a year and they realized they couldn't do without me."

"I don't know if the Richmond Heights Police Department is ever going to come to realize that."

"Well," she said, as the waiter appeared with their din-
ners, "at least I know it wasn't because you didn't like me."

"You don't have any worries there."

After the show they stopped at a place called The Bistro,
which catered more to the after-theater crowd.

Valerie informed Keough of Brady's progress.

"He's been placed in a foster home, for now."

"Do you still see him?"

She nodded. "From time to time, to check on him. Has
Detective Jackson made any progress?"

"He and I don't talk much."

"Don't get along?"

Keough shook his head. "He doesn't like New York detectives."

"And you don't like detectives from St. Louis?"

"On the contrary," Keough said, "he's the only one I've
met that I dislike. Most of the men here are all right."

"Does that surprise you?"

"No, why should it?"

"Well, being from New York . . ."

"Ah," he said, "why does everyone think that I came
here with an attitude?"

"Is the New York attitude a myth?"

"Probably not," he admitted, "but so far I'm very happy
here."

"Does that mean you like it better than you liked New York?"

"Not quite," he said, "but I'm willing to give it some more time."

After drinks at The Bistro they walked across the street to the parking lot where they had both left their cars. Keough found himself wishing they had come together, in one car. It would have made this part much easier.

"I had a great time," he said, when they reached her car. "Thank you for inviting me."

"I've made the first move," she said. "Next time you have to call me."

"Maybe I should just make the next move now."

He moved closer to her and kissed her. He meant it to be brief, but held it long enough to make it more meaningful.

"Well," she said, her eyes shining, "that's a start, anyway."

He opened the door for her and watched her drive off, then walked to his own car. He wondered if he should have made a stronger move, maybe suggesting a drink at his place or hers. He decided that he'd played it right. She was pleasant to talk to, and lovely to look at, but he really wasn't looking for a relationship at the moment. He was still too new to the city, and to his job. He still had lots of unpacking to do. He'd gotten all of his kites and paraphernalia out in the open, but hadn't had a chance to put any of it to use, yet.

That's what was missing, he thought, as he drove home.

He'd been finding of late that he was having trouble concentrating. In the past he'd always been able to put a kite in the air and take the time to sort things out.

It was September now, and he decided to spend his free time over the next couple of days tracking down a place to fly his kites. Then he'd be able to figure something out about these dead women, and the babies in the Dumpsters, and maybe he'd even devote some of that time to Brady Sanders, even though he was no longer officially involved.

Thirty-three

THE DEAD BABY showed up on Saturday.

Keough was up early that morning. It was his intention to find a kite shop and/or a club, and he was gathering together some of his kites, tails, and spools of string when the phone rang.

"Keough."

"It's Steinbach."

"I'm off today—"

"They found the other baby."

Keough closed his eyes.

"Dead?"

"You called it."

Now he opened his eyes and looked away from his kites. No relaxation today.

"Tell me where . . ."

Keough stood next to Steinbach and the two men looked down at the remains of the baby. Amidst the refuse it looked like a doll—a child's discarded, broken doll.

"It was a boy," Steinbach said.

"Yeah."

"Can we remove it now?" one of the coroner's crew asked.

They were all taking this badly.

"Go ahead," Steinbach said. He and Keough turned and walked away. All around them was trash, sorted into piles to be dealt with one way or another. It was while sorting the piles that the baby had been found.

"Okay," Keough said, "so the third baby has shown up. Now what about the third mother? Why is he keeping her so long?"

"Maybe he's not," Steinbach said. "Maybe she's just gonna be hard to find, or be found by accident, like this baby. Maybe the two women we've found are numbers two and three, or one and three, or . . . who the hell knows?"

Keough looked up at the sky and felt the breeze swirling around, carrying the stench of garbage with it.

"Today would have been a good day to fly a kite."

"Sorry," Steinbach said, "but I thought you'd want in on this."

"I do," Keough said. "I want in on the whole thing."

"You're gonna get your wish."

Keough looked at him.

"What do you mean?"

"A task force," Steinbach said.

"You're kidding."

"I'm not. My boss and your boss talked today."

"This early?"

"They were called even before you. They want a task force formed to find the other missing mother, and the killer, before he hits again."

"Who's on the task force?"

"You and me . . ."

"Good—"

". . . and Jackson."

"Oh shit."

"He's the top homicide man in the city, Keough," Steinbach said. "He's got to be on the task force."

"Who's going to be in command?"

"We'll report to my boss," Steinbach said, "Captain McGwire. We'll work out of our building, where we had the meeting."

"I'm not catching any cases in Richmond Heights?" Keough asked.

"Not anymore," Steinbach said, "not until we catch this guy. Looks like the brass believes you now, Joe."

"A serial killer."

Steinbach nodded.

"He's not just killing women, anymore."

"I'm not so sure."

"We've got a dead baby on our hands that says—"

"No, I mean I'm not so sure he killed this child on purpose," Keough said, cutting him off.

"You think this was an accident?"

"Well, look at the way the other two were found," Keough said. "Lying right on top of the garbage. What if this baby had been placed the same way, and somebody just didn't see it?"

"You mean somebody dumped some garbage right on top of this infant without seeing it, and it suffocated?"

"Something like that. Do we know how often they sort this trash?"

"No," Steinbach said. "Some of it came in today, some of it could have been here for weeks." He sniffed the air. "You can tell that."

"Yeah." Keough started to look back to where the baby was being bagged, then stopped himself. "Let's go someplace else and talk, huh?"

"Fine with me. How about the Parkmoor?"

Keough knew where the Parkmoor restaurant was because it was only about half a mile from the Richmond Heights station.

"Maybe by the time we get there I'll be able to keep some breakfast down," Steinbach added.

"Fine with me," Keough said. "I can stop by the station afterward."

"You need to follow me?"

"Naw, I'll find it."

"Okay," Steinbach said, "meet you there."

They went to their individual cars, left the garbage dump, and headed for Richmond Heights.

The Parkmoor restaurant reminded Keough of some he had frequented when he lived in New York. It was the closest he'd seen to a Brooklyn diner since his arrival in St. Louis. It had been a St. Louis landmark for over fifty years.

They got a booth in the back with a view of the intersection of Clayton Road and Big Bend Boulevard. They ordered coffee and breakfast, both opting for eggs and toast and whatever else came with it.

"Does Jackson know about the task force?" Keough asked when they each had coffee.

"Not yet."

"Who's going to tell him?"

"McGwire."

"When does this task force officially start?"

"Monday."

"Am I getting paid if I work the weekend?"

"Not if you're supposed to be off. You're back on salary Monday, like normal."

Great. If he wanted to work on the case today and tomorrow it would be on his own time. Getting a kite in the air was getting further and further away all the time.

"Did you get my message yesterday?" Steinbach asked.

"Yeah," Keough said, "I was going to try to return it today."

"After you flew your kites?"

"Something like that. Did you want to talk about the malls?"

"Yes," Steinbach said. "What did you find out?"

Keough told him what he'd found out, pausing only when the waitress appeared with their food. He finished up with his interviews with Deb Morgan and Kate Fouquet.

"A dead ringer?" Steinbach asked.

"Not facially," Keough said, "but physically, yes. They are all the same exact type."

They stared at each other for a few moments.

"Are you thinking what I'm thinking?" Steinbach asked.

"Decoy?"

"Uh-huh."

"Do we have a female cop who looks like that?"

"I'll have to check into it."

"What did you find out from the malls you visited?"

"Nothing from Mid-Rivers," Steinbach said, "but that might be too far away for him. A woman reported a man following her in the Northwest Plaza Mall."

"He didn't attack her?"

"No," Steinbach said, "apparently he followed her until she went into the covered parking, then broke it off."

"Covered parking," Keough repeated. "The women I talked to were attacked in the surface parking lots."

"Maybe he doesn't like covered parking."

"Maybe," Keough said, "and maybe it's even stronger than just not liking it."

"A phobia, maybe?"

"That's what I'm thinking."

Steinbach made a face.

"You've been through this task force stuff before," Steinbach said. "We're going to have to bring in a shrink, aren't we? And the Feebs?"

"The FBI would supply one of their shrinks or profilers, but yeah, you're right—although we could probably put it off for a while. Would Jackson go along with that?"

"To tell you the truth," Steinbach said, "I can't tell you what Jackson will or won't go along with. He and I usually go our separate ways. Why would you want to put it off?"

"I hate all that psychobabble," Keough said. "They usually tell you stuff you already know. He wet the bed, was abused by a family member—"

"—or a mother's boyfriend, or something like that."

"Right," Keough said, pushing his empty plate away. He had one last piece of toast and he started smearing grape jelly on it.

"What are you thinking?"

"Bear with me while I talk it through, all right?"

"Shoot."

"We got a man who likes blondes in their late twenties to middle thirties, good-looking blondes who are in shape, but who are also young mothers who are pushing their babies in strollers."

"Okay."

"He snatches them at malls, but he doesn't like covered parking lots. Maybe there's a little claustrophobia going on there."

"Okay," Steinbach said, again.

"He leaves the babies in Dumpsters, probably so they'll be found alive."

"Again, we're assuming this one died by accident."

"Right."

"Go on."

"This new one aside, why didn't he kill the babies? Why leave them alive?"

"Why not? They can't identify him."

"That's true, but I think it's something else."

"Like what?"

Keough hesitated, then said in annoyance, "I don't know. Some sort of—" He made a face. "Psychological explanation. Let's go onto the women. He keeps them a while, sexually assaults them, then kills them, leaving them in different places."

"He has sex with them alive," Steinbach added, "and dead."

That stopped Keough for a moment. "I didn't know that."

"It's in the report on the second woman."

"Bite marks?"

"Yep," Steinbach said, "he's a biter."

"What we don't know," Keough said, "is if he kills the women on purpose, or in the act of having sex with them. Maybe he doesn't mean to kill them."

"You're giving him a lot of credit."

"On the contrary," Keough said, "I think we're dealing with a stupid man here."

Steinbach sat up straight. "Oh, explain this one to me,

Sherlock. You mean you don't think we're dealing with an educated man? I mean, that's sometimes part of the profile, isn't it? Educated, thinks he smarter than the police? I've read some of the books, too, you know."

Keough shook his head, warming to his subject.

"No, I don't think he's smart at all, Al," Keough said. "If he was he wouldn't be taking the chances he's taking."

"Like what?"

"Well, like attacking the dark-haired woman because she got in his way," Keough said. "He followed her out to the parking lot just to hit her. That's not smart at all. I mean, he let her *see* him. If he was smarter than us he wouldn't have done that."

Steinbach rubbed his jaw.

"You're right about that. If he was smart he wouldn't let her see him and then leave her alive."

"Exactly—and that reminds me. We've got to get an artist with a sketch pad or an identikit to these women."

"I'll take care of that on Monday."

Keough sighed.

"I guess we'll have to meet with Jackson on Monday and fill him in on what we have."

"That should be interesting. You know, he's going to go one of two ways."

"How's that?"

"He's either going to want to be in charge—with Mc-Gwire as the figurehead—or he's going to want to go off on his own."

"That would suit me," Keough said. "I can work easier

with you than with you and him—and we've got a head start on this. Let him go his own way. Maybe he's good enough to catch this guy on his own."

"You don't want the credit?"

"I just want the crazy bastard caught, Al. Jackson can have the credit—or you. I'm not worried about that part of it."

They left the tip, split the bill two ways, and went up front to pay it. They paused outside in the parking lot.

"Is this task force going to make the papers?" he asked Steinbach.

"That's something we'll have to talk about on Monday with Jackson, and the captain."

"If he knows we're after him, he might stop."

"Isn't that good enough?"

"No," Keough said, "he's got to be caught. What if he moves to another city, or another state, and just starts again?"

"I see what you mean. All right, we'll talk about it Monday. Try and enjoy the rest of your weekend."

They split up and got into their respective cars. Steinbach drove off and at the last minute Keough decided not to go into the Richmond Heights station, but to simply drive home.

Thirty-four

WHEN HE READ about the dead baby in the Sunday paper, he sat down in the middle of the floor, crossed his legs, held his head in his hands, and rocked.

This wasn't supposed to happen. His mother was going to be very angry with him. He was supposed to be looking out for his little brother. How could he have let this happen? It wasn't his fault . . . it was the baby-sitter's fault . . . that little blond bitch . . . she was supposed to be watching . . .

Then, through tears of anger and frustration and fear, he suddenly realized the truth. He was not a child, he was an adult. His mother was dead, and his little brother was alive, living in another city, in another state, a very successful businessman.

This dead child was not his brother, was not even related to him. No one was going to scold him or blame him. It wasn't his fault the little boy was dead. He had disposed of him the same way he had the others, and they weren't dead. They'd been found, the way they were supposed to be. It wasn't his fault that something had gone wrong.

He stopped crying, stopped rocking, and got up off the floor. He took the newspaper to the sofa and read the article all the way through. Sure, he felt bad that the boy was dead, but it wasn't his fault.

It was everybody else's.

So there was no need for him to be concerned. He could continue to go out and do what he was doing, keep searching for the perfect woman, a cross between the women in the adult movies, and his mother.

He stood up and walked to the coffee table, where he had some framed photographs of his family: his dead father, his little brother, both as a baby and grown, and his dead mother. In the photo she was smiling, her long blond hair blowing slightly in the wind, and she was pushing a stroller, which held his little brother.

This was the only photo he had of his mother, because it was his favorite. She was never more beautiful than she was in this picture. He stared at the photo, touching the glass of the picture frame, and then frowning. This was his mother, wasn't it? It could have been the baby-sitter. No, no, what was wrong with him? This was his mother. The baby-sitter, though young and blond, had never been as pretty as his mother.

Never.

He put the photo back down on the table, next to the mail—there was another bill from the video place, again, for the tape he'd never returned—then turned and walked to the kitchen.

It was early, and now that he was over the initial shock

of the story about the dead baby, he could make himself something for breakfast.

His eyes still felt itchy from the tears he'd foolishly spent, but he tried to ignore them. He took out the milk and peaches from the refrigerator, added both to a bowl of cereal, then carried it to the TV. He had folded up his sofa bed, so he sat on the sofa and started the tape in the machine and ate his cereal while he watched his favorite movie.

Thirty-five

KEOUGH STOPPED INTO the Richmond Heights station early Monday morning just to verify what Steinbach had told him on Saturday. He got the word from Sergeant Bilcheck.

"Three-man task force, my friend, you, Steinbach, and Jackson—and good luck dealing with Jackson."

"What's the story on him, anyway?" Keough asked.

"Ego."

"Is he any good?"

"He's got the skills," Bilcheck said, "but that ego gets in

his way. Some people say he's got such a big ego you'd think he was from New York."

"And people say New Yorkers have an attitude."

"Do me a favor, will you?"

"What?"

"Catch this guy quick and get back here?"

"Will you miss me?"

Bilchek smiled and said, "I'll be a man short."

"Same thing," Keough said, as he went out the door.

Keough was ready to start his new assignment because on Sunday he had gone to Forest Park and finally put a kite in the air. It was a small thing, but it had cleared his head, and now that he'd done it once he knew he'd get into a routine.

When he reached the office of the Major Case Squad, Steinbach was already there waiting with a brown paper bag that said "Einstein's Bros. Bagels" on it.

"Coffee and bagel," Steinbach said.

"At least it's not a donut," Keough said.

"I don't deal in stereotypes. Pull up a chair, you can share my desk."

"That Jackson's?" Keough asked, indicating the other desk in the small room.

"That's right."

"There's nothing on it."

"He's a neat freak."

Steinbach took out two bagels.

"Butter or cream cheese? It's raspberry."

"I'll take the butter."

Steinbach handed it to him.

"Where's the boss?"

"He's got an office through there." He inclined his head toward a door set in the back wall. "He'll want to see the three of us in about fifteen minutes. Time enough to eat a bagel."

In fifteen minutes Jackson still had not arrived.

"This figures," Steinbach said, wadding up the paper his breakfast had been wrapped in and tossing it into the waste basket.

"What does?"

"Jackson. He's making a statement."

"Has he got that kind of pull?"

"Yeah," Steinbach said. "He solved a couple of cases last year, really lucked into the solutions, if you ask me. They put him at the top of the heap."

"Well," Keough said, "Us bottom-of-the-heapers better go and see the boss."

"I read O'Donnell's book," Steinbach said, as they stood up. "You're not such a bottom-of-the-heaper."

"O'Donnell made me sound good."

"Uh-huh," Steinbach said, but didn't pursue the matter.

They entered the captain's office after Steinbach knocked at the door.

"Have a seat," McGwire said. "Jackson won't be here, he's working on a lead."

Keough and Steinbach exchanged a glance.

"Am I to understand that you two have been working together already?"

"We've been comparing notes," Steinbach said.

"What are we looking at here in the way of more victims?"

"There's two definites, and a woman who's still missing," Steinbach said. "She may or may not show up as one of his victims."

"Was one of the Dumpster kids hers?"

"Yes." Steinbach had checked with the husband when they reunited him with the child, and the man verified his wife was still missing.

"Then she's dead."

"More than likely," Keough said.

"Then there's nothing else I can say but go out and catch this guy."

"We can do that, Cap," Steinbach said.

"Then do it."

Keough looked at Steinbach, who jerked his head and started to get up.

"What was that all about?" Keough asked when they were out in the hall.

"He's a man of few words."

"I'll say."

"He won't get in our way," Steinbach said, "that's what's important."

"Now if Jackson would do the same thing," Keough said, "we'd be in business."

Since they each had their own car they decided to split up.

"We'll cover more ground that way," Steinbach said, in the parking lot. "Plus, we're really not used to working with each other. We'd be spending too much time trying not to step on each other's toes. We can just keep doing what we've been doing—and now we don't have other cases getting in the way."

"That's fine by me," Keough said. "Since all of the victims that we know of have shown up, what we need to do now is try to get a witness to give us a good look at the perp."

"That's my job," Steinbach said. "I'll have an artist talk to the witness he hit—what's her name?"

"Marie Tobin."

"Right. Give me her address and I'll take care of it."

Keough tore out the page in his notebook with Marie Tobin's name, address, and phone number on it and handed it to Steinbach.

"I've still got to talk to a detective named Taylor," Keough said. "He works undercover for Narcotics in the Galleria. Maybe he saw something along the way that doesn't mean anything to him, but might mean something to us."

"That's fine," Steinbach said. "What do you say we meet back here about three this afternoon to compare notes? Do you have a radio?"

"No."

"Hold on," Steinbach said. "I've got two units in my car."

He retrieved the two radios and they made sure they were on the same channel. They also exchanged call numbers so they'd be able to identify each other.

"Okay, let's get the ball rolling on this," Steinbach said.

"See you back here at three," Keough said.

Steinbach went back inside to make some calls and arrange for an artist to visit Marie Tobin. Keough got into his car and drove out of the parking lot.

He couldn't help but think that now that he was off the chart, not catching any other cases, he might be able to sneak in some time on the Brady Sanders case. He still had it in his mind that there was something going on between Bill Sanders and the girl who worked at his office, Miss Bonny.

He hoped he'd be able to check it out without running into Ken Jackson.

Thirty-six

WHEN KEOUGH ARRIVED at the Richmond Heights station, there was a message telling him to be at the Galleria at two that afternoon to meet Detective Taylor. He was to sit on one of the benches outside Brentano's Bookstore, near the fountains.

Keough had time to kill before going to the Galleria and no other leads to pursue in the case of the—the what? What were they calling him? Since one of the children had shown up dead, maybe they should just call their man the Mother-and-Child Killer—or better yet, the Mall Rat.

That was it. He decided to think of the man from now on as the Mall Rat.

He decided to drive over to the real estate office where Sanders had worked and see what he could see. Maybe he could just shake Miss Bonny up a little bit, and see what fell out of her pretty head.

He parked right in front and went inside. Miss Bonny was at her desk, as she had been the first time he was there. She looked up and her eyes widened when she recognized him.

"Detective . . ." She groped for his name.

"Keough."

"Yes," she said. "Would you, uh, like to see Mr. Riverside again?"

"No," he said. "I came just to see you, Miss Bonny."

"Me?" she asked, looking astonished—or frightened. "Whatever for?"

"I was wondering if you'd heard from Mr. Sanders."

Her eyes darted around the room, a dead giveaway that she was about to tell a whopper.

"Why would I see him?"

To Keough it was a sure sign that someone had to lie but was desperately trying not to when they answered a question with a question, as Miss Bonny had done.

"I don't know," Keough said, "I just thought you might have been contacted by him. After all, you did say that you were friends, didn't you?"

"No, sir," she said, firmly, "I did not. I said nothing of the sort. I said we worked together, and that's all."

"Really?"

"Yes, really."

Keough contrived to look puzzled.

"Hmm, where did I get my information, then?"

"That's what I'd like to know," she said, suddenly indignant.

"I'll have to check my notes, won't I?" he asked her. "Thanks for your time, Miss Bonny."

"You're . . . welcome."

He left her looking dazed and confused. He was convinced now more than ever that she had a thing for Bill Sanders.

He got in the car and turned on the motor, then the radio, but did not drive off.

He considered following Miss Bonny when she left for lunch, but decided against it. It would probably make more sense to follow her in the evening, after work. If she were going to rendezvous with Sanders, night would seem most likely. She hadn't done it the other times he'd watched her, but maybe he'd get lucky.

In the end he started the car and drove straight down Clayton Road until he reached the intersection of Brentwood Boulevard, where the Galleria was. He was several hours early, but he decided to take a good look at the mall, and possibly even pick out some likely victims for the Mall Rat. Were they plentiful in malls at this time of the year? Or would the killer have to search for the right one to be his next victim?

He parked in one of the surface lots and spent the next

two hours girl watching. It was a hell of a way to make a living.

Two hours later he had seen one likely victim, a blond mother with an equally blond daughter in a stroller. He chose to do his watching from the same bench where he was supposed to meet Detective Taylor. While sitting there he started to think about the time of the year they were in. It was September, and the weather had been pretty mild since the beginning of the month. There were still lots of shorts and halter tops and tank tops in the mall, but there were also some people covering up a little more than they had during July and August.

Katherine Fouquet, the woman with the six-year-old, had been attacked in July. Marie Tobin had been punched in August. Maybe he'd take another victim in September. What would happen in October and then November when the weather got colder? Was he attacking women who not only looked a certain way, but dressed a certain way, as well? What would happen when the women began to cover up?

What if this wasn't the first summer this killer had struck?

His reverie was broken when a man sat on the bench with him, at the other end.

"I don't want it to look like we're together."

Keough looked at the man. He was dressed in jeans and a black Harley T-shirt and worn sneakers. He looked like he needed a shave, a haircut, and probably a bath.

"Taylor?"

"That's right. You're Keough. I've seen you around the station."

"I haven't seen you."

"I'm in and out," Taylor said. "Listen, I've got some information about a buy going down at the Dillard's end of the mall. Can we get to the point?"

"It looks as if women are being snatched from mall parking lots," Keough said. "I was wondering if you'd seen anything."

"When?"

"All summer, since July."

"Is this about the women who were found in the men's room and under the Dumpster?"

"That's right."

"They were grabbed from here?"

"I don't know if those women were grabbed from this location," Keough said, "but I do know that he tried for a woman in this parking lot in July and didn't get her."

"Why not?"

"She had a six-year-old who ran. Since then he's taken women with strollers."

"Jesus. Hey, the babies found in the Dumpsters?"

"Those are the ones."

"Bastard."

"We found another baby on Saturday."

"Saturday," Taylor repeated. "I didn't hear."

"At a garbage dump," Keough said. "Dead."

"Jesus."

"So think it over, Taylor," Keough said. "Maybe you

saw a woman being hassled, or followed. Maybe it didn't mean anything to you at the time."

"I'll give it some thought."

"Blond women," Keough said, "pretty, well built, pushing strollers."

"This guy's sick."

"Yeah, he is," Keough said. "That's why there's a new three-man task force setup to try and catch him."

"You and who else?"

"Detectives Steinbach and Jackson, from Major Case."

"Steinbach's okay, but Jackson . . ." He made a face and shook his head.

"I'm finding that out."

"I've got to go," Taylor said, looking at his watch. "Where do I call you if I remember something?"

"Leave a message at Richmond Heights, or call Major Case."

"Okay," Taylor said, and without further word got up and wandered off—at least, it looked like he was wandering off. He was shuffling his feet, and his head was down. Very few people were paying attention to him. Keough thought he was a little obvious for an undercover vice cop, but then maybe that was just his New York attitude.

Thirty-seven

WHEN KEOUGH GOT back to his new office there was a message waiting for him, relayed from the Richmond Heights station. He was to call Mrs. Valerie Speck at children's services. Not knowing if this was a business or pleasure call he decided to return it immediately.

"Oh God, I'm glad you called, Joe."

"What's wrong?"

"It's the foster parents I placed Brady with."

"What about them?"

"They called and said a man was hanging around the house looking inside."

"Was he looking for Brady?" Keough asked, wondering if the man could possibly be the boy's father.

"I don't know."

"Were the police there?"

"Yes."

"When did it happen?"

"Earlier today. I called your station around noon, but they said you weren't there anymore."

"I've been temporarily reassigned."

"Can you do something, anyway?"

"Yes, I'll take a ride, uh, out there." He pulled a pad over and asked her for the address. She gave it to him and told him it was in Florissant, then had to tell him where that was. It was well north of St. Louis, and she gave him directions.

"Why was he placed all the way out there?"

"Luck of the draw."

"All right," he said. "I'm on my way."

"Oh, thanks, Joe. They're real shaken up, and the police out there didn't do much to soothe their fears."

Keough didn't bother telling her there wasn't much the police could have done if the man was gone when they arrived. Unless . . .

"Did the man actually see or talk to Brady?"

"No," she said, "Brady was at preschool."

"Valerie," he asked, "did anyone go to the school to see if Brady was okay?"

"Oh God . . . I don't know. Lord, what if . . . Joe, the Goodmans weren't told about Brady's parents. We don't give out that kind of information. They wouldn't have any reason to think to go to the school—"

"Look," he said, "just relax. I'll take a ride out there, ask some questions, check on Brady, and then I'll call you tonight."

"Could we meet somewhere," she asked, then added, "I mean, to talk about it?"

"Sure, pick a place and tell me when I can call you."

"All right. Thanks for doing this, Joe."

"Hey," he said, "I'm concerned about Brady, too."

He hung up, wrote a note for Steinbach, and then left the building to drive to Florissant.

Keough found the neighborhood he wanted without much difficulty. Valerie's directions had been very easy to follow. He pulled up in front of one of many private homes on a block that reminded him of some parts of Brooklyn. He parked his car in front of the address she had given him, walked to the door, and rang the bell.

The woman who answered the door was in her thirties, plain-looking in a pleasant way. She was drying her hands on a dish towel.

"Mrs. Goodman?"

"That's right."

"My name is Detective Keough." He took out his shield and ID and showed it to her.

"Frank!" she called. "Can you come here?" She looked at Keough and said, "Frank is my husband."

Keough nodded and waited. Frank Goodman was also in his thirties, slightly overweight, soft-looking, with a receding hairline and a slack jaw. Together they looked at Keough's identification.

"What can we do for you, Detective?" Mr. Goodman asked, handing the ID back.

"I'm the detective who was originally working on Brady's case, Mr. and Mrs. Goodman. I—"

"Detective Keyhole!" Mrs. Goodman said, interrupting him.

"What?"

"That's what Brady calls you."

"It is?"

"That's right," Mr. Goodman said. "He's said it a few times. Keyhole. We weren't sure what he meant."

"May I come in and see Brady?"

"Of course," Mr. Goodman said, and they both backed up to let him enter.

"Brady has talked about you," Mrs. Goodman said. "He told us you gave him cookies."

"I did," Keough said. "Chocolate chip."

"His favorite."

"I didn't know that," Keough said. "It was all we had available at the station."

"What brings you here, Detective?" Mr. Goodman asked. "Are you checking on Brady?"

"Yes, sir," Keough said. "I wanted to see how he was, but I also spoke to Mrs. Speck and she, uh, told me about the, uh, incident."

"The man who was here," Mrs. Goodman said.

"That's right. Can you tell me what happened?"

"Well," she said, "I was in the laundry room and when I came out I saw this man looking in the kitchen window. I didn't say anything right away, just watched him. When he went to the kitchen door and tried to open it—well, I'm afraid that's when I yelled."

"Then what happened?"

"He ran off."

"And what did you do?"

"She called me," her husband chimed in, "and I called the police."

"Mrs. Goodman," Keough said, "can you describe the man?"

"I'm afraid I can't," she said. "Oh, he was white, and had dark hair, and I had the impression that he was about our age, but that's all. I didn't get a very good look at him, you see."

"I understand."

"Why are you here about this, Detective?" Mr. Goodman asked.

"As I told you, sir," Keough said, "I wanted to check on the boy."

"We don't know all the particulars about Brady's case, Detective," Mr. Goodman said. "We know about you finding him, and we know that he calls you Detective Keyhole, but that's about all. Is there something else we should know?"

"I'm sure if there was, Mr. Goodman, Mrs. Speck would have told you."

"Is there anything for us to be . . . concerned about?"

"No," Keough lied. "I don't think so." Keough didn't want to say anything to them without talking to Valerie first. He was of the opinion, however, that they should have been told more before they took Brady in.

"Can I see Brady before I go?"

"Of course," Mrs. Goodman said. "He's in his room. I'll get him."

"Why don't I just go and see him there?"

Brady's foster parents exchanged a glance and then Mr. Goodman said, "Well, I don't see why not."

"I'll show you his room," Mrs. Goodman said.

"Thank you."

She led Keough down a hallway and stopped at the first doorway they came to. Inside the room, which was furnished for a child Brady's age, the boy sat on the floor, playing with some interconnecting plastic blocks.

Brady looked up, saw Keough, and said, "Keyhole," with no expression, or particular inflection.

"Thank you," Keough said to Mrs. Goodman again, and she was intimidated enough by him to withdraw and return to the living room with her husband.

Keough moved into the room and crouched down on one knee.

"Hiya, Brady."

"Hi." The boy's eyes did not leave the blocks, which he was laboriously building into something Keough wasn't sure he'd recognize.

"What have you got there?"

"Legos."

"Ah." Keough had seen commercials, so although they had not been immediately recognizable to him, he did know the name when he heard it.

"How are you, Brady?"

"Fine."

"Brady," Keough said, "did a man come to school to see you today?"

"No."

"Did you see your daddy today, Brady?"

"No." The boy was still working on the blocks.

"Have you seen your daddy, uh, lately?" He wasn't sure the boy would know what "lately" meant. He didn't know how a child perceived time.

But the boy answered, "No."

At that point Mr. Goodman appeared in the doorway.

"Detective?"

Keough held up a hand.

"I'll see you soon, okay, Brady?"

At this point Brady looked at him and, without a smile, said, "Keyhole."

"That's right, Brady," he said, "I'm your friend, Keyhole."

Brady turned his attention back to the blocks.

"Detective?"

"Yes, sir." Keough stood up and followed Mr. Goodman back down the hall to the living room.

"Mr. and Mrs. Goodman," he said, before they could speak, "what school is Brady in?"

Mrs. Goodman answered immediately, before her husband could stop her.

"Florissant Nursery."

"Detective Keough," Mr. Goodman said, "this doesn't feel right to me. I don't think we want to answer anymore questions."

"That's fine, Mr. Goodman," Keough said. "That's your right."

"And I intend to call Mrs. Speck about you."

"Please do, if it will put your mind at ease."

"Please leave now."

"Frank—" his wife said, but he silenced her with a look.

"Of course," Keough said. "Thank you for letting me see Brady."

Keough went out the front door and walked to his car, realizing that he was leaving behind a very suspicious Mr. Goodman. He hoped that he hadn't caused problems for Brady with his foster parents.

Thirty-eight

"I WENT TO the school, not expecting to find anyone. Luckily, they have a conscientious director. She was working late."

"And?"

"She said the nursery school has very good security, because they've had to deal with divorced parents grabbing children in the past. She said that if anyone had been around the school looking for Brady, she would have heard about it."

"And do you think she would have?"

"She likes to think she has good security, but what she probably has is a couple of tired, retired cops, or worse, a couple of security guards with no experience at all."

"Is that what schools like that had in Brooklyn?"

"Was that my Brooklyn attitude coming through?"

"It was. In my experience, though, you hide it quite well most of the time—better than your Brooklyn accent, anyway."

"What's wrong with my accent?"

"Nothing," Valerie Speck said. "I think it's charming."

They were sitting across a table from each other in a chain restaurant called The Black Eyed Pea, which Keough had never heard of before he moved to St. Louis. This one was on Watson Road, in Crestwood, and served country-style food. Valerie had recommended a baked potato smothered in pot roast, as well as a vegetable he'd never had before: fried corn. She'd chosen this place because it was near her home, which he now knew was in Sunset Hills.

He'd never before had anyone tell him that his accent was "charming."

"Anyway," he said, "the school saw no one, Mrs. Goodman can't identify anyone, and Brady says he hasn't seen his father."

"Do you think Brady's telling the truth?"

"I think they're all telling the truth," he said. "I also think I may have caused some trouble for Brady."

She remained silent.

"Did I?"

"I'm afraid you did—although it's not your fault, Joe. I asked you to go out there."

"What happened?"

"They want to give him up."

"Can they do that?"

"They can."

"What happens now?"

"I'll have to find another home for him."

"And where will he stay in the meantime?"

She sighed and said, "He has to go back to a shelter. I'm going to pick him up tomorrow."

"Damn!"

"Not your fault, Joe," she said, again.

"Ah, I probably could have been more discreet." He was disgusted with himself.

"Families do this a lot, Joe," she said. "They take in children, then discover they didn't really want them, or they don't really want *this* one—"

"Or maybe some cop comes in and screws it up . . ."

"Try your corn."

He picked it up and bit into it, and was surprised at how good it was. It was a small ear of corn on the cob with a fried coating on it.

"Good." He put it back down on the plate.

"Do you think it was Brady's father?"

"It could have been," he said, "but how would he have found him?"

"I don't know."

"Could he have gotten the address from someone in your office?"

"I suppose that's possible."

"Well, if it was him he got it from somewhere, and if it was him it means he's still around."

"What can you do about that?"

"I can tell the detective in charge."

"Nothing more?"

"I've been reassigned, Valerie," he said, and went on to tell her about the new case.

"That's . . . disgusting," she said, when he was done.

"Yes."

"And the third woman, has she shown up yet?"

"No."

"Do you think she's . . . dead?"

"Yes."

"Those poor children . . . that poor baby."

He saw that her eyes were tearing up.

"Hey, hey," he said, "you're a professional, you deal with kids everyday."

"Not dead ones," she said, dabbing at her eyes with her napkin. "Bruised and battered ones, abandoned ones, but they're still alive. This poor child won't have a chance to grow up . . ."

"That's not necessarily a bad thing."

She stared at him.

"Sorry," he said. "Attitude, again."

"I know some children turn out to be . . . people you wouldn't want to know."

"That's such a nice way of putting it."

"But I think they all deserve the right to grow up."

"I agree, Valerie," he said. "I'm just as sick about that dead baby as you are."

"I hope you find the bastard," she said, fervently, "and I hope he suffers for what he's done."

"We'll find him."

Slowly her features relaxed and her eyes cleared. He wondered if that was what she'd look like when in the throes of passion.

"What about Brady?"

"I'll give Detective Jackson the information," he said, and then trailed off.

"What is it?"

He had just realized that if he'd been pulled off all of his cases to work on the Mall Rat case and Steinbach had also, then the same had to be true for Jackson.

That meant he didn't know who was working on the Sanders case, if anyone.

"Joe?"

"Just a thought, that's all."

"Must have been a heavy one."

He smiled.

"I'll talk to the detective working Brady's case, Valerie," he said. "And I'll keep an eye on it."

"You care about him, don't you?"

Keough hesitated, then said, "Yeah, I do. I care what happens to him. I also care about what happened to his parents."

"If that was his father out in Florissant, then where's his mother? Dead?"

"Maybe."

"Why hasn't her body been found?"

"I don't know."

"Poor you," she said, suddenly.

"Why?"

"You're waiting for two more women to show up dead," she said, reaching across the table and putting her hand on his. "That must be hard on you."

"Well . . . it isn't easy."

She left her hand there for a few more moments, then removed it.

"I appreciate being able to talk to you about this, Valerie."

"I'm glad you feel you can, Joe."

Aside from their business dealings, Keough quite liked this other game they were playing. It was more fun than just rushing to bed the first night they had gone out.

In the parking lot they stood by her car.

"I have to get up early," she said.

"So do I."

He kissed her, and she clung to him for a moment. As if she was a mind reader she said in his ear, "I like this game."

She got into her car quickly, and drove away.

Thirty-nine

"WHERE WERE YOU yesterday afternoon?" Steinbach said as Keough walked into the office the next morning.

"Had to run an errand," Keough said.

"Did it have to do with our case?"

Keough made a face. "Not exactly."

Steinbach gave him a look and said, "Maybe you should let me in on it."

Keough sat down and accepted the container of coffee Steinbach offered him. He proceeded to tell him not only about the errand, but about his whole day. The other detective listened intently and did not interrupt.

"So?" Keough said, when he was finished.

"So what?"

"So, who's taking Jackson's cases while he's working with us?"

"That's a good question."

"How do we find out the answer?"

"Well," Steinbach said, dropping his feet down off the desk, "we can ask him, or we can look at the files."

"Let's look at the files."

Steinbach went to a file cabinet against the wall—one of three—and opened it. He pulled a file out, opened it, and scanned it. His eyebrows went up and he looked at Keough.

"What?"

"The case is closed."

Keough sat straight up. "It can't be."

"It can, and is," Steinbach said. "No progress, he says. No body. Closed until further evidence arises."

"How can further evidence come to light if he's not looking for it?"

"You want to take a look?" Steinbach offered Keough the file.

"You bet I do."

He got up and took the file from Steinbach. "Shit," he said, and dropped the file on top of the file cabinet. Steinbach retrieved it and returned it to the drawer.

"What are you thinking?" he asked.

"He closed it prematurely," Keough said, "probably because of this task force thing. First he didn't think there was a serial killer, and now he wants the credit for catching him so bad that he'll shitcan some other cases."

"It's not some other cases you're talking about," Steinbach said. "It's this one in particular, the Sanders case."

"You're right."

"Is it the little boy?"

"Yes . . . partly."

"What else?"

"I want to know what happened," Keough said. "Don't you? Isn't that why we became detectives?"

Steinbach studied Keough for a few moments before replying.

"Joe, this is not New York. We don't have unlimited manpower. Sure, I'd like to know what happened to the Sanderses. I'd also like to know what happened to half a dozen other people who are missing, or who were killed. The simple fact of the matter is, I don't and I probably never will. I'm sure the same is true of you."

"In spades," Keough said, "but this is different."

"Why? Because it involves a little boy?"

"Because there are still avenues of investigation to be pursued, that's why. It's not ready to be closed."

"Take it up with Jackson, then."

"Sure," Keough said. "He'll welcome my input."

"The boss, then."

"I don't like Jackson," Keough said, "but I'm not ready to go over a fellow officer's head."

"Then what do you intend to do?"

Keough thought a moment, then said, "I don't know."

"If this task force thing is going to work we need to work together," Steinbach said. "I need to know you're with me on this, one hundred percent."

"I am," Keough said, "but what about Jackson?"

"He's the flavor of the month, Joe," Steinbach said, "the prima donna. He's off on his own, and if he catches the guy, fine, but I think it's you and me, working together, who are going to catch him—that is, if we're both committed to it."

"I'm committed, Al."

"All right, then," Steinbach said. "Let's work on it."

* * *

Working on it meant some brainstorming while they waited for a sketch of the suspect from Marie Tobin and Kate Fouquet.

"What have we got so far?" Steinbach asked.

"We've got a guy who has a mother fixation."

"I thought you didn't like psychobabble?"

"I don't," Keough said, "but hear me out."

"Go ahead."

He went through it all again. The young mothers who were pushing baby strollers, the mothers turning up dead. Was the Mall Rat killing his own mother? Was the third baby killed by accident?

Steinbach nodded during all this and waited for Keough to go on. Unlike Jackson, who resented Keough for his New York experience, Steinbach thought he could learn a lot from a man like Keough. He himself had rarely been out of St. Louis.

"We know he's working malls, and we know he prefers the surface parking lots to the covered lots."

"We *know* that?"

"I think we know that," Keough said.

"So we've got a guy who likes blond mothers, has sex with them, and kills them—"

"Sometimes he has sex with them *after* he kills them."

"—and takes the babies and leaves them someplace relatively safe."

"Right."

Steinbach shook his head.

"He thinks a Dumpster is someplace safe?"

"Well, two out of three times, it was."

"Joe," Steinbach said, "how do we know he'll do it again? After all, we only found two women."

"There's another one out there, Al," Keough said. "Three babies, three mothers. She just hasn't turned up."

"And she might never," Steinbach added.

"I know."

"Maybe he'll just stop."

"I hope not."

"What would be so wrong with that?"

"I want to catch him, Al," Keough said, "that's what would be so wrong."

"You take being a detective real serious, don't you?"

"Don't you?"

"It's a job," Steinbach said. "That's all. All I ever wanted to be was a policeman. When they promoted me to detective I took the job because it paid more. To tell you the truth, I'd rather be riding around the street in a car."

"Then why aren't you?"

"I've got a wife and two kids, remember?" Steinbach said. "My life's not my own."

They stared at each other for a few moments, then around the room, each alone with his own thoughts for a short while.

"Not much to do before we get the sketches," Steinbach said.

"I know," Keough said. "If the sketches match we'll be able to start showing them in malls."

"And if they don't?"

Keough shrugged.

"Lunch?" Steinbach asked.

"It's not lunch time."

"Let's fake it."

Keough shrugged. He'd eat something, only because there was nothing else to do—for now.

Forty

HE WAS BACK at Crestwood. Mid-Rivers had been a flop. He hadn't seen one woman there who had attracted him, let alone started his heart pumping the way it did when he *really* wanted one of them. Oh, there were plenty of women with strollers, but none of them were right.

So, back to Crestwood, to see if he could find the one who got away.

Crestwood had a Dillard's at one end, and a Famous-Barr at the other. Right in the center was a Sears. Crestwood resembled two shopping centers that had been connected and covered and made into one large mall.

Downstairs, on the Famous-Barr side, was an arcade and fun center that had everything from video games to bumper cars to virtual reality.

He'd been in there once and hated it. Boys with pants

that were too baggy and baseball caps worn backwards, weird haircuts, body piercings, and pretty young girls hanging onto them like they were the catch of the day. It disgusted him.

But the food court was down there as well, and he did get hungry or have to follow a pretty woman down there.

Crestwood had covered parking beneath the Dillard's side of the mall, otherwise it was all surface parking from one end to the other. He chose the times he went to the malls carefully. It was usually on weekends, when they were very crowded, because that's when he felt his prey would be out.

This time, however, it was between lunch and dinner on a weekday, and it was also the time of year when the kids were going back to school, so the mall was particularly empty. The weather would be changing soon, and the young mothers would start covering up. October, though, would bring Indian summer. He had until at least November before sweaters and long pants would be the uniform of the day.

If this was the Galleria he'd be sitting right about in the center of the mall, where FAO Schwarz and Kay Bee toys were located. Crestwood did not have a Schwarz, but they had a Kay Bee. He got himself a pretzel and a Coke and sat on a bench in front of some decorative plants where he had a good view of the toy store. He used to stake out the clothing stores, but there were more young women without babies shopping there. He'd finally realized that the toy stores were the places to watch, with the food courts a close second.

Unfortunately, sitting several doors down from the toy store put him right in front of a lingerie store. This distracted him. In fact, the photos in the window aroused him, but not in the way his young mothers did. Still, it was a distraction . . .

He was not a very smart man. It did not dawn on him that with the mall this empty he would stand out—especially in front of a lingerie shop. He usually wore torn jeans and a soiled T-shirt when he was doing what the psychologists called trolling for his victims. This mode of dress blended in very well with weekend crowds, but during the week, when the shoppers were dressed for work, the thin, dark-haired man with long, lank, dirty hair and a homeless-style wardrobe stood out like a sore thumb.

Which was why there was trouble.

Patricia Dey had been working in Frederick's of Hollywood for over a year. A fortyish mother of two teenage girls, she enjoyed her job. There was nothing in that store that she could ever wear. Not only was she too shy ever to wear these types of garments, but she was not built for them. Still, she had acquired the ability to match her customers with certain items, and enjoyed doing so. It made her feel useful, and that was the reason she had come to Crestwood Mall looking for a job in the first place.

She had also acquired the ability to spot certain types of men who habitually took up a station just outside the store. Most of them were husbands waiting for their wives, who were off pillaging the mall, and who figured this was as good a place as any to wait. They watched the women and girls who went in and out, and looked at the photos in the windows, but they were harmless.

Then there were the other types, the weirdos who not only watched the women, but fantasized about them and—eventually—made remarks to them as they went in and out, the occasional man who looked at the photos in the windows not as advertisements, but as something else, entirely—like entertainment.

There was a man like that sitting outside the store right now, and she decided to call security before the creep decided to make a move on one of her customers.

Gary Neibuhr had been a security guard at Crestwood Mall for about three months. He had no police experience whatsoever. He had come out of college with a degree in criminal law, and had not been able to get a job in law enforcement. He was on several waiting lists for city and state jobs, but in the meantime he had been able to get this job because they had been impressed with his degree.

Of course, his degree did not prepare him for the kinds of people he would have to deal with in mall security—especially a mall like Crestwood, which had a large teen population because of the arcade. Belligerent teens were the norm, as well as pickpockets, purse snatchers, and snatch-and-grab artists who targeted the big department stores.

And then there were people like this fellow sitting on a bench a few stores down from Kay Bee Toy Store.

Well, a few doors down from the toy store was a Frederick's of Hollywood store.

The call had come in from an employee in Frederick's who reported a suspicious man sitting outside her store. The man was suspicious, all right. He also looked like the kind who hadn't changed his underwear in three days.

Neibuhr had run this type off before. They were usually the same types who peeped in windows, and they rarely caused trouble when asked to move. He didn't anticipate any problem running this one off, either.

He didn't see the security guard approaching. His attention was split between the front of the toy store, and the photo of the full-breasted woman in the hot pink teddy in the window of Frederick's. He was also wondering if they'd give him a calender if he went into Frederick's.

"Hey, you."

He was startled by the voice. He looked up and saw a uniformed security man looking down at him. The man was not large, and was about the same age as he was. He was wearing a gun, and his hand was resting on the butt of it.

"Me?"

"What are you doin'?"

"Just sitting."

"Are you waiting for someone?"

He looked away and said, "No."

He was a bad liar. His mother had always told him that. He had *never* gotten away with lying to her.

"Are you here with someone?"

He looked at the guard this time when he said, "No."

"I think you better move on."

"I ain't doing nothing."

"I know," the guard said, "but you're botherin' people."

He shook his head, not understanding. "But I ain't doing nothing."

"You're just sittin' here," the guard said. "This is a mall. Either shop, or leave."

That was when he looked down at the toy store and saw her.

Kate Fouquet had spent the morning with the sketch artist, giving him a description of the man who had tried to grab her and her six-year-old daughter late in June. When they were done and the police artist had left, she suddenly felt better. She'd been a prisoner in her own home since the incident had occurred, but now that she had contributed something toward finding the man, she felt free.

She decided to go to the mall, and while she would not bring her daughter with her—she was not feeling *that* good yet—she decided to go to the toy store and buy something for her. The poor kid loved the Galleria and the Crestwood Mall and its arcade, and she did not understand why they had not gone there in three months. Luckily, the incident in the parking lot did not weigh heavily on her mind.

As she was entering the Kay Bee Toy Store, she noticed a security guard talking to a man on a bench—and she suddenly stopped, a cold feeling in the pit of her stomach.

It was him!

He recognized the woman, but it was not the one he had been looking for. In fact, he had never expected to see this woman again. She was still blond and pretty, a perfect specimen, but she had been the first woman he'd attempted to grab, the one with the daughter who had run off screaming. That had been a huge mistake. He had been so attracted to her that he ignored the fact that she did not have a stroller. It was later that he realized his mistake and corrected it.

Now, however, it seemed that the mistake might come back and haunt him, for she was looking right at him, and from her expression, she recognized him.

". . . got to get going—" the security guard was saying to him when he stood up.

"Hey!" the woman shouted. "Hey, stop him. Stop that man!"

"Wha—" the guard said, but suddenly he was in the plants behind the bench, pushed there by the man he'd been talking to, who was now running toward Dillard.

"Stop that man!" Kate Fouquet yelled again, and she was running toward the guard as he staggered out of the bushes, and as the running man disappeared around a corner.

Forty-one

DETECTIVES JOE KEOUGH and Al Steinbach were actually looking at the sketch supplied by Kate Fouquet when they got the call about the incident in the Crestwood Mall.

"I can't believe he came back here."

"I told you he wasn't smart," Keough said, as they parked in front of Chevy's Restaurant. "What I can't believe is that Kate decided to go to a mall today."

"Coincidence," Steinbach said, and both men shook their heads. Coincidence was the most unpredictable part of police work. You never knew whether it was going to help or hurt your case.

They entered the mall, walked past Dillard and the German chocolate shop. They turned the corner, went past the pretzel place, Hallmark, and Barnes & Nobles until they reached Frederick's. Kate Fouquet was sitting on a bench in front of the lingerie shop, with several mall security men and a couple of Crestwood cops. There was also a small crowd which had gathered to watch them.

Keough showed his badge and said his name, adding, "This is my partner, Detective Steinbach."

"I'm Officer Wells," one of the Crestwood cops said. "This lady says she knows you."

"She does," Keough said. "She's assisting us on a case."

"Do you need us for anything?" Wells asked.

"Yes," Keough said, and Steinbach produced photocopies of the sketch Kate Fouquet had supplied. They didn't yet have a sketch from Marie Tobin to compare with it.

"Just hold on a second," he said to the cops. He showed Kate the sketch. "Was this the man?"

"Yes," Kate said, "it was him. I recognized him. He was talking to this man." She pointed to one of the mall security men.

"What's your name?" Keough asked.

"Neibuhr," the man said, nervously, "uh, Gary."

"Gary, was this the man you were talking to?" Keough showed him the sketch.

"It looks like him," the guard said. "His hair was longer, though, and real dirty."

Keough turned to Wells and the other cop.

"I'd like you each to take one of these," he said, handing them each a sketch, "and separate. Each of you start at an opposite end of the mall and see if you can find this man."

"He's probably long gone," Wells said.

"I agree," Keough said, "but do it. He's already killed several women."

"Jesus!" the cop with Wells said, his eyes wide. He was about ten years younger than Wells, who was obviously the more experienced man.

"If you see him," Keough said, "don't try to apprehend him. Just get in touch with us."

Steinbach took out a radio and coordinated channels with the two uninformed cops, who then took off to do their search.

"What about us?" the other security man asked. He was older than Neibuhr, and not as nervous.

"Might as well," Steinbach said, and handed them each a sketch. "Check the parking lots and don't try to take him alone."

"Do you have other men you can use?" Keough asked the older man.

"Sure, why?"

"We want to talk to this man," he said, indicating Gary Neibuhr.

"Okay," the other man said. "I'll get on it. Uh, my name's Hartman, by the way. Pete."

"Get to work Pete, okay?" Keough asked.

"I'm going."

"You gonna stay with her?" Steinbach asked Keough.

"Yes."

"I'm gonna search, too."

"Go," Keough said, and sat down next to Kate. "How are you?"

"I can't believe it," she said, looking at him. She was wearing a pink sleeveless top that emphasized her full breasts and a pair of white shorts. "The first day I decide to go to a mall again, and there he is."

"What did you do when you saw him, Kate?"

"I yelled."

"Did he see you before or after you yelled?"

"I . . . don't know."

"Think."

She did, for a few moments, and then said, "Before. He recognized me. I could tell."

People were still stopping to look at them curiously. Keough wished he had told the security man to keep them moving, then remembered Neibuhr, who was still standing by.

"Can you get these people to move on?" Keough asked. "I'll talk to you in a minute."

"Sure," the guard said, happy to have something to do.

"Where's your daughter?" Keough asked Kate.

"I didn't bring her," she said. "She's in school. Jesus, I wish I hadn't come."

"Believe it or not, Kate, it's a good thing you did. It helps us. At least we know he's still out here, looking."

"And that's helpful?"

"It is to us," he said, lamely.

"Well, not to me," she said. "Look, I can't stop my hands from shaking."

Her hands were resting on her smooth, tanned thighs, palms up, and they were indeed shaking. He took them in his and held them.

"Take it easy, Kate."

"Can't you find him?"

"We're doing our best," Keough said. He couldn't help thinking that if he was in New York he'd have twenty cops searching the mall by now instead of two cops and some security guards.

"Can I go home?" she asked. "I don't think I ever want to go to another mall in my life."

"Did you drive here?"

"Yes."

"Where are you parked."

"Outside, over by the Pasta House."

"Okay," Keough said. "I'll walk you to your car. Just let me talk to this security guard first, all right?"

"Sure."

He released her hands and stood up.

"Gary, we've been looking for this man for a long time."

"He's a killer?"

"Let me ask you some questions first, okay?"

"Oh . . . okay."

"What was he doing?"

"Just sitting here."

"On this bench?"

"That's right."

"Why did you approach him?"

"We got a call from an employee in here," the guard said, indicating the lingerie store, "that he was ogling the customers."

"Did you see a woman with a stroller at all?"

"A stroller?"

"Right."

"With, like, a baby in it?"

"That's right."

Neibuhr frowned.

"I don't think so."

"What did he say to you?"

"Just that he wasn't doin' anything."

Keough looked up and down. From where they were he could see the front of many other stores . . . including a toy store. If the killer wanted to find a woman with a stroller, a toy store would be perfect—but there were no benches in front of it.

He had to sit someplace, and it was probably just a coincidence that he sat here. Meanwhile, somebody in the lingerie shop got worried and called security.

"How was he dressed?"

"Dirty," Neibuhr said. "Dirty T-shirt, torn, boat shoes, no socks."

"You're pretty observant."

The guard stood up straight.

"I was a criminal law major."

"Is that right?"

"I'm on the waiting list for, uh, several agencies."

"I wish you luck. Which way did he run?"

"That way," Neibuhr said, "toward Dillard. Probably out into the parking lot, or down to covered parking. There's a stairway just outside."

"No," Keough said, "not covered parking."

"Why not?"

"He doesn't like it."

"H-how do you know that?"

"I figured it out."

"Wow."

"Gary, I'm going to walk the young lady to her car. Would you wait here for my partner, please?"

"Sure, Detective."

"I'll be right back."

"I'll tell him."

"Kate? Come on, I'll walk you to your car."

"Th-thanks."

She stood up, then fell back down again onto the bench.

"Oh, wow," she said. "My legs are weak."

He took her hands again, drew her to her feet and said, "I'll help you."

Forty-two

RUNNING.

He didn't have far to run. His car was parked in the lot in front of Chevy's. He got in and backed up so fast that he smacked into the back of another car. Ignoring that, he put his car in drive and took off before anyone could come running out of the mall.

That goddamn bitch! He remembered her from the Galleria. What the hell was she doing here at Crestwood? Why did she have to come on this day? And what about that security guard? Why didn't he mind his own business?

He pulled out onto Watson Road and turned right, only because he could, and because he wanted to get away from there. He was heading west, not quite sure where he was going. He kept driving until he saw the strip mall on the left. There was an International House of Pancakes, a Friday's, a department store, a clothing store, and a Borders Books.

He pulled in, just to get off the street. Then drove around the parking lot until he reached the area in front of Borders—and that's when he saw her.

Forty-three

KEOUGH WALKED KATE Fouquet to her car and tried to reassure her. She was still visibly shaken when she drove away, and Keough wouldn't have blamed her if she kept her word and never went to another mall again.

Instead of walking back through the mall he walked along the outside. He watched the parking lot, wondering where the killer's car had been, which way he had gone. It never occurred to him that the man might have been on foot. Considering the crimes he'd committed, and the number of bodies—large and small—he had transported, there had to be a car.

He was walking in front of the Mexican restaurant, Chevy's, not looking in the windows at the diners, but out at the parking lot, when he saw a man holding his head and looking at the back of his car. Across from it was an empty parking spot. Obviously, the man's car had just been backed into.

He stepped into the parking lot and approached the man. "Can I help you?" he asked.

The man stared at him blankly. Keough took out his ID. "I'm a police officer."

"Somebody hit my car," the man said. He was a portly man in his late thirties wearing powder blue shorts, a white belt, and a shirt with orange-and-yellow flowers on it. Those clothes, Keough thought, should have been on a retired man living in Florida.

"Did you see who did it?"

"No," the man said. "I just came out and found it this way. Look, there's glass all over the ground."

The man's tail light had been smashed and there were pieces of red glass on the ground, but there were also shards of orange glass that had not come from this car.

As much as Keough didn't like coincidences, he loved hunches, and now he had one.

"Wait here," he said.

"But what—"

"Wait," Keough said "I'll have somebody come out and take a report."

The man opened his mouth, but instead of speaking he just grabbed his head and started dancing around, looking down at the rear of his car.

It's just a car, Keough wanted to tell him.

He found Steinbach inside with Neibuhr and told him his hunch. They found the uniformed cops and had them go out and take a report from the man in the parking lot.

"And I want the glass," Keough said.

"What?" Wells asked.

"The glass on the ground. I want you to collect it."

"Don't we need a lab—"

"Just pick it all up and put it in a paper bag. Take it back to your station and I'll get it later. Okay?"

"Whatever turns you on, Detective."

The two cops turned to leave.

"And get pictures."

"Of what?" Wells asked.

"The back of the car."

"With what?"

"Your station must have a Polaroid."

"It does," the younger cop said. It was the first time he'd spoken.

"Then use it."

Wells nodded and gave his partner a dirty look, and then they went out to the parking lot.

"Can I go?" Neibuhr asked.

"Can we get in touch with you here?"

"I guess—sure."

"Okay, go ahead."

As the guard walked away, Steinbach said, "What do you want to do?"

"Try another hunch."

"What do you mean?"

"Come on," Keough said. "I'll tell you on the way."

When they reached the street, Steinbach, who was driving, said, "Which way?"

"Right."

"Why right?"

"It would be easier," Keough said. "Remember, he's running. He's not going to wait to cross over and turn left. Right turn on red, remember? No waiting. He'd go right."

"And then where?"

"That's what we're going to find out."

They drove past some small shopping centers, but Keough didn't feel that the killer would have stopped at any of them.

"Why not?" Steinbach asked.

"A Toys'Я'Us maybe," he said, "but none of these. I don't think you'd normally find a mother with a stroller at Office Depot, or something like that."

"So he just keeps driving."

"I think so."

"Maybe he lives around here somewhere," Steinbach said. "Maybe he's already home."

"Maybe," Keough said. "Let's just go a little further. What's ahead?"

"Lindbergh," Steinbach said. "Also, he could get on the highway up here, forty-four."

They drove on, coming to the point where Lindbergh intersected Watson. "Stay on Watson, or take Lindbergh?" Steinbach asked.

"That looks like a large shopping center up ahead," Keough said. "Let's try that."

"I think I know what you're thinking," Steinbach said. "He was trolling and got interrupted."

"Trolling?"

"Okay, so I read some of the psychobabble."

"Go on."

"You think he's desperate for a victim because he was interrupted."

"I think it's possible."

"Only if his killing is a compulsion," Steinbach said, "and, at the moment, he's in the thrall of that compulsion."

"You really did do your homework."

They drove across Lindbergh and past IHOP, and Steinbach pulled into the parking lot near Borders Books.

Keough squinted. "What's going on over there?"

"That's a Sunset Hills police car," Steinbach said. "Something happened."

They drove over to check it out. Two uniformed cops were talking with someone. They couldn't see who because there was a group of people around them.

Steinbach stopped the car and they both got out and approached the assemblage. They confronted the two officers and showed their ID.

"Detectives Keough and Steinbach, from Major Case. What have you got here?"

He didn't really have to ask, though. He could see now that the policeman were talking to a young, blond mother dressed in shorts and a halter top.

"Some guy tried to grab this lady and her kid," one of the cops said.

"Where's the child?" Keough asked.

The woman said, "He's in the car. The man tried to push me into the car after I buckled my baby in."

"What happened?" Keough asked.

"I started kicking and screaming and he ran off."

"Did he get in a car?" Keough asked the woman.

"I—I think so. I'm not sure."

"Officer," Keough said, "we're in pursuit of this guy. Take a statement from the lady, a full statement complete with description, and send us a copy, will you?"

"Sure, but—"

"We've got to keep going," Keough said, cutting him off. "We may have a chance to catch this guy."

"If you do," the woman said, "I'll identify him."

"Thank you, ma'am," Keough said.

Keough and Steinbach ran for their car, with Steinbach getting behind the wheel again.

"Which way now?" he asked.

"Back out the way we came, then make a right?"

"But . . . that's really going back the way we came. Would he do that?"

"Right turn's the easiest," Keough said, "and then another right."

"Ah," Steinbach said, "south on Lindbergh."

They drove to the end of the shopping center and took the Lindbergh ramp. Now they were heading through Sunset Hills toward Mehlville.

"He's been out here before," Keough said.

"Sure he has," Steinbach said, growing excited for the first time. "The South County Mall's out this way."

"That's where he's headed," Keough said. "We've got to radio ahead, get somebody out there."

"That's the county," Steinbach said.

"Gardner," Keough said.

"Who?"

"Detective Barry Gardner," Keough said. "He caught the first baby in the Dumpster case."

Keough grabbed the radio. He had to get a message to Gardner to get out to the South County Mall fast.

Forty-four

BY THE TIME Keough and Steinbach reached South County, cops were there waiting for them. St. Louis County police and mall security shared an office on the southwest side of the mall. The entrance was outside.

Steinbach parked the car on the J.C. Penny side of the mall and he and Keough walked around until they found the security office.

"Detective Keough?" a uniformed cop asked. He bore the insignia of a St. Louis County lieutenant.

"That's right," he said. "This is my partner, Detective Steinbach."

"We've met," the lieutenant said. "My name's Marcus. You're with Major Case, right?"

"Usually," Steinbach said, "but we're attached to a task force now."

"What kind of task force?"

Keough looked around the office. There was another St. Louis cop, probably the lieutenant's driver, and a mall security man.

"It's okay," Lieutenant Marcus said, "we cooperate with each other. This is Captain Mason, South County Mall security."

"Captain," Keough said. "What I'm about to tell you all has to stay in this room, all right?"

"Of course," Lieutenant Marcus said, and the other two men nodded their agreement.

Keough told them about the killer, what he'd done, and what had happened so far on this day.

"So you think he's in our mall?" the captain asked.

"Yes," Keough said.

"Why . . . if you don't mind me asking?"

"Because I think he left the Crestwood Mall with a catch-the-tail attitude."

"Come again?"

"When a dog is chasing his tail he's just thinking, 'catch the tail, catch the tail,' " Keough explained. "I think this killer is thinking, 'find a victim, find a victim.' "

"I see."

"And we need to find him first—or, at least, get in his way."

"Do you have his picture?" Marcus asked.

"Yes, but not enough to go around," Steinbach said.

"How about a description?"

"We can describe him," Keough said, "but there's a quicker way to do this."

"How?" Marcus asked.

"We need to find any blond women—late twenties, early thirties—in the mall, pushing a stroller, and stay with them."

"What?" Captain Mason asked.

"He likes blond mothers with strollers."

"I don't—"

"Let's not ask anymore questions, Captain," Lieutenant Marcus advised. "Let's just do this before we're too late."

"All right," Mason said. "I'll radio my men."

"And I'll radio mine," Marcus said.

"How many men do you have?" Keough asked.

"Half a dozen," Mason answered.

"I've got another two cars at the other end of the mall with two men," Marcus said. "Also, I understand Detective Gardner is on his way."

"Okay," Keough said, "there's five of us right here, so that gives us thirteen until Gardner gets here. We need to cover all the major exits, just in case a woman fitting our description comes in or goes out."

Mason had just finished radioing his men.

"Captain, how many major exits are there?"

"There are four main mall exits," Mason explained, "several smaller ones, and then the entrances and exits to the department stores."

"Do you have any covered parking lots?"

"No," Mason said, "only surface parking."

"We'll have to check the lots. After that, we'll take a chance on the major exits," Keough said, "the ones directly accessible to the parking lot, and accessible to women with strollers. That means no steps."

"That cuts it down," Mason said. "I'll deploy my men."

"Okay," Keough said, "I suggest that we go into the mall and start looking."

"Let's do it," Lieutenant Marcus said.

They synchronized their radios so they'd all be on the same channel, and then went into the mall and split up.

They found two women in the mall who matched the description—four, actually, but two of them did not have strollers. One had a young child about five or six, and the other was childless, but walking with another woman who was older, darker, and pushing a stroller. Keough made the decision to cover them all.

The mall existed on three levels. One main level that ran north to south, and two secondary levels, upper and lower, running west of the main stem. When Gardner arrived, he coordinated with Keough, meeting him on the top level of the mall, near a McDonald's, Sbarro's and A&W's. There was a small food court set up, with tables and chairs. Keough had found one of the blond women there, one with a child in a stroller, had identified himself, and convinced her to sit at a table and wait. By the time Gardner arrived, the woman was becoming impatient.

"Can't you tell me what this is about?" she asked.

"In a little while, ma'am," Keough said, as he watched Gardner come off the escalator.

"I have to meet my husband—"

"I'll have to ask you to be patient just a little while longer, ma'am," Keough said. "I'm really sorry to inconvenience you."

"Am I in danger?" she suddenly asked.

"No, ma'am, not as long as you stay here."

That quieted her as Gardner reached Keough.

"What have we got?"

Keough took Gardner's arm and moved him away from the woman.

"We're watching four women, and we've got men on the exits, but we've been here close to an hour now. I think he's gone."

"Or he was never here."

"Shit!"

"What?"

"I should have thought of this before," Keough said. "I think our man backed into a car over in the Crestwood parking lot. I should have had mall security here check the parking lot for damaged cars."

"That might not have worked," Gardner said. "There's probably a lot of cars out there with the same sort of dent."

"Maybe so," Keough said. "It's just something I wish I'd thought of."

At that moment Keough saw both Steinbach and Lieutenant Marcus come off the escalator.

"Thanks for getting me such quick cooperation, Barry," Keough said, "but I think we're going to have to call it off."

"Anything?" Steinbach asked as he and Marcus reached them.

"No," Keough said.

Gardner and the lieutenant exchanged a wordless nod.

"How much longer do you want to do this?" Marcus asked Keough.

Keough appreciated the fact that the lieutenant had not tried to take over. It was quite a change from what would have happened in New York.

"I think we can call it off, Loo," Keough said. "I do think, though, that we should have these women walked to their cars."

"We can do that," Marcus said. "I'll radio the captain to have his men take care of it."

"Have him send a man up here, too," Keough said. "This lady's been real patient with us."

"I'll have my driver take care of her."

"Thanks, Loo."

The lieutenant got on the radio.

"What's next?" Steinbach asked.

Keough scowled.

"I think I've pushed this hunch as far as I dare to, Al."

"It was a good hunch, Joe," Steinbach said. "Look at what happened over by Borders."

"That might not have been him."

"It was him," Steinbach said. "I feel it, and you felt it."

"But he got away."

"He didn't get a victim, though."

"Not today," Keough said, "but he's got to be frustrated about it."

"Fuck 'im," Steinbach said. "Let him be frustrated. From the time we got the call from Crestwood you've been on his ass, and he didn't get one today. That's what matters, partner. We stopped him."

"She stopped him."

"Who?"

"Kate Fouquet," Keough said. "She spotted him, she got mall security to call us. Also, that security guard, and the woman in the lingerie store. They all stopped him."

"Hey," Steinbach said, "go ahead and give credit where credit is due, at least he was stopped."

Keough wished he could be as optimistic about the day's events as Steinbach was. Sure, the killer had been stopped today—unless he went right from South County to another mall and grabbed a woman there. Galleria? West County? Could they call all the malls and warn them? No, it wasn't feasible.

They had to hope that the killer was so frustrated that he left South County—if he was, indeed, ever there—and went back into his hole for a while.

Lieutenant Marcus' driver escorted the woman to her

car and Steinbach said to Keough, "Come on, partner. Let's go. We've got to backtrack and see if we can pick up some evidence."

Keough nodded, but he had the feeling that their opportunity had slipped away.

Forty-five

HE SLAMMED THE door of his apartment and stood with his back against it. He was covered with sweat, but unmindful of the fact. Neither did he smell his own sour, foul odor. All he knew was that he had escaped. He had seen the police in South County, knew they were looking for him. What he didn't know was how they knew he'd be there.

He'd been lucky to slip away, even with a guard on the door. Maybe they didn't have a description of him. Or maybe they weren't looking for him, after all. Could it have been a coincidence? Were they looking for someone else, entirely?

He smiled and then, moments later, laughter came bubbling out. He staggered into his living room, onto the sofa, and sat there holding his sides, laughing and laughing, not at all sure why. Maybe he was just relieved to have gotten away—but then the laughter stopped abruptly.

He had not found what he was looking for. That meddling guard had brought attention to him and that bitch from June, in the Galleria parking lot, had recognized him. He'd been forced to run.

He frowned, trying to remember his flight. He had no idea that he'd been in a sort of trance driving down Watson Road, pulling into the shopping center parking lot, spotting the woman with the stroller coming out of Borders Books. His knee ached, but he didn't remember her kicking him. In fact, he remembered little from the time he'd fled Crestwood up until the time he left South County. Everything in between was a blur.

All he knew for sure was that he was back home, and he was alone. He had gone out to find a victim, and had come back empty-handed.

And suddenly he wasn't laughing, anymore.

Forty-six

IT TOOK KEOUGH and Steinbach some time to return to the Major Case Squad office. They had to retrace their steps and pick up whatever information they could from the statements of witnesses—specifically the woman in the Border's parking lot. They'd had no time to question her, and the uniformed cop on the scene—not being a trained detective—had not asked all the pertinent questions. One of them was going to have to interview the woman the next morning. They also had to pick up the bag of broken glass from Crestwood.

When they got to the Major Case Squad office they found a surprise waiting for them.

"Gentlemen," Captain McGwire said, as they entered, looking haggard and worse for the wear, "it's about time you got here."

"Cap," Steinbach said, "we had some trouble—"

"I heard about your escapades today," McGwire said, cutting him off.

"From who?" Keough asked.

"I've been getting calls all afternoon," McGwire said. "I heard from the Crestwood police, the Sunset Hills police, the county, I've heard from the mayors of both Crestwood and Sunset Hills, I've heard from several other agencies—you got around today, didn't you?"

"We were tracking our killer," Steinbach said.

"Did you ever have him in sight?"

"Well, no . . ."

"And yet you instituted a search of the South County Mall, frightening many of their shoppers."

"Well . . ." Steinbach said.

"I heard from them, too."

"Captain," Keough said, "our man was spotted in the Crestwood Mall—"

"By who?"

"His earliest victim."

"I thought his earliest victim was dead?"

"It was an early attempt," Keough said, "back in June—"

"Never mind," McGwire said, "I don't want to hear it. I've got some people I want you both to meet."

McGwire stepped to his office door, opened it, and said, "Would you come in, please?"

Two people entered the room, a man and a woman. The man was in his late twenties, clean-shaven and well-dressed, average height and weight. The woman was in her late thirties, built sort of blocky, with short black hair and very little makeup on a face that sported a jaw just a shade too big. She was wearing a gray suit with a white blouse. Her shoes, Keough noticed, were sensible.

"These are Agents Hannibal and Connors," McGwire said.

"Thomas Hannibal," the man said.

"Harriett Connors," the woman said.

"FBI." Keough spoke with obvious distaste. His past encounters with the FBI had not left him feeling good about the feds. In the past he'd lost cases to them. McGwire hadn't taken the case away from them, but how long would it be before the federal agents would take over?

Agent Connors frowned.

"You say that like it's a bad word."

Keough did not reply. He remembered he was in St. Louis, not yet settled in to the point where he could complain to the captain. Hell, if he was going to complain about something it would have been having the Sanders case handed to Jackson.

Why complain about any of it? Why not just treat it all like a job, the way Steinbach did?

"I've called the FBI in to work with us," McGwire said.

"Cap—" Keough started.

McGwire held up his hand. "I want this guy caught."

Keough hadn't been about to complain. He was going to say, "Cap, that's fine with me," but he held it back now and waited.

"And you think they're going to catch the Mall Rat?" Steinbach asked.

"Mall Rat?" Connors asked.

"That's what Keough calls him," Steinbach said. "You think you can catch him?"

"We think we can work together on this, Detective," Harriett Connors said.

"Cooperate," Agent Hannibal said.

Keough and Steinbach exchanged a glance. Steinbach had never worked with the FBI before, but Keough had. It was his experience that they rarely worked "with" local law enforcement. They usually took over whatever case they were called in on, or they allowed you to "work" with them.

"Your captain has filled us in on the case," Agent Connors said, "and we've seen the files."

"What do you need us for, then?" Steinbach asked

Keough noticed that Agent Connors met their gaze head on. It was obvious she was the senior agent of the two.

"There are usually things that are not in the file," she said. "Aren't there?"

"Are there?" Keough asked.

"Intangibles," Agent Hannibal said.

"Work together," McGwire said, giving both men a hard look. "Catch this bastard, and do it without disrupting the entire city."

McGwire turned, went back into his office, and slammed the door.

"That's a tall order," Agent Connors said. "I mean, about not disrupting the city."

Keough looked at his watch.

"Got an appointment?" Connors asked.

Keough looked at her. "End of shift."

"I thought this was a task force," she said.

"So?"

"I thought task forces didn't work regular hours."

"We don't," Steinbach said. "But we've had a hard day."

"We know," she said. "We heard."

Keough watched her closely for a smirk, but there wasn't one.

"Whose call was it?" she asked.

"Whose call was what?" Steinbach replied.

"Today," she said, "chasing this guy's trail."

"Trying to," Keough said. He still felt bad, as if he'd missed something. They couldn't have gotten to Crestwood any faster, though. As soon as they got the call from security they were rolling. It was a lucky thing they were in the office to catch the call. But still, they had little to show for it . . .

"It was Joe's," Steinbach said, "and I think it was a good call, right down the line."

"So do I," Connors said.

"You do?" Steinbach asked.

"From what I heard, yeah." She turned her attention to Keough. "I read your book."

"It's not my book." He was tired of telling people that.

"It's about you."

"It's about two killers in New York."

"Whatever," she said. "It was good work, what you did in New York—if the book's accurate."

"It's accurate."

"I think we'll be able to work together."

"We can try," Keough said. She seemed okay, Agent Conners. Time would tell, though.

"You've worked with us before," she said. "The FBI, I mean."

"I have."

"Did you run this guy through VICAP?"

"We did." It was one of the first things Keough did when the task force was formed. He had been surprised that the FBI hadn't flagged it and shown up earlier.

"Anything?"

"No," he said. "No match on the MO."

"Well," Connors said, "mothers with children in strollers? I wouldn't think so. That's sort of . . . specialized."

Everyone had settled down. Hannibal was leaning against a file cabinet, Connors had rested a broad hip on one of the desks. Steinbach had taken a seat behind his desk, and Keough was leaning against the door.

"What can you tell me, Detective Keough?" she asked. "I understand you were the first to see the pattern."

Keough hesitated, then did a mental shrug and laid it out for the two agents.

"Well," Hannibal said when Keough was finished, "our course of action seems clear."

"Does it?" he asked.

Connors looked at Hannibal. Keough assumed there was something in the look that gave him the go-ahead.

"Sure," Hannibal said, "we've got to stake out every mall in town."

"Tomorrow," Keough said.

"Of course," Hannibal said. "If he's in a panic for a victim, as you suggest, he'll have to go out tomorrow to find one."

"So you're going to organize this by the time the malls open tomorrow morning?"

"How long did it take you to seal off that mall today?" Connors asked.

"That was one mall."

Keough moved to the desk and looked down at the pink message slips sitting in Steinbach's in box. One of them was for him.

"So," she said, "we'll take them one at a time. With the cooperation of the local police, mall security, and the agents that we bring in to oversee each action, we should be able to do it." She looked at her partner. "You and I will take the smallest mall."

Hannibal simply nodded.

"Why the smallest?" Steinbach asked.

"Well," Connors said. "I don't think he'll go back to either of the ones he was at today." She was giving them the benefit of the doubt, assuming that he actually was at the South County Mall.

"That still leaves plenty of others."

"Didn't you say he hadn't been to that mall yet?" she asked Keough.

"Not that we have a report of."

She shrugged. "We'll try that one."

Keough tucked his message into his pocket, then looked from Connors to Hannibal. It was the junior agent who had that We-*are*-the-FBI look on his face.

"Of course," Connors said, "we'll have your cooperation, won't we?"

Keough hesitated, then nodded and said, "My partner will be here bright and early tomorrow morning."

Steinbach's look asked, "And you won't?"

"I've got something else to do," Keough said, as if Steinbach had asked out loud.

"Something important?" Connors asked.

"Yes."

"More important than this?" She was frowning.

"I'll be around in the afternoon," Keough said. "If I'm lucky, you won't have caught him by then."

"We will have caught him by then," Hannibal said.

"Really?"

The man nodded.

"Going in," he said. "We'll nail him going in."

"I wish you luck," Keough said. "Al? I've got that thing in the car you wanted."

"What thing?"

Keough gave him a look.

"Oh, the thing!" he said, standing up. "Right. I'll come out with you and we'll, uh, put it in my car."

"Agents Connors, Hannibal?" Keough said. "We'll see you tomorrow."

"Detective?"

"Yes?"

Connors smiled. "We'll need one of you to let us know how many malls there are, and where they are."

"That'll be Al," Keough said. "I'm new in town. He'll, uh, be right back in. Just wait here."

Connors looked dubious as Keough and Steinbach went out the door.

Forty-seven

"WHAT'S GOING ON?" Steinbach asked, when they were outside.

Keough took the message slip from his pocket and handed it to Steinbach to read.

"This is what you'll be doing in the morning?" he asked, handing it back.

"That," Keough said, "and flying a kite."

"In Forest Park?"

"That's the place to do it."

"What about these FBI bozos?"

"What about them?"

"What if they actually catch our guy tomorrow?"

"They probably will," Keough said. "If they seal off all the malls, they probably will."

"If he comes out to play tomorrow."

"That's right," Keough said. "If."

"And if he doesn't?"

Keough shrugged.

"They can't keep the malls covered forever. It would tie up too much manpower."

"And if they do catch him?"

"Hey, that'd be great," Keough said. "I told you from the beginning, Al. I just want him caught."

"Seems to me, after all our work, you'd want us involved."

"I don't care who catches him," Keough said, putting his hand on his partner's shoulder, "as long as he's caught, and he doesn't kill any more women."

"Or babies."

"Right."

Steinbach sighed. "I guess you're right," he said. "That is the important thing, isn't it?"

"Yep."

"I'm just surprised you're taking this so calmly."

"You know," Keough said, "I'm a little surprised, myself. Maybe it's because they didn't come on like such assholes—at least, Connors didn't."

"She seems okay." Steinbach said. "The other one's a little bit of a prick, though, don't you think?"

"Maybe," Keough said. "You know, Al, I think you may be rubbing off on me."

"In what way?"

"You know, treating this as just a job."

"That's funny," Steinbach said, "I thought you were rubbing off on me."

There was an awkward silence between them that Keough broke.

"I'll probably be in a couple of hours after you, tomorrow. Just leave me a message telling me which mall you're at and I'll meet you there."

"Which one do you think he'll be at?" Steinbach asked. Keough thought a moment.

"Well, not Crestwood, and not South County."

"Galleria?"

"I don't think so. That's where he first encountered Kate Fouquet. After yesterday, I don't think he's going to want to see her again."

"That leaves West County, Northwest Plaza, Frontenac—"

"Which is the smallest?"

"West County."

"The bird mall?"

"That's right—or maybe Frontenac."

"Tell me about Frontenac."

"It's the classiest mall in town, with Saks Fifth Avenue and Neiman Marcus." He went on to explain that the clientele there was usually quite well off, and that it wasn't a mall that catered to kids of any ages, unless they were teenage girls with money.

"He won't go there," Keough said.

"Why not?"

"It's beyond both his means and his thinking," Keough said. "It won't even occur to him to go there."

"How can you be sure?"

"I'm not sure," Keough said, "but that would be my bet. Why don't you go to the bird mall," Keough said, "and I'll meet you there, in the security office. That's where Agents Connors and Hannibal will want to be. You stick with them."

"I never worked with the FBI before."

"It could be an education," Keough said. "Just remember to watch your back."

"I hope they know what they're doing."

"They usually do."

"I thought they were supposed to be a bunch of fuck-ups."

"In the movies, maybe," Keough said. "In real life they're generally pretty sharp."

"But you don't like them?"

"They're kind of like little kids, sometimes," Keough said.

"In what way?"

Keough put the message slip back in his pocket and said, "They don't always like to share."

"Hey," Steinbach called out as Keough headed for his car.

"What?"

"One of us should find Ken Jackson," he said. "He should be in on this."

Keough waved his hand and said, "Go ahead. He's not going to want to hear from me, anyway."

"He doesn't want to work with you," Steinbach said, "what's he going to think about working with the FBI?"

Keough opened his car door, looked at Steinbach, and said, "I don't give a fuck."

Forty-eight

DETECTIVE KEN JACKSON was arrogant. He knew that. He was probably a prick. He knew that, too. What he also knew, though, was that he was a good detective. He had a natural aptitude for it, and he had hunches that usually panned out—as this one had.

He'd followed a hunch for the past couple of days, and it had led him here, to this house in the Shaw section of St. Louis. Shaw was filled with one family homes built in the twenties for middle-income families. This house was on Klemm Street, behind the botanical gardens and right along Tower Grove Park. It was an end house, which gave it lots of privacy. Ideal, Jackson thought, for a killer who wanted his comings and goings to go unnoticed.

Jackson's hunch had directed him here, and he had no idea what had gone on during the day, because he had not been in touch with either Joe Keough or Al Steinbach.

"Mr. Eric Pautz," he said to himself, "get ready for an unexpected visitor."

He drew his gun and made his way to the back of the house.

He got into the house with no trouble. The back door lock was not that hard to slip. It was too bad somebody hadn't broken into the house and killed the fucker already.

He found himself in the kitchen and stopped to listen for sounds of movement in the house. When there were none forthcoming, he continued through the kitchen and into the rest of the house.

There was a living room and dining room, but what he was more concerned with was what was upstairs—the bedrooms. He made his way to the stairs and went up slowly, just in case the asshole was asleep. If he was he'd just screw his gun into the killer's ear and wake him up.

He reached the upstairs hall and found that the house had two bedrooms. Both doors were open, and they were both empty. One appeared to be a master bedroom, with a queen-sized bed in it, but the room looked unlived in.

The bedspread hadn't seen a wrinkle in years, of that he was sure. It was almost as if the room was being kept as some kind of shrine.

He went to the second bedroom and knew he had the right place. The bed was unmade, the sheets soiled with what he didn't care to think about. There was a TV and VCR setup at the foot of the bed, and a couple of stacks of tapes on either side. He put his gun away and took out his pocket flash. Using the light he read the titles of the tapes. The stack of the right were Westerns: *Unforgiven*, *Wyatt Earp*, *Tombstone*, and others. The stack on the left, though, had titles like *Bad Girls IV*, *Wet Nurses*, *Spandex Sex*, and others. One in particular caught his eye. It was on top, and instead of a box with pictures on it, it was in a black rental box, the kind you got from the video stores. The title stamped on the side was *Strolling Blondes*. The box was empty, and since there wasn't a tape lying around, he assumed it was in the machine.

He found the remote control, which operated both the TV and VCR. He turned both of them on, then hit the play button. Seconds later he was watching a blond girl with an incredible body pushing a stroller with a small child in it. Abruptly, she was stopped by a man who engaged her in conversation. There was a choppy scene change usually evident in these kinds of movies, and the man and woman were suddenly naked on a bed, apparently in a motel. While they were exploring each other avidly with hands and mouths the stroller was propped next to the bed. It was apparent the child in the stroller was a rubber doll, but of course, within the contents of the "plot" the woman was probably cheating on her husband with her child right next to the bed.

He turned off the VCR and put the remote down on the bed. He shone his flash around the room, preferring not to turn the lights on in case Pautz came home while he was there.

He started going through the dresser drawers. One was filled with porno magazines, another with underwear which he assumed to be clean. When he got to the bottom drawer, he found it filled with a different kind of clothing— ripped and torn women's clothing. He took some of it out and held it up to the light. There were panties, a sundress, a pair of shorts, all of which showed the stress of having been forcibly removed. This idiot not only kept souvenirs, he kept them right in his house. He was either arrogant or stupid.

Jackson dropped the clothing back into the drawer and closed it. He shone the flashlight around the room once again and stopped when he saw a door, presumably a closet. Lord knew what he'd find in there.

He crossed the room to the closet. It was a single door with a knob, not a sliding door like you saw in a lot of homes. Maybe it was a bathroom? Only one way to find out.

He reached for the knob with his right hand, holding the flashlight in the left, opening the door slowly. As his light illuminated the interior he saw that it was indeed a closet, with clothing hanging in it. As he opened it wider he became aware of someone in the closet, sitting on the floor. He shone the light downward and saw frightened eyes staring up at him, a man's eyes. He was cowering on the floor, his knees drawn up to his chest, obviously scared out of his wits.

"D-don't you hurt me," the man said.

"I'm not gonna hurt you," Jackson said. Could this be the dreaded killer they were looking for? A male victim? Or simply another resident of the house?

"Come out of there," Jackson said, softly. "Come on. I'm a policeman. I'm not gonna hurt—"

"Yes . . . you . . . are!" the man suddenly shouted, and as he lunged Jackson knew he had made a terrible mistake. His hand streaked for his gun, but already he knew it was too late. He felt the knife go into his belly, the impact driving all of the air from his lungs. His legs went dead, and as he was falling to the floor he was vaguely aware of the man still shouting at him, of the knife being withdrawn, and then he was being stabbed again . . . and again . . .

Forty-nine

AT SEVEN THE next morning Keough was in Forest Park flying a kite. This wouldn't be quite the relaxing experience it usually was, though. The kite was a cover.

It was seven-fifteen when someone came up beside him. There were some runners in the park, but no one else was flying a kite. Keough was pleased with the breeze that morning, and had actually gotten into what he was doing, enjoying the loops and whirls of the kite and its tail. When she appeared she almost startled him.

"Good morning, Miss Bonny."

"Detective."

"Do you have a first name?"

She hesitated, then said, "Angela."

"May I call you Angela?"

He looked at her then. She was dressed for work in a suit, the skirt of which hung several inches below her knees, and high heels. For someone who wanted to meet him here instead of the office—he supposed to avoid being seen—she was dressed oddly for a walk in the park.

"Why did you leave me a message to meet you here?" he asked.

Her message had been clear: "Please meet me in Forest Park near the running track. It's urgent. Be discreet." It also contained detailed directions, or they never would have found each other in the sprawling expanse of Forest Park.

Keough still didn't know who had taken the message, but that didn't matter. When he got home and read it again, he thought about his kites and that it was time to air them out. He decided he'd take a simple one with him to the meeting, just to finally get in some air time.

"Do you do this a lot?" she asked. "Fly kites?"

"Yes."

"Why?" She actually sounded interested, and a bit puzzled.

"It's relaxing."

"I thought flying kites was for kids."

He was used to that attitude.

"It is," he said, "it's for kids, and for adults. Do you know that stunt kites can fly at sixty miles an hour?"

"I . . . didn't even know there were stunt kites."

"And they're entirely under your control—if you know what to do with your hands."

"I see."

He sensed he was losing her, and they hadn't come to talk about his kites, anyway. The one he had in the air now was a simple line kite, so he took his eyes off it and looked at her.

"What did you bring me here to tell me, Angela?"

"Well . . ."

She paused as a runner went by.

"Nobody's going to listen to us," he said. "Go ahead."

"It's . . . it's about . . . about Bill Sanders."

Big surprise. He waited.

"I don't know where to start."

"Maybe I can help," he said. "Were you having an affair with him?"

She hesitated, then nodded.

"Have you seen him since he and his wife disappeared?"

"No," she said. "Honestly. I thought I would, but . . ."

"Then why did you want to meet me here?"

"I'm worried about him," she said. "I thought . . . I thought if I told you the truth it might help you find him."

He wondered how to play this, and decided to scare her. Why let her off easy?

"It might have helped," he said, "if you had told the truth earlier, like in the beginning."

"I . . . I don't understand. This doesn't help?"

"Well," he said, "for one thing, I'm no longer on the case. You have to talk to Detective Jackson."

"Him!" she said, spitting the word out. "He's . . . rude."

"Yes," Keough said, "that's our Detective Jackson, but you see, it's his case, now."

She shook her head.

"I won't talk to him."

"You won't have to," Keough said. "I'll give him the information, but I don't know how much help it will be . . . now."

She looked at the ground.

"All right," she said, "I deserve this. I know I should have told the truth in the beginning, but . . ."

"But what?"

"I was afraid," she said. "I didn't know what had happened to Bill, but he always said we had to be . . . discreet."

"Discreet," Keough said. "Did you think that no one in the office knew about you?"

She frowned at him and said, "No one did."

"I sensed it when I first met you." Keough grinned. "Don't you think other people could? People who knew the both of you?"

She stood frozen for a moment, then said, "Oh, God. Do you think . . . they all knew?"

"Not all," he said, "but somebody must have."

"But . . . but what if someone told his wife?"

"What would have happened?"

"Anything could have happened," she said. "After all, she's—she was—"

"She was what?"

She firmed her chin and said, "She was a bitch. She used to . . . to hit him."

"Hit who? Brady?"

"I imagine she hit Brady," Angela Bonny said, "but she also hit Bill."

"Wait a minute," Keough said, "let me get this straight. *She* used to hit *him*?"

"That's right."

"And did he hit her back?"

"He didn't dare."

"Why not?"

"Bill would never hit a woman."

Now Keough frowned. Had he gone about this all wrong from the start? Could it have been *Mrs.* Sanders who killed *Mr.* Sanders? But what about the man who had shown up at Brady's foster home? A stranger? A coincidence that someone happened to be peeping in the window of that house?

"Angela, you've got to tell me the truth now," he said. "It's very important."

"I will."

"Have you heard from Bill Sanders at all since he disappeared?"

"No, I haven't," she said. "I—I swear it."

Keough stared at her for a moment, then took a small pair of scissors from his pocket and cut the string on the kite. Immediately the colorful paper soared higher and further. ~~farther~~

"Why did you do that?" she asked.

"I like flying them," he said, "but I hate reeling 'em back in."

"What . . . what can I do now?"

"Nothing," he said. "Go to work, Angela. I'll be in touch."

"You will?" she asked. "Not that . . . that other detective?"

"No," he said, "not the other detective. Me."

"Thank you, Detective Keough."

He nodded and she walked away.

"Hey, mister," a boy of about eight or nine called out to him. "Your kite's gettin' away."

"I know," he said.

"Ain't you gonna chase it?" the boy asked. "It'll probably come down someplace else in the park."

"I'll tell you what," Keough said. "If you can catch it, it's yours."

"Really?" The boy's eyes widened.

"Really."

"Cool!" the boy said, and took off running.

Keough made his way back to his car and drove home. Approaching the house he looked up at the three-story brick-and-slate structure and wondered, as he usually did, how anyone could live in such a big place when all the rooms were open, and not just in three or four rooms, as he was. The message light on his phone was blinking twice, indicating two messages. He debated whether he should pick them up or not. He already had two things he wanted to do today: question the woman who had almost been grabbed yesterday in the Border's parking lot, and check into some information regarding the Sanders case. If one of the messages was from Steinbach, though, telling him that the FBI had caught the killer, it would save him from wasting time.

He walked to the machine and pressed play.

Beep.

"Joe, it's Valerie. Please call me."

No note of urgency in her tone. No way to tell if her request was business or pleasure.

Beep.

"Keough, it's Captain McGwire. Get your ass in here. Ken Jackson was found dead this morning!"

He clipped his holster to his belt, pulled on a windbreaker, and left the house.

Fifty

JACKSON WAS FOUND in the trunk of his car, wrapped in a sheet. He'd been stabbed seventeen times then driven out to South County and left on Lemay Ferry Road, out past Butler Hill Road, near some open land. His badge, ID, and gun were still on him.

Keough found this out when he got to the office, filled in by Captain McGwire.

"Where's your partner?" McGwire demanded as Keough entered.

"He's with the FBI," Keough said, "staking out malls."

"Oh, yeah," McGwire said, passing a hand over his drawn face.

"Are you all right, Cap?"

McGwire dropped his hand and stared at Keough.

"I've never had one of my men killed before, Keough. I'm afraid I—I don't quite know how to react."

Keough had seen his fair share of dead cops in New York, but he kept quiet. McGwire seemed stunned, which was a perfectly natural reaction.

At that point McGwire explained how Jackson was

found by a passing St. Louis County police car who noticed Jackson's unmarked car parked by the side of the road.

"What made him check it?" Keough asked.

"There aren't that many cars parked on the side of the road out there," McGwire said. "He saw the radio in the car and knew something was wrong. Why would an unmarked police car just be parked out there like that?"

"Who responded?"

"St. Louis County detectives went to the scene, and then they called me. I went out there myself."

"When was this?"

"Daylight," McGwire said.

Just when Keough was leaving his house to go to Forest Park. He wanted to ask when McGwire left the message on his tape machine, but decided not to. He didn't want to have to say what he was doing when McGwire was viewing the body of one of his men.

"Where is he now?"

"The morgue. Do you want to see the body?"

"Uh, no, why would I?"

"Because you're in charge of this case."

"I see," Keough said. "Does that mean I'm off the Mall Rat case?"

"Yes," McGwire said. "Steinbach can handle that."

"He'll be a one-man task force."

"So what?" McGwire snapped. "One of my men is dead, Keough, and you're the only man with the experience to handle this case. You've handled this sort of thing in New York, haven't you?"

"As a matter of fact, Captain, yes," Keough said, "I have."

"Then it's yours."

"If you don't mind me saying so, Cap," Keough said, "I think I should stay on the serial case, as well."

"No," McGwire said. "Besides, the Feebs will probably catch him today."

"I don't think so, Cap."

"You think the killer is going to get in and out of one of those malls without getting caught?"

"I don't think the killer will go to any of the malls today."

"Why not?"

They were standing in the squad room, and McGwire was fidgeting, moving from side to side, almost swaying.

"Can we go in your office, Cap? Maybe have a cup of coffee?" Keough had brought two containers of coffee in with him.

McGwire heaved a big sigh and stopped swaying.

"Yeah, okay," he said. "I could use a cup of coffee."

"And I think you should sit down."

McGwire rubbed his jaw, which was covered with stubble, and said, "Yeah, okay. Come on in."

They went into the captain's office, and Keough took the two coffees out and put one on the man's desk. McGwire sat in his chair and closed his eyes for a moment, then opened them and reached for the coffee.

"I hope black's okay," Keough said.

"Fine."

Keough sat across from McGwire, holding his own coffee.

"Okay," McGwire said, after a sip. "What's on your mind?"

"Cap, Jackson was working on just one case, the serial killer—the Mall Rat."

"I know that."

"It stands to reason that he was killed because of that." McGwire leaned forward.

"You're saying that the same killer got him?"

"I'm saying that Jackson was a good detective, maybe as good as he thought he was. Maybe he got onto the killer, found him, and came out on the short end."

"Jackson's put a lot of people away, Keough," McGwire said. "What makes you think his death is connected to the task force?"

"Call it a hunch," Keough said, "or say I don't believe that much in coincidence. Neither Steinbach or I knew what Jackson was doing. He was keeping to himself."

"So he found out something you fellas didn't know, and moved on it himself."

"That's what I'm saying, sir," Keough said. "Maybe if he'd filled us in he'd still be alive."

McGwire put his coffee down carefully on his desk.

"So his arrogance finally got him killed."

Keough didn't respond.

"All right," McGwire said, "keep working on the serial killer, but work on Jackson's killing, too."

"Both of us?"

"Yes. Of course, if the FBI get him today—"

"They won't."

"Why not?"

"He's not the smartest guy in the world, Cap, but if he killed a cop last night I don't think he'll be going out trolling today."

"You think killing a cop satisfied his . . . his obsession?"

"Probably not," Keough said, "but maybe it scared him enough to keep him inside."

"What are you going to do now, then?"

"Well," Keough said, "I don't think I'll be any help at any of the malls. I'd like to go through Jackson's things."

McGwire picked up the phone.

"I'll have his personal effects brought up here."

"I'll want everything, sir," Keough said, "everything he had on him, and everything that was in his car."

"Done."

"I'll also want to check his home. Was he married?"

"Yes," McGwire said, putting the phone back down for the moment, "and he had two kids."

"Can you arrange for me to get inside his home?"

"I think so."

"Preferably with no one else there," Keough said.

"Why?"

"It would just be easier to go through his things without someone looking over my shoulder."

McGwire toyed with his coffee container.

"I know his wife," he said, finally. "I think I can arrange it."

"Okay. Is that it?"

"For now."

McGwire picked up the phone again.

"I want this son of a bitch caught, Keough," he said, dialing.

"That's my intention, Captain. There's one other thing—you don't have to hang up."

"What is it?" McGwire asked, as the phone rang in his ear.

"Just keep the FBI off my back as much as you can," Keough said. "Like I said, I work better without anyone looking over my shoulder."

"I'll do what I can—yeah, hello. This is Captain McGwire. Who is this?"

Keough tuned out the captain's end of the conversation as the man arranged to have all of Ken Jackson's personal effects brought to the office. Keough wondered what was going on at the malls. He felt pretty sure that the man who had killed the women and placed the babies in the Dumpsters was the same man who had killed Ken Jackson. It just made sense to him. It also made sense that the killer wouldn't be cruising any malls today. Having killed women in the past—and one child, probably by mistake—at the moment, he was probably trying to deal with the fact that he had killed a man, a policeman.

At least, Keough was hoping that this was weighing heavily on the man's mind—so heavily that maybe he'd make a mistake.

Fifty-one

ERIC PAUTZ WENT out to buy a newspaper. Clutching the *St. Louis Post-Dispatch* in his hands, he made his way back to his house in Shaw. He did not look at the newspaper until he was inside. He needn't have bothered, there was nothing there about a policeman being killed. It had been discovered too early that morning.

That stupid cop had to come blundering into his house last night. Lucky for him he was coming out of the downstairs bathroom as the cop forced the back door. He had gone right into the kitchen, grabbed a knife, and then hid in the closet. At least he thought he hid in the closet. He wasn't quite sure what had happened until he realized that he was stabbing the man over and over again.

In truth the killer had panicked. After grabbing a knife from the kitchen he had run up to his room to hide. He became confused, cowering in the darkness as he had done many times as a child, when his mother was angry with him. The closet had always been his safe place. It was quiet, and the walls seemed to hold him, comfort him.

Then the door opened, and the light came streaming into his safe place . . .

It wasn't until after he had stabbed the man a dozen times that he realized what he was doing. Still, he went on stabbing five more times before he stopped and stared.

He had never killed a man before. He stood looking down at him, and realized it didn't give him the same pleasure as killing a woman.

He flipped on the bedroom light, turned the man over, and went through his pockets. He found the gun first, and then he found the badge and ID.

He panicked again, but just for a moment. He went to the front window to look out, but didn't see anyone. He stepped out the front door to take a better look, but still saw no one.

The cop had come alone.

It didn't take long to find the man's car. He knew the cars usually parked on the block, and he found it down the block and used the cop's keys to drive it to his house with the lights off. He drove it up the driveway to the side of the house, and from there on it was the same as with the women. He had wrapped up the cop in a sheet, and dropped him into the trunk. As an afterthought he put the man's badge and ID back because he didn't need them. It never even occurred to him to take the gun.

He changed his clothes and drove the cop as far away from his house as he could think, to South County. He stopped the car by the side of the road and just walked away. He walked until he came to a street where he could catch a bus. It took him most of the night to get home, and when he arrived he just sat in the living room, still dressed, and waited for daylight. When the sun came out he went and bought a newspaper.

What was he supposed to do now?

Fifty-two

AS REQUESTED, EVERYTHING that was on Jackson or in his car was brought to the office—even the sheet he was wrapped in.

"Why would he leave the sheet?" Keough wondered.

"Maybe he knows there's nothing on it to give him away," McGwire said.

Keough checked the sheet and didn't find a monogram, or a laundry mark.

"See?" McGwire said.

"No," Keough said, shaking his head, "he left it because it never occurred to him to take it back with him."

"Why not? Is he that dumb?"

"I don't know if he's dumb, or just not smart."

McGwire blew some air out of his mouth.

"How could he be stupid and get away with these murders?"

"Because he's been lucky up to now, Cap. Look at last night. He drove Jackson's car all the way to South County and just left it. After that he had to walk a ways before he could take a bus or catch a cab. Nobody saw him."

"How do we know that?"

"We don't, for sure," Keough said, "but let's have county send a couple of cars out there to canvass the area. I bet we don't find anybody."

"You're saying that this guy has just been lucky?"

"Look at what he's done," Keough said. "He's gone back to malls where he's already grabbed somebody. That's not smart. He let a couple of witnesses see his face, so that we now have a sketch." Keough reminded himself that there was still another sketch to pick up.

"So he's been leaving witnesses alive."

"Right."

McGwire ran his hand through his thinning hair.

"Then he is dumb—and lucky . . . but his luck's got to run out."

"Maybe it did," Keough said, "last night. Jackson found him."

"Unlucky for Jackson," McGwire said.

"Of course," Keough said, "but if Jackson found him, then he can be found."

"Maybe he'll move."

"I doubt it," Keough said. "That's not the feeling I get from him. I just don't think this is going to scare him away.

There won't be anything in the paper to frighten him. He's going to think he got away with it."

"But . . . surely he won't go out and grab another woman?"

"Yes, he will," Keough said. "That urge has to be getting greater and greater."

"The urge to kill?"

Keough nodded.

"But he has killed."

"A man," Keough said. "He's killed a man. It's not the same thing."

While he was talking Keough was going through the stuff that had been dumped on one of the desks. The lab had already gone through it.

"I wonder what the FBI is doing?" McGwire said.

"Twiddling their thumbs, I hope."

"Maybe we should let them know what's going on."

"Not yet, Cap," Keough said. "Let's let them sit at the malls a little longer. Maybe I can find something . . ."

"Like what?"

"I don't know," Keough said, fingering Jackson's ID case. Keough backed away from the desk, frustrated.

"There's nothing here. Which desk does Jackson use?"

"That one," McGwire said, pointing to the other desk.

Keough went over to it, sat down, and began going through the drawers.

"You're good at this, aren't you?" McGwire asked.

"I like to think I am," Keough said, continuing to search the drawers.

"Jackson was good, but too arrogant about it," Mc-Gwire said. "How come you're not?"

"Arrogant?" Keough asked. He looked up at the Mc-Gwire. "You mean, since I'm from New York?"

"New York's got nothing to do with it," McGwire said. "I was just wondering."

"I think I had the arrogance knocked out of me," Keough said, going back to his task.

"By the Kopykat case?"

"You read the book?"

"Yes," McGwire said.

"Yeah, well, maybe that had something to do with it. Hello, what's this?"

"What?"

Keough pulled a 9 x 12 inch brown envelope from the center drawer and put it on the desk. He reached in and pulled out some newspaper clippings.

"How do we know that has anything to do with the case?" McGwire asked.

"We don't." Keough upended the envelope to see if anything else would fall out. When it didn't he started going through the clippings.

"What are they?"

"Pages," Keough said, "whole pages, folded in half, not clippings."

"From what paper?"

Keough turned one page sideways.

"The *Riverfront Times*."

"That's one of those giveaways—"

"I've seen it around since I've been here," Keough assured McGwire.

The captain moved closer and looked over Keough's shoulder.

"What are they?"

"They look like ads . . . for clubs . . . Are they strip clubs?"

He held one of the pages up for McGwire to look at.

"Oh yeah," he said, "those clubs are across the bridge, in Sauget, Collinsville, even Brooklyn."

"Brooklyn?" Keough looked up, surprised.

"You didn't know there was a Brooklyn, Illinois?"

"No."

"Sure," McGwire said, "it's full of those adult bookstores and video shops . . . you know, the one with the booths in the back? Also a few clubs. It's the center of the adult entertainment community around here."

"What about this side of the bridge?"

"In Missouri? Don't make me laugh. They resisted riverboat gambling for a long time, even though it would bring tons of jobs with it. You think they're going to go for topless joints?

"Is there anyplace in Missouri to buy these movies?"

"Ah, I see those commercials at night for one of those kinds of stores, but mostly they're in Brooklyn."

Keough continued looking through the ads. There was a big photo on one of the pages of two adult film actresses who were set to appear at one of the clubs together. Not being a student of the adult film scene he was unaware they did that. He thought the girls in the clubs and the girls in the movies were different. Now he knew there was some crossover.

"Cap, was Jackson into this sort of thing? Adult videos, strip clubs?"

"Naw, I don't think so," McGwire said. "He was pretty much a prude when it came to these things. Took being a father and husband seriously, you know?"

"Then why would he have this stuff?" Keough asked.

McGwire shrugged. "Who knows?"

"Was he working on some vice business?"

"No," McGwire said, "Ken was our homicide man, period."

"Then this stuff has to do with a homicide," Keough said, "and the only one he was working on was the Mall Rat."

"How's this stuff connected to our Mall Rat?" McGwire asked.

"I don't know," Keough said, "but I know where to go to ask."

Once again Keough decided not to try to get in touch with Steinbach. That would only alert the FBI that something was brewing. Certainly, they must be aware of Ken Jackson's death, but there was no reason for them to connect it with the search for the serial killer—not unless Steinbach made the connection and spoke up.

Keough had learned years ago that a detective had to rely on hunches. He had a hunch that he should follow up these newspaper ads without giving the FBI a chance to get in his way. If he came out of today with nothing to show, then he wouldn't mind sitting down with them and brainstorming. He had a healthy respect for the FBI. There were plenty of agents who knew what they were doing. There were not enough agents, however, who reciprocated. He felt that simply by virtue of being an FBI agent, a certain degree of arrogance crept into the picture.

Keough didn't think of himself as arrogant. Maybe other people did—maybe everyone in St. Louis did, since he was from New York—but he thought of himself as a good detective who ought to follow his hunches wherever they led him.

And right now they were leading him to Brooklyn, Illinois, a place he previously had never even heard of.

Fifty-three

HE'D LEFT A message with the captain for him to give Steinbach, and he asked that McGwire not do it in front of the two FBI agents.

"Why do you want to keep this from the FBI?" McGwire asked him.

"Just until tomorrow, Cap," Keough said. "I want to move on this myself before we bring them in on it. I just need the rest of today."

McGwire had finally agreed, since Keough had more experience as a detective than he did, despite the difference in rank. Keough had come to respect McGwire more for the man's reaction to the killing of one of his men—and turning the investigation over to him was a main part of that. McGwire was not about to let his own ego get in the way of catching a cop killer. He decided that utilizing Keough's experience was better than trying to deny it, or top it, because of his superior rank. In truth, McGwire was an administrator and had never been a detective.

"But tomorrow we take the FBI into our confidence," he'd added before Keough left the office.

"Agreed," Keough said.

McGwire had arranged for Keough to get into Ken Jackson's house while no one was around, as Keough had requested. Keough was putting off going across the Mississippi to Illinois and the strip clubs and adult bookstores until later in the evening, when there would be more people to talk to and show the sketch to.

Keough spent an hour inside Jackson's house. The man kept an office there, but had very little in the way of files. As spare as his desk was at work, it was sparer still at home. In the end there was nothing in the house that could help, and Keough had to go back to the newspapers he'd found in the man's desk at work.

He still felt the only reason Jackson would have kept

them was if they were important. After all, Jackson kept very little in his desk.

Keough took the newspapers home with him and saw his message light blinking three times at him. He hoped one of the messages would be from Steinbach.

He pressed play and listened.

Beep.

"Joe, it's Valerie. Please give me a call when you get a chance. Thanks."

Damn. He hadn't had a chance to call her back.

Beep.

"Hey, partner, it's me. Nothing much happening at the mall. Thought I'd check in with you. See you at the office."

Obviously, that message had been left earlier in the day.

Beep.

"Jesus, just heard about Jackson. Captain McGwire gave me your message after the FBI left. Boy, are they pissed. I'll meet you where you said. See you then."

Keough checked his watch. He'd told McGwire to have Steinbach meet him at Culpepper's again, but that wasn't for two hours, yet.

Keough went into the kitchen, skirting some boxes in the hall that he still hadn't emptied. For the most part everything he'd brought with him had been put away somewhere, but there was still some things that didn't have a place.

He pulled a Pete's Wicked Ale from the fridge and sat at the table with the newspaper pages. He shuffled them and turned them over to see if maybe there wasn't something he was missing. There wasn't, that he could see. All they had in common were the ads from the strip clubs and adult stores, so he felt he had no choice but to drive over there and see what he could find out. Now that Steinbach had returned his message, he knew they could go together, or split up to cover more ground. He'd discuss it with his partner at dinner.

He thought a moment about Ken Jackson's murder. He certainly hadn't liked the man much, but he was sorry as hell that a fellow cop was dead. In New York cops took this sort of things personally. It would be interesting to see the reactions of the other cops in town.

He had to admit that he still was not comfortable with his life in St. Louis. He wasn't ready to pronounce the experiment a failure, yet, but he hoped things would change within the next few months. He needed a little more stimulation in his life. It was an awful thing to admit but up to today he hadn't felt the kind of adrenaline rush he'd felt while going through Jackson's desk and finding these newspapers, not even while he and Steinbach were chasing the killer the day before. Hadn't *that* turned out great? And now that the FBI was involved they'd probably be calling the shots on the serial case—unless he could come up with something across the river. Even if they took the case over, however, he still had a connection because he was running the investigation of Jackson's murder. No matter what the FBI said, that was a local case.

He finished his beer and decided to answer Valerie's call before she started to think that he was avoiding her. He also had to decide what he was going to do about the

Sanders case, now that Jackson was dead and no one else was working on it.

A check of the clock told him she'd probably still be at work, and he called her there.

"Joe," she said, sounding very glad to hear from him, "I'm glad you called before I left."

"Is something wrong?"

"No, I—I just wanted to tell you that we've placed Brady with another family."

"That's great. Where do they live?"

She told him. The neighborhood meant nothing to him, but he didn't ask where it was.

"Joe?"

"Yes?"

"Is something wrong? You seem preoccupied."

"You'll read about it in the newspapers eventually," he said. The body had been found too late for it to make the papers that day. "We lost a man."

He explained it to her and she listened in silence until he was done.

"I'm so sorry," she said, finally. "So you're in charge of this case?"

"Yes."

"What about the man who's killing the women, and the babies?"

One baby, he thought, but he didn't correct her.

"I think they're connected."

"Really?"

"Jackson was working on it at the time of his death."

"And you think the same man killed him?"

"I think so," he said. "At least, I'm going to work on that premise."

"Can you—would you like to, um, do something, or would you rather be alone?"

"I'd love to do something, but I'm going to be working tonight." He decided not to tell her that he was going to be going to strip clubs that night. It didn't seem the kind of thing you should tell a woman who was interested in you—or who you were interested in.

"We've got some leads we have to follow up," he said, "and I need to talk to my partner. I haven't seen him all day."

"Of course," she said. "I, uh, hope I'll be able to see you fairly soon. I mean, I know this case will take up a lot of your time . . ."

"I promise," he said. "I'll call you soon. Good news about Brady," he added, before she could respond. "Are they a nice family?"

"Yes," she said. "I interviewed them myself."

"Good," he said. "I hope the little guy is happy. I haven't given up on his case, you know."

"You haven't? In spite of everything?"

"I'd still like to know what happened to his parents," he said. "I think he'll need to know, won't he?"

"I think so," she said. "And there's something else I think."

"What's that?"

"That you're a pretty great guy."

"I thought you knew that already."

She laughed and said, "I suspected, but now I know for sure."

"Glad to hear it," he said. "Well, I've got to go back to work."

"Me, too," she said. "I'll talk to you soon."

" 'Bye, Valerie."

He hung up and checked his watch. He certainly would rather have been doing something with her than meeting Steinbach at Culpepper's. There was still a hell of a lot to do, though, before he could do even think about his private life.

He went upstairs to shower before meeting his partner for dinner. He was also aware that he'd probably be talking to a lot of women that night. He didn't want to do that in the same clothes he'd been wearing all day.

Fifty-four

THEY TALKED ABOUT the FBI stakeout of the malls and Jackson's murder over dinner at Culpeppers. Steinbach explained that nothing had happened all day.

"Connors was cool," he said, "real patient, very professional. Her partner, though, that Hannibal, he was real antsy."

"What was the mood when they finally called it off?" Keough asked.

"Except for Hannibal everybody took it in stride. Agent Connors said she'd see us in the morning at the office. She's really sort of okay, Joe."

"That's good. We'll have to explain Jackson's murder to her," Keough said, "if she doesn't see it in the newspapers first."

While neither man had been crazy about their dead colleague, Ken Jackson, Steinbach had worked with him for several years and had been shocked at the news of—and conditions surrounding—his death.

"I can't believe it," he said. "He always acted like he was indestructible."

"I've know a lot of cops like that," Keough said. "They usually find out the hard way that they aren't."

"He found out the hard way, all right."

Keough explained to his partner his theory about the killers being the same.

"Well, it makes sense to me," Steinbach said, "but what if we work that angle and we're wrong?"

"McGwire gave me the lead in this investigation, Al, and I think the cases have to be connected. I mean, what else was he working on?"

"That's just it," Steinbach said. "No one ever knew."

"Well, we know for sure he was working on the dead blondes, and the baby, so I think we've got to make a decision whether to go that way or not."

"Hey," Steinbach said, "I'm glad McGwire gave you the lead. I'll follow it."

They both followed it, over to the Illinois side of the Mississippi River.

The first place they tried was called the Emerald Club, in Sauget. Immediately they heard the music playing, although it wasn't loud enough to assail their ears. They were stopped just inside the door by a well-dressed bouncer type who asked them for five bucks each.

"Will this do?" Keough asked, showing the man his badge.

"Aw, what's this about?" the man asked. "I thought we had this taken care—"

"We just need to ask a few questions," Keough said, stopping the man before he said something he'd regret. "We're looking for a man."

"Nothing but ladies here, gents," the man said, spreading his hands.

Keough took out the sketch they had of the killer.

"This guy look familiar?"

"He looks like a lot of guys who come in here," the man said. "Could I pick him out of a crowd? No."

"Look again."

The man obliged, but said, "Officer—"

"Detective," Steinbach said.

"Sorry," the man said. "Detectives, unless the guy's like a regular, I wouldn't know him."

"What about the girls? The bartender?"

"Same thing," he said, "but feel free to ask. Just don't scare the customers, okay?"

Keough looked around. There were three stages, two of which were being used by girls at the moment. At each stage there was maybe one or two guys sitting, and there was a guy at the bar.

"Doesn't look like you've got too many customers," Keough said.

"It's early," the man said. "In a few hours we'll be packed. We got the best-looking women around here."

"Uh-huh," Keough said, and he and Steinbach walked deeper into the place. They were immediately accosted by a waitress wearing fishnet stockings, black bikini bottoms and a lowcut top. She was about five four and very well endowed.

"Drinks, gentlemen?" she asked, brightly.

"Not tonight, sweetie," Steinbach said.

"Didn't he explain to ya that there's a drink limit?" she asked. "You can have—"

"Talk to him about it, darlin'," Steinbach said. "He'll explain."

She frowned at them, then walked over to the guy at the door, who talked to her very animatedly for a few seconds.

"Gotta give the guy credit," Steinbach said.

"For what?"

"Look at those two girls. They're not bad."

His partner was right. One of the girls was a tall redhead who had already stripped down to a G-string. She had beautiful skin and small, well-shaped breasts. The other girl was shorter, blond, her breasts large and firm looking. She was holding them both in her hands, at the moment, flicking her nipples with her thumbs.

As the two detectives watched the waitress went to both girls and told them something that caused them to straighten up and look over at them.

"Uh-oh," Steinbach said. "Busted. There goes our chance of seeing them go bottomless."

"Not what we're here for, anyway, partner."

"Hey," Steinbach said, "I don't mind a bonus or two during my work day."

"As long as your wife doesn't find out?"

"You got it."

"Let's show the sketch and get moving," Keough said, "before one of us falls in love."

They decided to lay off the customers. Word could spread like wildfire that a couple of cops were haunting the clubs, and it might get back to the wrong person.

They talked to the bartender, a tall, full-breasted gal who looked like she belonged up on stage—maybe she took her turn, who knew?—and showed her the sketch. She claimed not to know who it was. They tried the waitress, then a couple of girls who were not on stage at the moment.

"How long before they finish up?" Keough asked one of the girls, indicating the blonde and the redhead.

"Coupla minutes," she said. She was a brunette, too thin for Keough's taste. He wondered how the customers would react when she got up there after those two. "I got a set comin' up. Why don't ya stay?"

"Some other time, maybe," Keough said.

"What about you?" she asked Steinbach. "Want a lap dance?"

"Not tonight, thanks."

"Suit yourself," she said. "You don't know what you're missin'."

A minute later they watched her swish her way to the stage where the blonde was finishing up and change places with her.

The blonde approached them, carrying part of her outfit in her hands, but not bothering to cover her breasts which, Keough noticed, were quite extraordinary in spite of the fact that he doubted they were natural.

"Can I help you fellas?" she asked.

Up close she was beautiful, and Keough noticed that Steinbach was having a problem concentrating on the task at hand. Hell, so was he, and she knew it.

They showed her the sketch and asked if she's ever seen the man.

"Don't you have a picture?"

"Sorry," Keough said, "just the sketch."

She took it from him to take a closer look. He noticed the sweet smell of whatever body lotion she was wearing. He wondered if they all wore the same scent.

"No," she said, handing it back, "I don't know him. Maybe Candy does."

"Candy?"

"The redhead. She's a slut. Maybe she went to his car with him, or something."

"What's your name?" Keough asked.

"Blondie."

"Sure."

"Sorry I couldn't help you."

As she walked away Steinbach said, "Who says she didn't help us? I feel a lot better than I did when I came in."

"Come on," Keough said, as the redhead came off her stage, "let's talk to the slut."

The redhead also claimed not to know the man in the sketch, so they went on to another club, and then another, with the same results. The only thing that changed was the music, and the fact that the clubs were starting to fill up.

"They all wear the same scent," Steinbach said. "Did you notice that?"

"Yeah, I did."

"Stripper smell."

Keough figured that was as good a name as any.

At one of the clubs Keough had been surprised to find the girls hopping into the laps of the men who were sitting at the stage. They'd gyrate for a while, some of them getting pretty gymnastic about it, then stand and encourage the men to stuff some money into their G-strings.

"You know," Steinbach said, "we should come back to these places some night when we're off duty. You know, like a guy's night out?"

"It's a thought," Keough said.

They were sitting in the car in the parking lot of the fourth club they had hit.

"What's next?" Steinbach asked.

"I think it's time to check out what Brooklyn, Illinois, looks like."

"I'm with you," Steinbach said. "You haven't steered me wrong, yet."

Fifty-five

FOR THE NEXT two days they hit the stores during the day and the clubs at night.

Brooklyn was filled with adult bookstores, video shops, and toy stores that sold every sexual device imaginable. They were right along Route 3, which Steinbach told Keough was also called the River Road, and then deeper into town. Brooklyn, Illinois, was certainly nothing like the Brooklyn Keough had left behind. It was a small town whose primary industry seemed to be geared toward adults—although Keough was certainly willing to admit that there could have been much more beyond what he was seeing today.

They stopped in front of one place and looked in the window.

"The laws sure are different on this side of the river,"

Steinbach said. "I can see three or four things in this window that would save my marriage."

"Does your marriage need saving?"

"Naw," Steinbach said, "just maybe some livening up."

This place seemed to carry everything, while some of the others they'd been to specialized only in books and videos. It also promised live action in the back booths.

As they entered Steinbach said, "There's more rubber and vinyl in here than I've seen in my whole life."

"Maybe you've led a sheltered life."

Steinbach ducked away from a dildo hanging from the ceiling and said, "Maybe I have."

"Welcome to the Hot Box, gentlemen," a man behind the counter said. "What's your pleasure? Books, movies, tasty playthings, or we've got some hot flesh in the back.

The man was in his forties, with long, lank black hair, a safety pin in his nose, several gold studs in each ear, and a Metallica T-shirt. His chin was covered with dark stubble that didn't quite hide a big red pimple.

"Don't make a scene," Keough said, as he showed the man his badge and ID.

"About what?" He barely seemed to have looked, but his next words assured them that he had seen all he needed to see. "That's a Missouri ID, pal. You got no jurisdiction here."

"I could call for some Illinois cops with no problem, friend," Keough said, "but we're only here to ask a question or two, not to make any trouble."

"I can handle the local cops," the man said, "but you

know what? I'm feeling good tonight. Go ahead and ask."

"We appreciate it. What's your name?"

"They call me Father Bill."

"Why do they call you that?" Steinbach asked.

"I was gonna be a priest once," Father Bill said. "Even did some time in the seminary."

"Quite a career change," Steinbach said.

"That's what makes life interesting."

Keough took out the sketch and passed it to the man.

"This scumbag?" the man said. "There was one of you guys in here last week askin' about him."

"One of us?" Keough asked. He and Steinbach exchanged a glance. "You mean, a Missouri cop?"

"A Mizzou detective," Father Bill said.

"And you told him who this was?"

"Told him," the man said, "and gave him an address."

"How do you happen to have his address?" Steinbach asked.

"We got it on file. We got addresses for all our members."

"Members?"

"Of the video club," the man said. "We don't just give our videos away, ya know."

"So this man in this sketch is one of your clients?"

"Was," Father Bill said. "If he ever comes in here again I'll wring his neck."

"Why's that?" Keough asked.

"He owes me," the man said. "He took out a video and never brought it back. We been sending him bills, but . . ."

"What was the video?" Keough asked.

"His favorite," the man said. "He used to rent it all the time. I guess he finally decided to keep it."

"What was it?" Steinbach asked.

"*Strolling Blondes,*" the man said. "Not one of our better numbers, but he likes it for some reason."

"What was it about?"

"Beats me," the man said with a shrug of his bony shoulders, "but I could probably guess."

"Yeah," Keough said, exchanging a glance with Steinback, "so could we."

"Were going to need his address," Steinbach said.

"Why can't you get it from the other cop?"

Keough described Ken Jackson to the man who nodded and said, "That's him. Boy, did he have an attitude. Threatened to tear off my head and shit down my neck if I didn't cooperate, so I did. Can't you get it from him?"

"No," Steinbach said.

"Why not?"

"He's dead," Keough said.

"No shit!"

"Can you get it for us?" Steinbach asked.

"Sure, sure," the man said, "no problem."

While they waited Steinbach asked, "Now how do we play this?"

"Not the way Jackson said," Keough said.

"Jesus," Steinbach said, "he walked in there alone, with no backup, and this guy got the drop on him. That arrogant son of a bitch. You know, the moment he got stabbed must have been a shocker to him."

"I'd guess so."

"No," Steinbach said, "I mean to his ego, man. Jackson's arrogance went way beyond normal. To be taken out that way must have been a helluva shock."

Father Bill came back with the name and address written down on an index card.

"Eric Pautz," Steinbach said.

"Where's that address?" Keough asked. "Klemm Street?"

Steinbach thought a moment and then said, "That's Shaw, I think."

"Where's that?"

"Behind the botanical gardens," Steinbach said, "not that far from the West End."

Keough looked at Father Bill.

"Thanks for the information."

"Is somebody else gonna come lookin'?" Father Bill asked. "I mean, I can have some cards made up, ya know?"

"Nobody else," Keough said. "We're going to close this son of a bitch out."

"Good luck."

As they were heading for the door Father Bill called out, "Hey, if you get him, do I get my video back?"

Fifty-six

THEY DISCUSSED THEIR course of action on the way back to St. Louis. Driving over the bridge Keough couldn't help but admire the way the Arch looked in the moonlight. St. Louis had a pretty skyline. The Arch was impressive, day or night. Sometimes he wondered what held it up. He half expected it to just tip over.

"So what do we do?" Steinbach asked. "Head for this guy's house? Call for backup?"

"Let's think this through, Al," Keough said. "If we go and get him, what do we get him for?"

"Murder."

"Whose? The women? The baby? Jackson's?"

"All of 'em."

"How do we prove it?"

"We . . . I don't know. What about the Fouquet girl?"

"We can get him for simple assault. That's not going to do anybody any good, expect him. A good lawyer and he's out."

"So what do you suggest?"

"I think we've got to watch this son of a bitch," Keough

said. "Keep an eye on him and wait for him to make his next move."

"What about the FBI?" Steinbach asked. "Are they going to cooperate?"

"They've got to," Keough said. "What could they get him for? No, I think when we explain this to Agent Connors she'll see the sense in it."

"We'll have to explain it to McGwire first," Steinbach said. "He wants this guy's ass bad."

"We'll talk to him first," Keough said. "He won't be in the office now. Do you know where he lives?"

"No," Steinbach said, "but we can find out. Just drive to the office."

When they got to the Major Case office, Steinbach found McGwire's home phone number and called him. It was nearly ten, but there was a good chance he'd be awake, depending on what kind of lifestyle he had.

He wasn't.

"Sorry to wake you, Cap," Keough said, "but we got him."

"You got who?"

"The killer."

"You've *got* him?"

"Well, we don't physically have him," Keough said, "but we know who he is . . . maybe."

There was a heavy sigh on the other end of the line.

"Where are you?"

"The office."

"Stay there," McGwire said, "and get some coffee. I'm on my way."

Keough hung up.

"He's on his way," he said, "and he wants coffee."

"So do I," Steinbach said. "I'll be right back."

By the time Steinbach returned Keough had found something in their in box.

"What is it?"

"The other sketch," Keough said. "The one from Marie Tobin. Look." He laid the two sketches side by side, the one from Marie Tobin and the one from Kate Fouquet. "See?"

"It's the same man," Steinbach said, putting bags of coffee and donuts on the desk. "It's him."

"Now all we need to do," Keough said, "is make sure that this is Eric Pautz."

"It's him," Steinbach said. "It's got to be."

"Got to be who?" McGwire asked, entering at that moment. He had obviously dressed haphazardly, his topcoat buttoned to his neck, his hair probably combed back with his fingers, a pair of old loafers on his feet.

"Hello, Cap," Steinbach said. "Sorry to get you down here at this time."

"Is that coffee?"

"Yes, sir." Steinbach took out a container and handed it to his superior. McGwire removed the plastic top and took a grateful sip. "Is this our man?"

"Yes, sir," Keough said, pushing the sketches closer together. "These are the two sketches our witnesses came up with."

"Hmm," McGwire said, "subtle differences, but I'd say it's the same guy."

"I agree."

McGwire looked at Steinbach. "You were saying a name when I came in?"

"Yes, sir," Steinbach said. "Pautz, Eric Pautz."

"Pautz?" He looked at Keough. "Is this on the level?"

"Yes, sir," Keough said.

"How did you get a name at all?"

"Maybe we better sit down."

They all took seats and Keough ended up behind Ken Jackson's desk. McGwire listened while Keough told him what they had found out. Steinbach quietly devoured a donut and watched.

"How did Jackson get to that store?" he asked when Keough finished.

"I don't know, Cap," Keough said. "Maybe he played a hunch."

"You know about hunches, huh?"

"I know something about them, yeah," Keough said.

"What's your next move, then? Pick him up?"

"No. We can't get him on anything but simple assault," Keough said. "What we've got to do now is make sure that Eric Pautz matches these sketches, and if he does, watch and wait for him to make his next move."

"What about the FBI? Gonna let them in on it?"

"Sure," Keough said. "Why not? The more the merrier. They can watch with us."

"And when he makes his next move on a woman, we'll have him."

"Right."

"But will we have him for Jackson's murder?"

Keough tossed a quick look at Steinbach, who raised his eyebrows.

"Well have to wait and see, Cap," Keough said.

"Because as much as I want him for the murders of these women, I want the man who killed one of my men. You said it was gonna be the same guy."

"I still think it is, Cap," Keough said. "Once we grab him, we can go into his house and look around, then we can interrogate him. Maybe he'll confess."

"And if he doesn't?"

"Well, maybe we'll find something in his house. We're just going to have to take it one step at a time—that is, with your permission."

McGwire finished his coffee, crumpled the cup, and dropped it in a nearby waste basket.

"I gave you the lead, Keough," he said, finally. He got to his feet. "We'll play it your way. Be here early in the morning and we'll talk to the FBI together."

"Yes, sir."

He started for the door, then turned and looked back at his two men.

"You did good work," he said, and left.

Keough took the top off his coffee and sipped it. It was lukewarm, but tasted good.

"Donut?" Steinbach asked.

"Sure."

Donuts were cliche where cops were concerned, but the truth of the matter was that they were quick to buy and quick to consume. They often satisfied the hunger gnawing at a cop's belly when he didn't have time to stop to eat, or when he was on stakeout.

Steinbach tossed the bag over to Keough, who deftly caught it with one hand. There was one donut left, a plain one, which suited him fine. He took a bite, then sipped the coffee. That was the other thing about donuts. They improved the taste of coffee—even brought good coffee up another level.

They drank their coffee and ate their donuts for a few moments before Steinbach broke the silence.

"So, what do we do next?"

Keough swallowed the last of his donut with the last of his coffee, then dropped the cup into the trash and rubbed crumbs from his hands.

"Go home, Al," he said. "Go home to your wife and kids. Starting tomorrow we'll be on a stakeout that might last a long time. Have your wife cook dinner for you, too, because we might be eating a lot more donuts."

"Fortunately," Steinbach said, standing up, "I like donuts. I'll see you in the morning."

"Early," Keough said, "around nine. The FBI should be here by then."

"Okay." He started for the door. "You comin'?"

"I'm going to sit here for a few minutes," Keough said. "I'll see you tomorrow."

"Joe," Steinbach said, "uh, the way you put this together, it was really, uh . . ."

"I know," Keough said. "Thanks, Al. See ya."

"Uh, yeah, okay."

Steinbach left, pulling the door shut behind him. Keough didn't want any congratulations, yet. Once this all worked out, then he'd take any accolades that came his way. For now he just hoped they'd find that Eric Pautz resembled the sketches, and that he'd make a move soon so they could pick him up. He wanted to verify that Pautz had done those women, killed the baby—albeit accidently—and then killed Jackson. When they put all of that on him, and it stuck . . . then what? Would he go back to being . . . complacent about his life here in St. Louis? He had to admit that this was the only time he had really come alive during his time here. And it would go on for the next few days—or weeks—of staking Pautz out, trying to put their case together and seeing it stick. Also, he still had the Sanders case to look into. Little Brady Sanders, at some time in his life, was going to want to know what happened to his parents, so there was still that matter to be put to rest.

But what then? What happened after that?

He passed a hand over his face and realized he was tired, and hungry. The donut had only served to show him how hungry he was. He decided to pick up takeout on the way home—maybe Chinese—and see if he could get some sleep. Tomorrow he'd have to try to get the FBI to agree with his assessment of the case—of the cases. From what he had seen of Agent Connors so far, he thought he'd be able to do that, but he wanted to be well rested when he tried.

As far as the other stuff, the personal things, he could put them aside until everything else was settled.

Fifty–seven

"WHY DIDN'T YOU tell us any of this before?" Agent Connors asked.

There were five of them in the Major Case office; Keough, Steinbach, Captain McGwire, and the two FBI agents, Connors and Hannibal. Spread out on the two desks were paper bags of bagels, donuts, and containers of coffee.

Keough had just finished explaining his theories to the FBI agents, who had listened intently, with less-than-happy looks on their faces.

"I had to move on my information fast," Keough said. "Besides, you were busy with your mall stakeouts." They had extended them for two days.

"Yeah," Hannibal said, derisively, "that was a waste of time."

Keough looked the younger man in the eyes and said, "It wasn't my idea."

"Hey, the mall business—"

"Can it, Tom," Connors said, and the younger agent closed his mouth.

"I'm spinning a theory here, Tom," Keough said, as if he was speaking to a dense child. "Nobody says you have to buy it." He looked at Connors again. "What would you have said if I told you I found some newspaper ads in Jackson's desk?"

"I don't honestly know what I'd have said," Connors replied.

"You sure as hell wouldn't have abandoned your mall stakeout, would you?" Keough asked. "Not on the basis of that."

"Probably not."

"So I had to come up with something more," Keough said, "and I have."

There were a few moments of silence while everyone took a bite or a sip of something.

"And now you've laid it all out for us?" Connors asked him.

"I have."

"And we're supposed to go along?" Hannibal asked.

"Or come up with a better idea, Agent Hannibal," Captain McGwire said, before Keough could answer. "Do you have a better alternative?"

"Well . . ." Hannibal said, slowly, "we could just go in and grab him."

"Bad idea," Steinbach said.

"I agree," Connors said. She looked at McGwire. "We'll go along with Detective Keough's plan, Captain." That drew her a look from her partner that she pointedly ignored. Keough had an idea there was trouble in paradise. Over the mall situation? Or this? Or something else, entirely?

"Here's what I suggest," Keough said. "We send somebody in to positively ID our perp. Once we know that Eric Pautz is the man in the sketches we can start to watch him and run a computer check."

"And how long do we watch him?" Hannibal asked.

"Until he makes a move."

"That could take months."

"It probably still wouldn't use as much manpower as yesterday's little exercise did, would it?" Keough asked him.

"Look—" Hannibal started, but Connors cut him off.

"Here's what I suggest," she said.

"Go ahead," Keough said.

"Once he's ID'd, we break into teams of two," she said. "I'll work with you, Keough, and Agent Hannibal can work with Detective Steinbach." She looked around and her eyes stopped on her partner. "Any objections?"

"No," McGwire said, immediately. "I like the idea of mixing and matching partners. Keough?"

"I don't have a problem, Cap."

Hannibal and Steinbach both looked unhappy that no one had consulted them.

"Okay," McGwire said, "then our next step is who should go in and ID our man?"

"I'll go," Keough said. "I want a good, long, close look at him."

"Any objections?" McGwire asked.

There were none.

"Let's do it, then," Keough said, and the meeting was adjourned.

It was decided that Keough should disguise himself as a UPS man. They went so far as to contact UPS and get one of their uniforms and trucks.

"What do we send him?" Steinbach asked.

"I've got an idea about that, too," Keough said.

"What do you have in mind?" Connors asked.

"You'll see."

The street Eric Pautz lived on, Klemm, dead ended against Tower Grove Park. For that reason Keough decided that they should stake him out with a car just off his block.

"If we stay on Botanical," he reasoned, "he has to drive past us to get out, either on Klemm, or a block to the west on Tower Grove Avenue, which runs right along the back of the botanical garden. Eventually he'll get to Shaw Boulevard, at which time he'll have to turn left or right. We can have a secondary car there, but I think we should stay on Botanical."

He was showing Connors, Hannibal, Steinbach, and McGwire a map to illustrate his point.

"Why don't we just take over a house on his block?"

"Because this is an old neighborhood with old residents," Keough said. "We've already found out that Pautz inherited the house from his mother. His family has lived there for years. The community is too tightly knit. Word will get around."

"I'll go along with this," Connors said.

"Do you need to okay this with anyone?" McGwire said.

"No, sir," she said. "I have complete autonomy where this case is concerned."

"That's impressive," McGwire said.

"Because I'm a woman, sir?"

This was the first hint Keough had that Connors might have some sort of chip on her shoulder.

"No," McGwire said, "I didn't mean that at all."

Connors seemed to believe him.

"Then we're ready to go?" Keough asked.

"UPS is on the way," Steinbach said.

"Let's do it, then," McGwire said.

Fifty-eight

KEOUGH DROVE THE UPS truck right up to the front of Eric Pautz's Klemm Street residence, put the brake on, and stepped out, carrying an 10 x 13 padded envelope. In the envelope was all of the pornographic material they could find, mostly catalogues for videos and toys to enhance someone's sex life. He figured Pautz, with his taste in videos, would never question this sort of a gift horse.

He walked up to the door and rang the bell; his heart started to pound immediately. In a matter of seconds he could be face-to-face with the killer of two or more women, an infant, and a cop. He wondered if he'd be able to keep from going for the man's throat.

He only had to ring the bell once, and the door was opened moments later. He was face-to-face with a man who very strongly resembled the two sketches they had.

"Eric Pautz?" he asked.

"That's right."

"This is for you."

Pautz appeared to be in his twenties, tall but very slender, almost skinny. Keough thought he would have trouble overpowering women like Kate Fouquet and Debra Morgan if it wasn't for the threats against their children. He seemed capable of sucker-punching Marie Tobin. He was wearing a soiled white T-shirt, and his hair was long and filthy.

"What is it?"

"I just deliver 'em," Keough said. He extended the new digital board that UPS was using and said, "Sign here." He'd gotten a quick lesson in how to use the device.

Pautz signed his name, still frowning.

"Have a nice day," Keough said, and forced himself to walk away from the man without putting a bullet between his eyes. Behind him he heard the door close.

He got into the UPS truck and drove it to Botanical Avenue, making a left and stopping halfway between Klemm and Tower Grove. There was a real UPS man waiting there to take the truck, and they made the exchange of positions smoothly. Keough immediately joined Agent Connors in the car which had been supplied by the FBI, getting into the back seat. Once inside he stripped off the UPS uniform.

"Is he our man?"

"He's our man."

She nodded and used her radio to quietly notify her other men that they had the right perp.

As an afterthought they had not only placed a secondary car on Shaw Boulevard, between Klemm and Tower Grove, but a third car on Arsenal Street, on the other side of Tower Grove Park, just in case Pautz decided to leave his car, scale some fences, and run through the park to Arsenal.

They were all in position.

Pautz did not come out of his house that first day, but on the second, during Keough and Connors' watch, he drove his car along Klemm to Shaw and made a left. They followed, Connors behind the wheel, doing a good job of tailing, never getting too close.

Pautz did not search for a victim that day, however. He did some grocery shopping, stopped at a chain bookstore, and then returned home for the day.

On the third day Connors and Keough sat in the car, looking over the file which had now been prepared on Eric Pautz.

"He's too clean," Connors said, as she and Keough passed some pages back and forth.

"He's on lots of mailing lists," Keough said, "which is why our UPS trick worked."

"No record," she said. "How can that be? Usually these types move up the ladder from petty crimes to major ones. This guy looks like he went right to kidnapping, rape, and murder first shot out of the box."

Keough was going over Pautz's vital statistics. He was six one, weighed in at 140, was twenty-nine, had only a high school education, and barely that. He seemed to have been left enough money so that he only worked when he had to, and that at odd jobs.

"He's been fired a lot," Connors said, reading to him from the sheet she had.

"I saw that."

"Personality conflicts," she said. "That follows the pattern."

The psychobabble pattern, Keough thought.

"He has a younger brother," she said.

"Uh-huh."

Abruptly, Connors put down the sheets she was reading and looked at Keough.

"If I remember correctly from your book," she said, and he didn't bother to correct her, "you don't believe in the psychological aspect of catching the serial killer."

"I just don't like giving these scumbags excuses," he said.

He was aware, for the third time, of the scent of Connors's perfume. It was hard not to be in the close confines of a car on stakeout. He'd been on stakeouts with women before, and he usually splashed on some extra cologne, as he had done this morning. Her scent, however, was sweet—sweeter than he would have imagined from her appearance. It was almost what Steinbach had called "stripper smell" the other night, but not quite. He couldn't remember having smelled it on her in the office. Had she, too, splashed on some extra?

"It works, you know," she said, "the psychological profiling."

"It has worked," he said. "I know, but not every time."

"Nothing works every time," she said.

"Exactly."

"Especially hunches."

He looked at her. She was staring straight ahead. Her profile was strongly cut, as if out of a mountain. She had a straight nose, a square jaw, and thin lips, but her mouth was far from unattractive. He had the feeling that with some makeup and a different hairdo she'd be a handsome woman.

"Don't tell me you've never worked a hunch," he asked, looking behind them.

They alternated looking front and back, at Klemm and Tower Grove, although the first time Pautz had come out he'd used Klemm.

"No," she said, "I haven't."

"You go by the book, huh?"

"I do," she said. "I believe in it."

"Bullshit."

"What?" She looked at him quickly, then away.

"You're working my hunch right now."

"The way you explained it was logical," she said. "I wasn't aware that we were playing a hunch."

"Well, we are."

"Well . . . it makes sense, that's all."

He looked back at the file in his lap and said, "It's still a hunch."

"Fine," she said.

"Fine," he said.

Fifty-nine

ON THE THIRD day Connors had shown up with Mike O'Donnell's book on the Kopykat case.

"I thought you read that" Keough asked.

"I'm reading it again."

"Why?"

"Because now I know you," she said, "and I'll read it with different eyes."

"It's not going to change."

She put the book down in her lap. Keough was looking toward Klemm Street, casting an occasional eye toward Tower Grove. By this time they were spending most of their time watching Klemm. If Pautz happened to get past them, the secondary car would alert them. By playing it this way, both of them didn't have to be so alert all the time. They were able to spell each other and take breaks, and during her breaks Connors was rereading the book.

"I'd think you would be proud of what you did," she said.

"Proud?" he asked. "I ended up without a job."

"You could have stayed in New York."

"Not and still be a cop."

"You could have done something else."

"Like what?"

"Gone private?"

"I'm not a private eye, Connors," he said, "I'm a cop."

"In St. Louis."

"St. Louis is all right," he said.

"I didn't say it wasn't."

"It's fine," he said. "It's got a lot going for it."

"Except for one thing," she said.

"What's that?"

"It ain't New York."

She turned her attention back to the book.

On the fourth day he found himself telling her all about the Sanders case.

"Sounds like you reconstructed it right," she said, when he was done. "All you have to do is wait for the woman's body to show up."

"Like the third woman in this case."

"Right," she said. "Eventually the bodies turn up. Almost always."

"Uh-huh."

"Are you worried about the boy?"

"Brady? Sure, I'm worried about him. At some point the kid is going to want to know what happened to his family—if he ends up being adopted permanently. Don't all adopted kids end up looking for their real parents?"

"No."

Keough stayed quiet.

"I never did."

"You were adopted?"

She nodded.

"I was about five."

"And what about your birth parents?"

She shrugged and said, "I guess they didn't want me."

"But you don't know for sure?"

"I don't care," she said. "I had parents. They raised me and I love them. There's no need for me to go looking for the people who gave birth to me. That doesn't make them my parents."

"Well . . . maybe Brady won't be as well adjusted as you obviously are."

They sat in silence for a while and then she said, "It's . . . nice of you."

"What is?"

"Wanting him to know," she said. "It's . . . decent."

"Thanks."

"So this case is keeping you from working on that?"

He explained that the Sanders case had been taken away and given to Jackson.

"The detective who was killed?"

"That's right."

"But I thought he was part of your task force."

"He was."

"Then . . ."

"Nobody was working on the other case," Keough said.

"I guess you want to get back to it, then."

"I will," he said, "right after we catch this Mall Rat."

She went back to the book, which she was almost finished rereading, and he went back to watching Klemm Street.

On the fifth day, he got an idea.

"A decoy."

"What?" Connors asked

"We looked into using a decoy, but we don't have anyone who fits the description."

"Not even with a wig?"

"No."

"Well, what would you do with a decoy, anyway?" she asked. "I mean, which mall would you place her in?"

"Whichever one he happens to be going to."

"Explain."

"If we had a decoy we could keep her on alert, ready to go at a moment's notice to whatever mall he's heading for at the time."

"And how would you know where he's headed?"

"We could figure that out easily enough," he said. "The

important thing would be to keep her ready to go in an instant."

She read the last page of O'Donnell's book then put it in the back seat.

"That could work," she said.

"Sure, it could—if you have someone who matches our victim profile."

"I'm sure we could come up with someone who fits the description," she said, grabbing the radio. "What is it, exactly?"

"Blond, caucasian, late twenties to early thirties, and in incredible physical condition."

"These are mothers we're talking about?"

"Yes, but mothers who keep in shape. They run, they work out. They dress to show their bodies off."

"This leaves me out," she said, wryly, "but I can get somebody."

"How soon?"

"She'll be here tomorrow."

For the first time on stakeout Keough was hoping that Pautz wouldn't move today.

Sixty

TRUE TO HER word Agent Harriett Connors had a decoy in the Major Case office the next morning.

"This is Agent Angela Tompkins," she said, making the introductions to Keough and Captain McGwire. "What do you think?"

"She's perfect," Keough said, and she was—in more ways than one.

Angela Tompkins was tall, blond, in her late twenties, and about as physically fit a female as Keough had ever seen.

"Has everything been explained to you, Agent Tompkins?" he asked.

"Call me Angela, please," she said in a throaty, sultry voice that completed her picture of perfection. "And yes, Harriett explained my job. I've brought along the right kind of clothes."

"We'll have to get her a stroller," Keough said.

"And a baby?" McGwire said.

"A doll would probably do," Keough said. "Just bundle

it up." Keough turned to Angela. "Can you manage to look like a young mother?"

"I think so. I have a three-year-old of my own."

"Good." McGwire turned to Keough and Connors. "You two better relieve your partners. I'll take care of Miss—uh, Agent Tompkins."

"Her partner should be here any minute," Connors said. "And we have a car for them. Just give them a radio and we should be all set."

"I hope this works," McGwire said. "I'm getting tired of the waiting."

On the way out to their car Connors said to Keough, "*He's* getting tired?"

Steinbach and Hannibal had not been getting along as well as Keough and Connors. In fact, after the second day they were barely speaking to each other.

"What about you and Connors?" Steinbach had asked.

"We're engaged," Keough said.

"Yeah, well," Steinbach had replied, "don't invite me *and* Hannibal to the wedding."

Now when they relieved the two mismatched partners, they explained to them about the decoy.

"Tompkins?" Hannibal said. "Do I know her?"

"No," Connors said, "the computer came up with her from the Denver office."

"How is she?" Steinbach asked Keough."

"She's perfect," he said. "You'll see when you get back to the office."

"Let's break this up before we attract too much attention," Connors suggested.

She and Keough walked back to their car as Steinbach and Hannibal pulled away in theirs.

"Maybe we should switch places with them," Keough said, as they settled in. "They're not getting along."

"It wouldn't help," she said. "You wouldn't get along with Hannibal, either."

"What's his problem?"

"What else?" she asked. "He's young."

"We should all have that problem."

"We have," Connors said, "and we managed to live through it."

"Think he will?"

"Only if I don't kill him first," she said.

After a full week Keough and Connors started their eighth day on stakeout with a bag of donuts to celebrate what Keough called their first anniversary.

"How sweet," she said, digging into the bag. "What's your record?"

"For what?"

"For a stakeout," she said. "What's your record?"

"Twenty-two days, when I was working vice."

"I was on stakeout for three months, once," she said. "Ninety-six days, to be exact."

"Never had that much time to devote to one case in New York," Keough said. "I'm sort of glad of that."

"I was a lot younger," Connors said. "I had better kidneys."

They drank their coffee and ate their anniversary donuts and then Connors said, "Eight days, Joe. What's this guy thinking?"

"I don't know."

"Maybe he's going to stop," she said, looking at Keough. "It's happened before, you know, like Zodiac."

"I hope that's not it, Harriett," Keough said.

"You really want this guy, huh?"

"He's killed women," Keough said, "beautiful, vibrant women, a baby, and a cop. Yeah, you could say I want him."

"Then maybe he knows we're onto him," she said. "Maybe he knows we're here."

"I'd prefer that."

"Why?"

"Because then he'd still make a move, eventually," Keough said, "and I think we've got him covered."

"I think so, too."

"But I don't think that's it."

"Why not?"

"He's not smart enough to know that we're onto him."

"Oh, that's right," Connors said, "I forgot. You think we've got a killer on our hands who's been operating on pure, blind, dumb luck."

"That's right."

"I still disagree," she said. "I don't think a serial killer can be dumb."

"Your profile, again?"

"That's right."

"Well," Keough said, "what about the organized and disorganized killers?"

"You *have* read all the material, haven't you?"

"How else would I know that I don't buy all of it?"

"But you do buy the organized/disorganized theory?"

"One of the killers in New York was disorganized, this one more so."

"I think you're confusing disorganized with unintelligent," Connors said. "Maybe you should do some more reading."

"Maybe we'll just find out when we catch him, huh?"

"That's what we're hoping."

Sixty-one

HE COULDN'T WAIT any longer.

Killing the cop had scared him. He'd been scared when he heard the man break in, scared when he realized he was killing him, and scared after he dumped him, scared that he'd be caught.

But he hadn't been.

Nobody had come looking for him but a UPS man, and even that had scared him.

But he wasn't scared, anymore.

It had been long enough. He was no rocket scientist, he

knew that, but he was smart enough to know that if the police knew he'd killed a cop they would have come for him by now. He'd watched enough *NYPD Blue* and *New York Undercover* to know that.

He looked at the pile of catalogues the UPS man had brought him a week ago. He'd never gotten anything from UPS before, and he enjoyed leafing through the catalogues. A couple of them sold porno movies, but he didn't see any titles he liked. Still, even the pictures in the catalogues had been enough to remind him he had a need that had to be taken care of.

Eight days was too long.

The last time he'd gone out looking, though, he'd almost gotten caught. And then the thing with the cop happened. He decided just to go to his favorite mall, take his time, pick himself out a good one, and go slow.

It was time.

Sixty-two

"HE'S ON THE move," Connors said, and then, "He's on the move."

The first had been to alert Keough, who had his eyes

closed, and the second was into the radio to alert the other cars.

"Let's stay with him," Keough said.

She started the car, drove to Klemm and turned left. It was seven blocks to Shaw Boulevard and then he turned left.

"It's going to be up to you to guess which mall he's heading for," Connors reminded Keough. "Let's see if this plan of yours is going to work."

Pautz, driving a four-door Dodge Dart that seemed to be held together by dirt and rust, passed Vandeventer Avenue and continued to Kingshighway. He took Kingshighway to Highway 40 and headed west.

"Galleria," Keough said.

"How can you be sure?"

"He could get off sooner and go to Crestwood, or he could pass it by and head for West County," Keough said—this case had made him nearly an authority on St. Louis malls. "But I think he's heading back to the Galleria."

"Back?"

Keough nodded and said, "Back to where it all started, Harriett."

"Okay," she said, picking up the radio, "it's your call. Let's get our decoy over to the Galleria."

As they approached the Brentwood Boulevard exit of Highway 40, Keough held his breath. If Pautz went by it would mean he might be going to West County— Keough's bird mall—and Keough didn't know if they'd be able to get their decoy over there fast enough. To his relief Pautz pulled his Dodge Dart Dirt Machine off Highway 40 and onto Brentwood Boulevard.

They followed him into the parking lot. It was early, and there were spots. They parked one aisle over from him and followed him in on foot, Connors on her hand unit the whole time. Keough told her to have the decoy meet them near the St. Louis Bread Company.

Keough and Connors followed Pautz into the mall through the door that was below FAO Schwarz. The secondary car pulled into the parking lot after them and the agents were just a few seconds behind them. Keough grabbed one of the men as he came through the automatic doors.

"Stay with him, and stay on the radio."

"Right."

The man was FBI so Keough said, "Mall security is on the same frequency. They'll be working with us."

"I understand."

Keough turned to Connors.

"Let's go meet the decoy."

"Right."

She had been on the radio with the decoy all the way to the mall.

"She's just a few minutes away," she said. "We just have to hope he doesn't pick a victim before we're ready to go."

"If he picks a victim," Keough said, "we'll have to be ready."

Keough checked in with the FBI man who was following Pautz, wishing that the man knew the mall.

"Where are you?" he asked.

"We're walking past a bookstore."

"Which one?"

"Waldenbooks," the man said, "on the first level."

"Stay with him."

"Right."

"And let me know if you see a woman who matches his type. Got it?"

"I understand."

Keough called in to mall security then and asked for the captain to meet him at the St. Louis Bread Company with some men. He also asked for the Richmond Heights man who was on duty to meet with them.

By the time the decoy came in with her stroller through the doors near the St. Louis Bread Company, Keough and Connors had been joined by Captain Battle of mall security, two of his men, and Officer Hartley from Richmond Heights. Add to that the FBI man who had driven the decoy, and they had a nice crowd.

"If he sees us he's going to get spooked," Connors said. "There's too many of us."

"You're right," Keough said. He spoke into the radio to the man tailing Pautz, the Mall Rat. "Where are you?"

"Second level," the man said, "passing a bookstore for kids."

"He's walking in this direction," Keough said to Connors, "but two sections away and upstairs. We've got a few minutes."

Keough used those few minutes to explain things to Hartley and to the mall security captain.

"What do you want my men to do?" the captain asked.

"Just be ready," Keough said. "Walk the mall like normal, but don't pay any undue attention to our man until you hear from me."

"Do you want the exits covered?"

"Have you got enough men?"

"To cover the main exits, yes," the captain said, "but not to cover the exits to the covered parking."

"Our man won't go there," Keough said. "Just cover the exits."

"And grab him if he tries to leave?"

"No," Keough said, "not unless I say so. There are two reasons he would leave the mall. First, if he's got a victim and he's following her to her car, and second, if he gives up."

"He shouldn't give up," Tompkins, the decoy said, "because we're giving him a victim."

She had gone all out, wearing a spandex running suit that showed off the flesh of her legs, abdomen, shoulders and arms—all *well* toned—as well as her taut butt. It was a little cool for such an outfit, but Keough hoped the killer wouldn't mind.

"If he doesn't go for you," Keough said, "he's crazier than I think."

She smiled at the compliment.

The stroller she had was an umbrella type, very common these days, and in it was a doll, bundled up to—hopefully—resemble a baby.

"Where should I set up?"

"Come with me," Keough said, grabbing her arm. Connors followed.

Keough pulled her to the center of the mall, where the fountains were, speaking into the radio.

"Where are you?"

"He's looking in FAO Schwarz," the FBI responded.

"We've got time," Keough said. "If he stays on the second floor we can catch him at the coffee stand."

"Where?" Tompkins said. "We just left the coffee—"

"There's one on the second level. Come on, we'll take the escalator." He turned to Connors. "You're going to have to coordinate everyone. I'll stay with Tompkins."

"Okay."

"Let's go," he said to the decoy.

"Can I have a latte?" she asked.

"I'll buy you anything you want," Keough said, "if it'll catch the bastard."

Sixty-three

HE WAS TAKING his time, actually browsing as he walked through the mall. He had decided, upon entering, to turn right, walk to the end of the mall, then take the escalator to the second level and walk back again, all the way to the other end, where Famous Barr was. From there he'd come back down and walk the downstairs before finally checking the food court, which was at the center of the mall, downstairs from where he first entered.

He stopped for a moment at FAO Schwarz to see if there were any mothers shopping in there. There were, and one was his type, but she had a toddler with her, holding it by the hand. There was no stroller in sight, so he moved on.

He walked past Barnes & Nobles and kept walking until he could stop and look down at the fountain. Sometimes young mothers with their babies in strollers would stop and look at the water. He stood that way for several minutes, but did not see anyone, and moved on.

When he got to the coffee place on the second level he almost stopped short, she was that perfect.

She was wearing her long blond hair in a ponytail and was clad in a tight-fitting running suit. The firm flesh of her legs, arms, and tummy was bare, and he felt the heat in his groin. He continued to walk past her, slowing to look her over as she sat with her coffee, leaning over every so often to check the baby in the stroller.

Perfect.

Keough watched with satisfaction as Pautz slowed when walking past Agent Tompkins. He had taken up position in the Museum Store, which was diagonally across from the coffee place, in a branch of the mall that led to covered parking. The killer slowed, but didn't stop, and eventually walked past the Museum Store. Keough could see clearly the hungry look on the face of the Mall Rat.

They had dangled the bait, and he had obviously seen it. Now they needed to wait for him to make a move.

"Connors," he said into the radio, "he's seen her."

"What's he doing?"

"Nothing yet. Stand by."

Instead of continuing on, the Mall Rat began to walk in a circle, bypassing the escalators. Eventually he was right across from Agent Topmkins, he on one side of the downstairs fountain, and she on the other, in a position where he could still watch her, but far enough away not to be seen—he thought.

"Come on, come on," Keough said to himself.

"Can I help you, sir?" a middle-aged female clerk asked him.

"Huh? Oh, no, just looking."

"Just let me know if I can—"

"I will," he said, annoyed at the interruption, "thank you."

She frowned and moved away, watching him suspiciously.

Keough saw the FBI man who had been tailing the killer as he walked past the decoy. The man spotted him in the store, but to his credit did not break stride. He kept walking and entered a clothing store across the way. From there he watched, as did Keough, and waited.

"What's he doing?" Connors' voice came over the radio anxiously.

"He's watching her."

"Come on, come on," Keough heard Connors say into the radio, "make a move . . ."

"Be patient, Harriett." He said it before he could stop himself and then thought maybe he shouldn't have used her first name over the radio.

Things started to happen, then, things he would think about later.

First, Pautz was coming around again, to walk by Tompkins for the second time. Maybe he just wanted a second look at her.

"He's moving toward her again . . ."

Tompkins got up and dropped her empty cup in a trash can, then started walking with the stroller. She was walking toward Pautz, so that she'd be sure to pass him. Keough was certain she didn't know she was doing this.

"She's getting up."

"I'm coming up," Connors said.

Keough stepped out of the Museum Store so he could keep her in sight. Pautz came around into her line of sight—and Keough's—and he saw Tompkins break stride for just a moment, and then keep walking. She was stiff, though, and he hoped the killer wouldn't notice it. Come on, he thought, swish your ass, relax . . .

It was inevitable. She and the Mall Rat were going to pass very close to each other. If he was going to take the bait he'd probably pass her, then turn around and follow her. This was it . . .

That's when Keough saw the kids. They were teenagers, probably fourteen or fifteen, two white kids with baseball caps on backward, jeans halfway down their hips, two white kids who thought they were gangster rappers from Compton. They were running, pushing each other, knocking into other people.

Tompkins and Pautz finally passed, and Keough saw Pautz turn to watch her.

At that moment the two teenagers converged on Tompkins, playing their game, and they must have been so impressed by her looks that they sort of staggered. One of them tripped over the other one's feet, and Keough knew there was no way to avoid it. He fell right into the umbrella stroller, knocking it over with enough force to have ejected a real baby.

He certainly hit it hard enough to knock a *doll* out of it, and that's what happened. The doll hit the mall floor and skidded *toward* Eric Pautz, who jumped back as if scalded, and then stopped and stared . . .

The last thing that happened was Steinbach and Hannibal appearing from the opposite direction, coming toward Tompkins, who was confused now. She didn't know what to do. How could she continue to play her role when her "baby" lying on the floor, plain as day, was made of plastic?

It all happened so fast . . .

He couldn't believe his eyes. The baby had fallen out of the stroller and it wasn't *real*. It was a *doll*. What was she doing with a doll?

He looked at her and their eyes locked, and he knew something was wrong. Suddenly, he felt cornered. He looked past her and saw the two men coming, one grabbing the other's arm, that one shaking it off and still coming.

Something was very wrong here . . .

Sixty-four

KEOUGH SAW STEINBACH try to grab Hannibal's arm, but the younger man wasn't having any of it. He was heading right for Eric Pautz.

"Shit."

"What's going on?" Connors asked, coming up next to him.

"Your partner's about to blow it," Keough said.

"I can stop him—"

"It's too late," Keough said. "Pautz sees him."

And then to compound the error Hannibal suddenly shouted, "FBI! Put your hands up!" and produced his gun.

Pautz looked around frantically for someplace to run, and Keough suddenly had an idea. They had to force him into the section of stores that led to the covered parking lot.

Steinbach came forward and now had a firm hold on Hannibal's arm.

"Al," Keough said into his radio, hoping that Steinbach had a unit, "herd him into the covered parking."

"He won't go in covered parking," Connors said, "you said so."

"He will if he has nowhere else to run."

And he didn't, unless he wanted to go into a store and take a hostage, but he didn't think like that. Keough was sure that Eric Pautz's thoughts would be of flight, not of hostages.

The Mall Rat turned to run and saw both Keough and Connors.

"We can't grab him," she said. "We don't have anything on him."

We don't have a choice, now, Keough thought, thanks to her partner, and thanks to circumstances.

The two teenage boys scrambled out of the way, not knowing what was going on, but knowing that something serious was happening.

Pautz turned again and saw Steinbach and Hannibal closing in now, along with Tompkins.

He looked around frantically. There was only one place to run, and he went for it.

He started running down the hallway toward the entrance to the covered parking lot. Keough didn't know if Pautz knew where he was going, or if he was just looking for a way out.

As the five of them followed, Keough shouted into the radio, "We need to seal off covered parking."

"Which area?" a voice came back.

"I don't know," Keough shouted, angrily. How could he know how they divided the area up? "Seal it all off."

Pautz went through the door, leaving Keough worried because he didn't know how big the covered parking lot was.

Eric Pautz ran toward the only door he could see. He heard shouting behind him, and running, but he didn't dare look back. His heart was pounding. If they caught him they were going to punish him. If his mother found out . . .

He ran through the door and he had the choice of going up a short flight of concrete steps, or down. He chose down, and then right. He started to run, and then suddenly he realized where he was. The ceiling seemed impossibly low, there were too many vehicles. A car drove up behind him, then sounded its horn. It echoed off the concrete ceiling and walls; Pautz put his hands over his ears to try and block it out. He broke into a cold sweat and suddenly the floor seemed slanted as his senses were assailed by a bout of vertigo.

Suddenly, he fell to his knees . . .

"What's going on?" Hannibal asked, aloud.

"Everybody stay where you are," Keough said. "It's the confined space."

"He doesn't have a weapon," Hannibal said. "Let's get him."

At that point Captain Battle of the mall security and Officer Hartley came through the door behind them, both with their guns drawn.

"Put those away," Keough said, as another horn sounded. A second car had come up behind Pautz, who was still on his knees, blocking the aisle.

"Get out of the way!" the driver yelled.

"Captain," Keough said, "get that car to back up, but walk all the way around our man. Don't go near him."

"Right."

"What are you going to do?" Connors asked.

"If we grab him now we've got nothing on him beyond flight to resist arrest. I've got to get him to confess."

"Confess?" Hannibal asked. "How—"

"That's the only way we can take him for the murders," Keough said. "He's got to confess in front of allof us."

Keough didn't know what a defense attorney's psychiatrist would do with this sort of confession, but he couldn't worry about that now. They simply could not let the man get away.

"Just stay back and let me talk to him," Keough said, starting forward.

"Let's move around and surround them," Connors said to the others as Keough started walking. "We don't want him getting away."

"Right," Steinbach said, and they all started circling with their guns still holstered.

Still holding his hands over his ears, Pautz saw the man coming toward him. The second horn seemed to be echoing inside his head now, and he still felt as if the floor was slanted. Tears mingled on his face with beads of sweat, and his skin felt prickly.

"Eric?"

The voice was muffled. He was surprised that the man knew his name.

"Eric? I want to help you."

"Get me out of here!" Pautz screamed, startling both Keough and himself.

"I can get you out of here, Eric," Keough said, "but you've got to do something for me first."

"What?" Pautz asked. A spit bubble formed on his mouth and popped. Tears and mucus streamed into his mouth. "What do I have to do?"

Keough came closer. The car behind Pautz backed up. Slowly, the Mall Rat removed his hands from his ears so he could hear what he had to do to get out of the parking lot.

"I need you to tell me about the women," Keough said, "and the babies, Eric."

"The babies . . ." Pautz repeated.

Once again it occurred to Keough that the baby they found dead had met its end accidently. He decided to use that.

"Why did you kill one of the babies?" he asked.

"The babies . . ."

Pautz looked confused, his hands hovering inches away from his ears, ready to clap back over them if the need arose.

"The babies . . ."

"You killed one of the babies, Eric," Keough said. "We found the other ones in the Dumpsters, but you killed one of them."

"I . . . I didn't . . ."

"Yes, you did."

Pautz shook his head violently.

"Didn't . . . wouldn't kill the baby . . . I took care of him . . ."

"You took care of the first two," Keough said, "but the third one died."

"I took care of him," Pautz said again, and Keough wasn't sure they were talking about the same thing.

"The women, Eric," he said, "you killed the women . . ."

"Yes," Pautz said, "I killed the women."

"Why?"

"They weren't . . . right," he said. "They weren't the right ones . . . I thought they were."

"And the babies?"

"I didn't hurt the babies," Pautz said. "I put them where they would be found."

"Except for the third one, the one that died."

"No," Pautz said, "I didn't . . . I *put* him in a Dumpster, like the others. It wasn't my fault nobody found him . . . not my fault . . ."

"But the women," Keough said, wanting him to say it again, "you did kill the women?"

Pautz looked directly at Keough and said, "I . . . I killed them . . ." His eyes were wild, showing whites all the way around, and he looked around him without moving his head, just his eyes, so that they seemed to be rolling in his head.

"Can you let me out? Can you let me out . . . now?"

"One more thing, Eric."

"I have to get out," Pautz said, and it came out in an anguished whisper.

"One more thing."

"W-what?"

"The policeman."

Pautz closed his eyes.

"I didn't mean it," he said. "He scared me."

"He scared you?"

Pautz nodded.

"I hid in the closet, but he found me."

"You had a knife."

Pautz nodded.

"And you stabbed him."

Another nod.

"Because he scared you?"

"Yes," he said, "he broke into my house, and I was scared." His eyes pleaded with Keough. "Can you take me out of here now?"

"Yes, Eric," Keough said, walking to him and reaching down, "I can take you out now."

He took Pautz by the arm and lifted him to his feet. The man's hands were still hovering near his ears. He looked at Keough, eyes wild, and said, "Mister?"

"Yes."

"About the baby?"

"What about the baby?"

Pautz finally moved a hand, wiping some tears and mucus from his face, and said, "Don't tell my mother?"

Sixty-five

"THERE ARE SOME things I don't understand," Steinbach said.

It was three days after the Mall Rat was apprehended. The newspapers had even used the name, which they had apparently gotten from someone. Steinbach? Hannibal? Perhaps by accident, someone letting the name slip? It didn't really matter.

They had taken Eric Pautz from the Galleria to the nearest police station, that being Richmond Heights. He was be held there until the FBI could arrange transportation, which they did, later in the day. The Mall Rat was no longer Keough's concern. The FBI had taken over, had gone through Pautz's apartment, and was now trying to ascertain where he had hidden the body of the third woman and if he had committed any other murders that they didn't know about, either in St. Louis or someplace else.

"There are always things we don't understand," Connors said, "or that we can't explain."

They were all there: Keough, Steinbach, Connors, Hannibal, and McGwire. The decoy, Tompkins, had been sent back to Denver with the assurance that she had done her best, and had actually been a help.

"What's not to understand?" Keough asked.

"Well, why was he taking blond mothers and children, for one thing?" Hannibal asked.

"There was a photo in his house," Connors said.

"Of who?"

"A blond woman."

"Who was she? His mother?" Steinbach asked.

"We're not sure."

"What do you mean, you're not sure?"

"Well," she said, "according to him, it's either his mother, or his baby-sitter."

"What? He doesn't know—"

"He's a little confused," she said.

"He's a lot confused," Hannibal said.

"Apparently his mother was a pretty blonde, but so was his baby-sitter when he was a child. Also, there's a younger brother he used to care for, and apparently there was some transference going on when it came to the babies. He used them to get the mothers to do what he wanted, but he never meant to hurt them. He thought he'd get in trouble if he did."

"He was killing women," Steinbach said, "but thought he'd get in trouble if he hurt the babies?"

"That's about it," she said.

Steinbach shook his head and looked at Keough, who rolled his eyes. Keough was not interested in the psychological reasons for Eric Pautz's crimes. He was satisfied with getting him off the streets.

"Are the charges going to stick?" he asked.

"I think so," Connors said. "He repeated his confession under much calmer conditions. I think we can make it stick."

"What about the closet?" Steinbach asked.

"What about it?" Connors asked.

"Well, he was afraid of the covered parking, right? Like, claustrophobic, right?"

"Right."

"Then how could he wait for Jackson in a closet?"

"Apparently," Connors said, "he considered the closet his safe place. This was a holdover from his childhood."

"And what about the porno movie? *Strolling Blondes*?"

"We screened it," Hannibal said, making it sound like a Hollywood premiere. "It's about blond mothers having sex with . . . whoever."

"I don't get it," Steinbach said. "Did he kill these women because they looked like his mother? His babysitter? Or the women in the movies?"

"Yes," Connors said, and before anyone else could speak the phone rang.

"Major Case," Captain McGwire said, picking it up. He listened for a moment, then held it out to Keough. "For you."

"Thanks."

Keough stepped away from the others as Steinbach kept asking questions, and said, "Hello?"

"Joe, it's Valerie."

"I've been meaning to call—"

"It's happening again, Joe," she said, agitated.

"What is?"

"Brady," she said. "There's a man hanging around his foster home."

"Now?"

"Yes."

"Give me the address, Valerie," he said, grabbing a slip of paper . . .

He didn't tell anyone where he was going. He still hadn't told McGwire that he had continued to work the Sanders case, even now that he was the fair-haired boy.

The foster home was in Sunset Hills this time, a nicer neighborhood, where people were concerned about strangers hanging around. He wasn't sure why the foster parents had called Valerie and not the police, but that didn't matter. He hoped that whoever the man was, he'd stay around long enough for Keough to catch him.

On the way he wondered—if this was indeed the same man—how he had managed to get the addresses of both the foster homes that Brady had been put in. He also hoped that this second incident wouldn't cost Brady his second foster home.

Sunset Hills was filled with residential neighborhoods, some better than others, but none of them below the lower rung of upper-middle class. People who owned homes there cared about them, kept up the appearance of their property, and chipped in for neighborhood security. Keough knew that because as he pulled up in front of the house he saw a private security car also parked there.

The man was just getting out of his car. Keough approached him, flashing his ID.

"What was your call?" he asked.

"A Peeping Tom," the man answered. He was young, so Keough doubted he was an ex-cop.

"What address called you?"

The man told him, and it matched Brady's address.

"Do you automatically put in a call for the police?"

"No, sir," the man said, "not for a call of this nature. Do we, uh, need backup?"

"I don't think so. What's your name?"

"Henry Deavers, sir."

"Henry, why don't you go around the right side of the house and I'll go around the left and we'll see what we can find."

"Okay."

He saw the man put his hand on his gun.

"Keep your gun holstered, okay? I don't think you'll be needing it."

"Yes, sir."

"Let's go."

This appeared to be one of the better Sunset Hills neighborhoods. The homes were large and well built, with driveways and two-car garages. Keough thought that this place was actually more like the home Brady had lived in with his parents than the one in Florissant had been. The little guy was probably comfortable here.

He was aware that many foster families took children in because they would then receive a monthly stipend to care for them. He was also aware that, at least in New York, many of those families then had their own uses for that money. He hoped St. Louis was different. Somebody, somewhere, had to be taking these kids in simply because they wanted to help, or because they loved children.

Keough circled the house, his eyes sweeping the yards alongside and behind as he went. As he got to the back he heard voices and knew that he was in time—maybe just.

". . . away before I call the police. I've already called security, and the social services woman."

He came around the back and saw the man. He was dark-haired, dressed in jeans and a sweatshirt, but he looked smaller than Keough would have thought Bill Sanders was.

"Bill Sanders?" he called.

The man turned toward the sound of Keough's voice and his eyes widened when he saw him.

"Police!" Keough said.

"No," the man said, "you don't understand." Only it didn't sound like a man's voice.

"Stop there."

"No," the man said again. He looked into the house, said, "Brady," and then turned to run.

"Don't run," Keough said, as the security man came from the other direction.

The man ran toward the back of the yard, where there

was a high wooden fence. Keough ran after him, as did the security man. He thought the fleeing man might vault the fence, and then they'd be in for a chase, but he stopped short, as if unwilling to make the jump.

As Keough reached him, the man turned and pointed a small pistol at him. Keough's thoughts went back to the day Brady had walked into the police station, the day he'd walked through the Sanders house and found an empty holster in one of the night tables.

He'd guessed a small-caliber pistol, and he'd been right.

"Mrs. Sanders," he said, "Marian, you don't want to do this."

It was Marian Sanders, all right. Even with the short black wig he recognized her from the photos he'd seen in the living room of her home. He also realized that a lot of this trouble could have been avoided if he had asked Brady in Florissant if he had seen his father *or* his mother.

"I just wanted to see my son."

"I understand that—" Keough started, but he was cut off by the arrival of the security man.

"Hold it!" he shouted, pointing his gun at Marian Sanders. "Throw the gun away."

"Put your gun up, Henry," Keough said, as calmly as he could.

"But . . . but, Detective—"

"Put it away," he said, again. "Mrs. Sanders doesn't want to shoot me."

"*Mrs.* Sanders?" the man said. He holstered his gun and

looked closer at the *man* holding the gun, and saw that it was, indeed, a woman. "You know her?"

"I do," Keough said. "Go and talk to the woman in the house. Tell her everything is all right."

"But detective—"

"Go on, Henry," Keough said, "do as I say."

Reluctantly, the security man obeyed and walked away. Meanwhile, Marian Sanders kept a tight, two-handed grip on the gun and kept it trained on Keough.

"Marian," Keough said, "why don't you give me the gun."

"You don't understand."

"About your son?" he asked. "Or about killing your husband?"

"It was a fight," she said, "and it got out of hand. I was so . . . angry. All the late nights, all the women . . ."

"And he hit you, didn't he?"

"We . . . we used to hit each other," she said. "It was a . . . a *sick* relationship."

"Why'd you stay married to him?"

She shrugged and said, "I loved him—and he loved me. I know he did. He just couldn't . . . s-stop . . . I couldn't take it, anymore."

"So there was an argument, and it escalated into a fight. Who got the knife?"

"I did," she said. "I stormed out of the bedroom, went to the kitchen, and got the knife, just to scare him."

"And it got out of hand."

"Yes," she said, tears sliding down her face, dropping

from her chin to the ground. "I s-stabbed him . . . he chased me down the hall into the living room, bleeding, and I stabbed him again . . . and again . . . and he was dead."

"What did you do then?" Keough asked. "Panic?"

"No," she said, wiping the tears from her face with a forearm while continuing to train the gun on him, "that's the odd part. I was very calm. I knew I had to do something with him so I wrapped him in an old blanket, dragged him to the garage, and put him in the trunk of the car. H-he wasn't very heavy, and he wasn't much bigger than me."

It had been easy to mistake her for a man not only because of the wig, but because she was a tall woman, perhaps five eight or nine.

"What about Brady?"

"Brady he came into the bedroom while I was getting the blanket. B-Bill . . . Bill's body was in the living room. I convinced Brady to go back to his room to wait for me. After I put Bill in the trunk of one car, I put Brady in the other car and took him to the only place I could think of."

"The police station."

She nodded.

"I knew they'd take care of him there."

"I did," Keough said. "I got there just as Brady walked in, Marian, and I took care of him."

"Th-thank you . . ."

"My name is Joe Keough," he said, "and I want to help you, the way I helped Brady."

"I just wanted to see him," she said. "When I went out to Florissant I didn't mean to scare anyone . . ."

"I know," he said, "but how did you find him both times?"

"I have a f-friend who works for the city," she said. "She helped me. I've been s-staying with her until I could figure out what to do."

"Does she know about your husband?"

"No," Marian Sanders said. "I just told her I had to hide from him."

That could have been true, or she might have been protecting her friend from being an accessory. It really didn't matter.

"Okay, Marian," he said, "now we've come to the point where you either have to shoot me, or give me the gun. Which is it going to be?"

She didn't respond right away.

"Brady's in the house, Marian," he said. "Maybe he's watching. What do you want to do?"

Marian stared at him for a few moments, and then suddenly all of her muscles relaxed and she slumped, dropping the hand with the gun to her side. With her other hand she slid the black wig off, revealing her own blond hair, which had been hastily chopped short. Keough moved then, taking the gun from her and helping her to her feet.

"Time to go, Marian. It's all over."

They started walking back to the house. Keough could now see a woman and Brady standing at sliding glass doors looking out at them. Henry, the security man, was standing just outside.

"C-can I see Brady before I go?" Marian asked.

"Why don't we wait until you can see him when you're looking more like his mother, huh?"

"When will that be?" she asked.

"I don't know, Marian," he said, "I honestly don't know."

Sixty-six

THE PLACE WAS called *A Taste of Manhattan*. It was in Clayton, and had been opened by some guys from Brooklyn. Valerie had brought him there as a surprise, but she needed him to tell her if it tasted like real Brooklyn pizza.

"God," he said, closing his eyes at the first bite, "it's perfect."

The slice was cut in a triangle, and he folded it lengthwise, the way they did in Brooklyn. He turned to Joey, the man behind the counter, and saluted him with the slice. According to Joey, this was the first of many Brooklyn pizzerias he and his partners were going to open.

St. Louis was getting better and better, and that was due, largely, to the woman sitting across from him.

"You know," she said, "I'm originally from Chicago, and this really can't stand up to a Chicago pizza."

Okay, so she wasn't perfect.

It had been a week since he'd brought Marian Sanders in for the murder of her husband. She had driven his body out to Riverport and dropped him into a construction site where they were building some new casinos.

That same day he had called Valerie, met with her at Dressel's for dinner, and explained a lot of things to her. After he covered the problems of the Sanders family he explained something that he himself had only just become aware of.

"I haven't been sure that I was going to stay in St. Louis," he said. "I think I was pushing you away so we wouldn't get involved. That would have made my decision harder. I needed to figure it out myself, with no distractions."

"I'm a distraction?"

"Definitely."

"And now you have it figured out?"

"Yes," he said. "I'm going to stay. In fact, Captain McGwire has offered me the position of lead homicide investigator at Major Case, and I'm taking it."

"And now you can deal with me?"

"If you'll let me," he said.

She'd frowned at him from across the table.

"I sort of like the romantic notion that you might decide to stay because of me," she said.

"Valerie—"

She held up her hand and he stopped.

"But I agree with you," she went on. "You needed to

make this decision on your own, without any help—or hinderance—from me."

"Then we can start over?" he asked.

"Oh, no," she said, "not over. That would waste all the time we've already invested—and I can't afford that. I've become . . . impatient to move to the next level."

"Which is?"

She smiled and said, "You live walking distance from here, don't you?"

They went to bed together for the first time that night, and had seen each other almost every day since. McGwire had given him a week off before he started his new job, and there was only Saturday and Sunday left.

They had started Saturday by going to Forest Park to fly some kites, and then she'd taken him for a surprise Brooklyn pizza.

He checked his watch and said, "We have time for another slice."

"Not me," she said, "but you go ahead. When do we have to see your friend?"

"He's signing from four to six," he said. "Plenty of time."

"I'm looking forward to meeting someone who's known you for a long time."

"Well," he said, "Mike qualifies."

Mike O'Donnell was signing copies of *Kopykat* at Big Sleep Books in the Central West End; he and Keough had agreed to have dinner afterward. Keough told O'Donnell he was bringing a new friend.

Big Sleep Books was on Euclid Avenue, just a couple of blocks from Keough's house. He had finally unpacked the last of his boxes, and now thought of the house as home.

He'd heard about the bookstore previously from Al Steinbach, but had never gone inside himself until now.

He and Valerie entered the small store and saw O'Donnell sitting at a table in the back with a handsome, slender, elegant-looking woman in her early sixties.

"Keyhole man!" O'Donnell said, and rose to give his friend a bear hug. O'Donnell, once a reporter for the *New York Post*, had written several true crime books before *Kopykat*, the first of which had made the best-seller list. The subsequent books had not done as well, until *Kopykat*, which was presently on many of the lists, including number nine of *The New York Times* list.

"You've gained weight," Keough said.

"Prosperity," O'Donnell said, touching his slightly swollen belly. He had also let his hair grow a bit longer, and shaggier, and had gotten somewhat grayer.

"Mike O'Donnell," Keough said, "meet Valerie Speck."

"Ah, I've heard about you," O'Donnell said, "we've got a lot to talk about."

"I'm looking forward to it."

"Joe, Valerie, this is Helen Simpson. She owns the store."

"So, you're Joe Keough," Helen said, shaking Keough's hand. She had a disconcerting way of looking right into his eyes when she spoke to him. It was disconcerting because not many people did it, these days. Keough liked it, and instinctively liked her. "I've been looking forward to meeting you ever since I read your book—and then Mike told me you lived here! Why have you never come in?"

"Well," Keough said, "I don't write, and I haven't been reading much, lately—"

"You could have come in and signed copies of *Kopykat.*"

"Why would I do that? I didn't write it."

"I, uh, told Helen that you were, uh, pretty active in the, uh, preparation of the book."

"That may be true, but I can't sign copies—"

"Of course you can," she said, "and you can start now."

There was no way out, he could see, so he signed a few for her. He had the feeling she usually got what she wanted.

"Now you can tell us about your newest case," Helen said, afterward.

"What case is that?" O'Donnell asked.

"It was in the papers," Helen told him. "He caught the Mall Rat."

"The Mall Rat?" O'Donnell said. He looked at Keough. "That sounds interesting."

"Maybe you could write that case as a book, also," Helen said, as if it was a wonderful idea.

"I need another book," O'Donnell said, looking at his friend. "My publisher's pushing me. Is there something to this Mall Rat case?"

"It's very interesting," Valerie said.

"You guys could write it together," Helen said. She was not shy with her suggestions.

"Joe—" O'Donnell started.

Some people came into the store then, and Helen got

up to greet them. Keough said, "Why don't you keep busy selling this one, Mike, and we can talk at dinner later, okay?"

"Okay," O'Donnell said, as Helen led the people over to meet the "famous" true crime writer and the "famous" detective, "but I really want to hear about this." He looked at Valerie and asked, "Help me with this guy, will you?"

"Oh, I don't know," she said, taking hold of Keough's arm, "I rather think you're the one who's going to have to help me. After all, we're right at the beginning of something."

As O'Donnell rose to talk to the prospective customers he said to her, "We'll help each other. We have tonight and all day tomorrow."

"Two against one," she said in Keough's ear. "I like those odds."

Keough wondered, idly, if he could go into work tomorrow, a day early.